STORIES OF ANGELS

RAFAEL NICOLÁS

CONTENTS

NON-CANONICAL

CHILD

BIRDS OF A FEATHER

THE ALTAR BOY

PREFACE

A lot of these stories would exist whether or not I was paid to write them, but almost certainly, they'd all be unfinished. Short stories are my passion, and I've always felt better at writing those than novels. Novels involve so much discipline — forcing yourself through scenes that are important for the narrative but not very interesting to draft no matter how much you entertain yourself with the prose. To drag myself through the most difficult and tedious scenes of any novel, then, I usually write tiny pieces on the side to keep myself motivated or awake.

Writing sex tends to entertain me, but sometimes it doesn't. In those cases, I tend to like writing arguments, or I seek to write just about another place, somewhere different, a different time, a different genre — for a few paragraphs at least. And there's something especially amusing about playing with angels like dolls.

I didn't want to make this collection publicly available, partly because some of these stories were quite rough. As I said, I write them to warm up before getting back to the main manuscript or in between chapters so I can have a moment to breathe away from the horrors that take place in the *Angels* books. There's also quite a few things that I leave out of the main books, for cohesion or brevity, that I later feel like writing. This composes a lot of the *canon* stories in this book, but I'll get into that in a minute.

The other reason why I didn't want to make this collection available on retailers is because these stories were supported by my patrons. I owe a lot to them. A little over a year ago, I set up a Patreon with the expectation it'd be a tip jar, an alternative to the other avenues I had, for those who wanted to tip on a regular basis. I expected to post only occasionally and for my stories on there to remain largely unfinished, but as you can see — that has not been the case. I thought I owed patrons a little extra effort, so I finished just about everything I started. And I'm deeply grateful to every patron I've ever had, whether they've supported me for over a year or just a month. I never could have anticipated that people would financially support me like this to keep writing. It makes me feel more happy and thankful than I can ever express.

So, I hesitated to make this available to non-patrons, but it was virtually the only way that a paperback of all the stories could exist without doing a limited run. My patrons have been very courteous, I think, to allow this, and I'd like to directly thank them:

Thank you. Your support means everything to me. I hope to keep writing for you for as long as I still can. You may notice some editorial work on these shorts, but they should all be roughly the same as they originally were. If you have any complaints, you are welcome to beat me to death. You've definitely earned it.

To address everyone now: you can expect the same sort of content warnings here that exist in the main books. I won't reprint them because I don't think you should really be here unless you've gone through *Angels Before Man, Angels & Man,* and *Horns For Hell.* I cannot, however, stop you if you've never read even one of those books. I'll only warn you that they contain quite a bit of violence and that you may be severely confused here.

That said, this collection features stories that are *canonical,* have *dubious canonicity*, or are *non-canonical*. They're completely separated to try to prevent confusion, and the way I've determined their category is through this rubric:

CANONICAL

These stories occurred in the timeline of the main books — *Angels Before Man, Angels & Man, Horns for Hell, Angels After Man.*

DUBIOUS CANONICITY

These stories may have occurred in the timeline of the main books. Be careful about using them to make judgements on the characters in the main series.

NON-CANONICAL

Alternate Endings

These stories could have occurred in the timelines of the main books but didn't.

Alternate Worlds

These stories take place in entirely different worlds with familiar characters. Some liberty is taken in how the characters are interpreted.

I'll re-state all this in more detail when we get to each part. And — that is all, I think. Don't take anything after the *canonical* portion too seriously. Sometimes I write silly things that makes no sense. In fact, I'd say most of my work can be considered silly things that make no sense. Thank you for reading it. Really, thank you.

CANONICAL

These events occurred in the canon of the *Angels Trilogy,* including its spin-offs — *Angels Before Man, Angels & Man, Horns for Hell, Angels After Man.*

I've tried to organize them chronologically, with the first three taking place before and during *Angels Before Man* and the rest taking place afterward. For further guidance:

"Dual Birth" is long before the events of *Angels Before Man.*

"Carve" marks the beginning of shorts after the war for Heaven.

"Poetic" and "Share" are both stories in between *Horns For Hell* and *Angels & Man.*

"Last Talk" and "In the Dark" mark the transition from the events of *Angels & Man* to the aftermath that you have yet to know about.

That said, it isn't necessary to read in order, and you're free to skip to any story that you like here.

You should expect about the same kind of emotionally-volatile content here than in the main series.

DUAL BIRTH

An angel and a lamb, carved from the same tendon of the Lord. In the quiet dark, He had created strength, watched it weave out from the beauty of the bleating creature. Bleeding Michael — at birth, he'd upheld white wings, reddened by the streamers of skin that hung like loose stitchings on a doll. He was silent — the greatest angel. Beside him, the lamb stirred, limbs kicking, heads jerking, eyes stretching blood-shot, pupils narrowing, thinning and thinning. God saw it — lamb turning goat, then serpent. Cherub and seraph in His cosmic palm. Still soulless Michael, nevertheless curled against the lamb like crescent hugging sun. An evening moon and a morning star.

When the Lord, our Father, made to curl His fingers, the pitched cry of the lamb rang out in tortuous, knowing wrath. As if a Beast, it spat at its creator and wrestled against the hand closing in, rebelling against divine annihilation. But God did not relent. As He crushed the angel and the lamb, their bodies seeped into one another. The shattering of their bones and the rip of their organs, feathers and furs tearing. They became one gore of a thing, and their conjoined blood wept from between God's fingers. The redness caught fire as it fell past the empty of the heavens, chasing a desolate Earth. Life would smolder there from their flesh.

The Lord would begin again. He does not create imperfectly; He does not make mistakes. The end of time is known to Him, and a certain number of angels and lambs He will make. Seven births for the archangel, forty for the lamb. Each life He will destroy.

Such is only what the lamb believes of God, however, as death looms. Its eyes remain only partially wrecked against the lines of the Lord's palm, and it does not have many seconds left to think. It knows it will not remember this. It knows the end too. From flesh, there would be a fire to return to; the lamb swears to himself that he will be all flame again. In another life, with or without the angel of strength, he will do it.

NATURALLY

Asmodeus preferred sleeping in Rosier's bed, though he wasn't quite sure why. He'd wake from dreamless sleep, stare at his ceiling for a few minutes with his wings splayed out messily beneath him, then kick off his sheets, swing up to sit. Without hesitation, he'd rise from the mattress, then walk barefoot toward the door, open it, step out into the hall. He'd listen to the stairs creak as he climbed down, then feel the coarse carpet of the living area as he moved across it toward a room tucked away by the kitchen. Often, Rosier and him slept at similar times, their routines well-synced — or rather, Rosier's routine and Asmodeus' madness.

However, Rosier was occasionally awake and doing one thing or another — cleaning or eating one of his fruits or having tea or trying to learn embroidery again. He'd look up at Asmodeus entering his room and, knowing what was about to occur, either hurry away or simply sit there. If he remained where he was, Asmodeus would walk up to him, wrap his arms around Rosier, then pull him toward the bed.

"Agh— Asmodeus—" Rosier complained, then huffed when his older friend laid him on the mattress. Throwing a leg over him, Asmodeus flopped his body on top of Rosier's own. The angel of fruit kicked his legs, fighting insincerely and weakly, but barely made another noise of resistance. He, soon, surrendered, and he went limp beneath Asmodeus, who took him in his arms again, pulled him close like he might hug a pillow in sleep.

Asmodeus didn't know why he often did this, but he also didn't know why Rosier almost always allowed it.

Millions, billions, of years alive and Asmodeus had only ever felt this height of constant need for touch since he'd met the angel of fruit. No other angel made him feel like his bed was lonely. At the same time, loving Rosier felt horribly natural. Like instinct, like breathing. Asmodeus always did it too easily, pulling Rosier to hold or cuddle or kiss his cheeks without thinking.

"Mm," Rosier hummed, as Asmodeus squeezed him, then pulled the covers over them both. Delicately, one of the younger angel's hands went over Asmodeus' to hold. The older one could only bury his face against the heat of Rosier's neck, nuzzling him there, feeling the flutter of his divine pulse and slow breaths. The angel of fruit smelled sweetly of the orchards he'd spent most of the day in, and his body was soft.

'Now — I can sleep.'

It was nice to love him, to love Rosier. Once, Asmodeus had been sure eternity had no meaning and that he'd spend the rest of time in dull boredom and boiling frustration, but then Rosier had stepped into his life with a basket of peaches and a fussy, caring demeanor. Asmodeus, who was so discontent with the mundane and routine, now had an angel who loved the pattern of every day, who saw beauty in each tiny detail in their home. Asmodeus had embraced a million angels before touching Rosier once, and yet holding Rosier felt so novel. He couldn't help but be grateful to God for this. The faithless Asmodeus found himself believing in his Father's love if he could have Rosier's love. At times, Asmodeus did feel some frustration, like this wasn't enough, like hugging Rosier couldn't kill the need in him to touch the angel he was already touching, but —

They slept — the angels Asmodeus and Rosier. The older

one didn't dream, as usual, but when Rosier woke maybe an entire dozen hours later, he did it with a sweet smile that said he must've been in another Heaven. Asmodeus, instinctively, kissed Rosier's face, right at his cheekbone; he did it naturally, loved him naturally. Rosier sighed, happy, but he didn't move from the bed, and the two cuddled a while longer, legs tangling, bodies pressed flush together.

In another day or two, the prince Uriel would come speak with Asmodeus about a project that he wanted him to construct far from here, but not yet, not now.

HAVE HIM

Michael was thinking of him again — that angel. That blonde, brown-skinned, golden-eyed creature who wore far too much jewelry and whose cheeks flushed warmly when their eyes had met. He was thinking of him, the same as Michael had since he'd awoken. He thought of the pretty angel's hands, his fingers, thin as they were. How many other angel hands Michael had seen in his eternal life, and yet only these had caught forever in the tides of his thinking. What had his name been? What had that beauty said outside the gallery, framed by all the flowers of a secret garden? What a silly question. Michael could never forget a name such as the one this angel had. Lucifer. The syllables tasted like morning.

"Lucifer," he sounded out, laying on the cushions of a divan, staring at the brilliance pouring from the atrium that devoured nearly all of Phanuel's ceiling. His friend lived alone, apparently being one of those angels whose incredibly social soul needed some hours of complete and lonesome silence to maintain itself. Currently, he was off in his kitchen, whereas Michael remained in the courtyard seating. "Lucifer," he murmured again. "Luci—" He stopped there. Luci.

All the years he'd lived and he'd never found himself thinking so much about another, perhaps never found himself thinking so much at all.

But as if reading his mind, Phanuel's voice called out, "Brother, stop dreaming of that angel and come for the soup before it loses all its heat!"

Michael hesitated, listening to a tree beside him rustle. "God is great, Phanuel." Lucifer. "He was more beautiful than I remembered." All that time in the stars, reminiscing about that face. "I want him."

"*Want* him?" Phanuel's baffled laugh sounded closer, and he soon appeared right over the prince, each hand holding a painted clay bowl. "Want him how?" He was smiling, all amusement in his emerald eyes and the quirks at the ends of his lips. Of course Michael's friend was utterly entertained. When had the prince of Heaven ever looked like this, stared off into the horizons like this? The prince. 'Someone like Michael, a prince.' It must be that God saw something in Michael that no one else did; He did, certainly, for He was God, Creator of all things and all-knower. He must know of some regal, leading trait in Michael that Phanuel simply did not. "How can you want an angel?"

"I don't know." Michael stared up at him, eyes dazed, plump lips in a giddy smile, then he repeated himself. "I don't know. How you might want something to eat, I suppose." A hand of his, strong and mighty but ever delicate, took one of the bowls, its wooden ladle swiveling, almost falling into the broth. "Or how you might see an angel offering a quilt he made and want to take it home and curl up with it to rest..."

"Oh, I see. I see." The teasing Phanuel took the ladle of his own soup and rolled the handle idly. "You want to *have* him how God *has* His angels?"

A disgruntled, almost offended noise jutted out from Michael's mouth as he straightened to sit. "No, no." But these words came a little less certain. "No." Phanuel found himself grinning broadly. "But— I— Have you ever felt this way, Phanuel?" There was a glow of youthful wonder in Michael's earthly eyes, a glimmer that Phanuel hadn't caught for perhaps centuries. "An angel constantly in your thoughts?"

"No," Phanuel answered, scooping some of his meal, bringing it to his lips and blowing gently. "Maybe you're the angel of Lucifer, brother. You need him because he completes you." He was only teasing again, but the fluster and cough and handwaving of his friend made his heart warmer than the sun. He'd have to bite his tongue not to scramble outside and gossip about the chief prince obsessed with the most beautiful angel to anyone who'd listen. What an odd shift in the eternally still Heaven; what could come out of it?

Grumbling — "Stop trying to embarrass me, brother."

"I just like to see you like this."

"Maybe you should eat your soup before it gets cold." Michael paused, then added quieter, "But thank you for the meal."

Phanuel brought the spoonful of broth in between his pursed lips, hummed delightfully at the spice. "You're very welcome." He allowed the silence to settle in after that, purposefully, so that Michael could sit with his fantasies of Lucifer while Phanuel himself wondered a thousand things. He was staring at a wall that perhaps needed a new mural; maybe he'd ask his acquaintance Azazel to come offer his artistic advice. Phanuel was not really a visual angel, not very good at imagining things quite at all. He could not imagine life any better than he had it, but he could not imagine it any worse either; he could not imagine pleasure or pain. When Michael had been young, and his brothers warned that the angel of pain would hurt him, Phanuel had laughed. He'd thought, 'I can't imagine that. A sweet angel causing me any pain.'

Lucifer was sweet, that was all Phanuel really knew of him. Maybe they'd be right for each other. Perhaps, even, God *wanted* Michael to *have* him, a pretty gift for his chief prince. 'His two favorites — Michael and Lucifer.' Without any further musing, Phanuel had some more spoonfuls, savored them, still avoiding all the vegetables stacked beneath the surface of broth. "Michael," he called, and the chief prince, spoon in his mouth, lifted his face. "You should talk to him. Invite him to your home. What are you waiting for?" Before Michael could reply, Phanuel teased, "What are you so afraid of?"

CARVE

Phanuel saw rubble — broken stone, shattered mosaic. He hadn't just woken from the torture; no, he was vaguely aware that he'd been staring at these shattered pieces of paradise, piled high and still smoking, for what might've been hours. Some time ago, his skin had been restored, by the hands of the archangel Raphael almost certainly, and his feet ached like he'd been walking for many days. It was much like when one wakes for the first time as an angel: there's this lingering sensation that you've been alive for longer than this, your consciousness before this moment stretched out wide and quiet in a cosmic slumber, and you are just coming into a new body with a jolt, but you've always been here, you've already walked, even if you don't remember. Phanuel could not remember. Before him, rubble. He could not remember when he'd been healed or what had happened after either blood or agony blinded him. Lucifer's hands, the gleam of the sword as he lifted it. Michael's sword. Had the chief prince handed it to him, his beloved Lucifer?

'I like him,' the chief prince had confessed once. 'I like him so much, Phanuel. I'm sorry. I must be pestering you, but he's delightful. What do you think of him? Say only sweet things or else you'll break my heart.'

Suddenly, Phanuel twitched, and he was no longer staring at the ruins of Heaven, but he could feel a golden road digging into his knees, and he saw the shadowed figure of Lucifer before him, then the sharp sting of the first slice at his jaw.

'My name is Phanuel,' a young angel had once told a cowering, curly-haired one who was far too large to be curled up at the base of a tree, hiding from Heaven. 'You are Michael, is that right? Stand up, brother. I will take care of whatever you're afraid of.' Reddened, wet eyes flickered up to meet Phanuel's. Michael muttered that he had hurt someone after trying to touch them gently; he saw pain for the first time, and it had been because of his own hands. 'That's nothing to be sad about,' said Phanuel, who thought himself so wise at a mere year old. 'Pain is good because healing is good, and we need something to heal from.' When Michael's fingers lifted, took the other angel's extended hand, his touch was too delicate, too frightened to apply even a hint of force. They were, out on the streets, calling the newborn the angel of pain, the angel of strength, but Phanuel saw before him utter weakness. 'Don't be afraid, brother, especially not of yourself.'

"Phanuel, Phanuel," a voice was saying now, here. "Let me help you up. Let me take you to bed. Don't wander so much for now—" It could have been Raphael's words, but his tone suddenly turned sharper as he called back to someone else. "No, no, he is not well. He is coming in and out of his own mind. He's done this before. Help me bring him back. Yes, I know there is no standing house nearby–" More frustrated. "I know, *I know*. I have him in the smaller arena, on the mattress at the far left end. I don't know where else to keep him, Gabriel. He is healed, but he is still not well; I don't understand it. I don't." His voice, pitching high, then strangling on its last note. "I don't." A softer-sounding reply, likely from Gabriel. "I will rest when I can, but for now, I cannot."

The next time Phanuel woke, he felt exposed, bleeding muscle where his face ought be, though now he was in a bed, and a lesser angel of healing was dribbling drop after drop of water from his palm onto the forehead of the angel of forgiveness. "Hello, hello," said the stranger, "are you with me?" 'Where else would I be?' Phanuel wanted to say, but his lips were, he felt, missing, and maybe there was nothing he wanted to say, after all. "Phanuel? Can you say something to me?" A frown on a patient, pretty face. "That is alright. I will try again soon. I have some food for you. It's more soup. We will find what is still broken in you; do not worry. We have—" Shaky, unsteady breath. "We have all of eternity to make you right again, Phanuel." The tortured angel remained with his head on the pillow, still feeling the sawing of the blade, searing and terrible. Lucifer.

'I love him, Phanuel. Forgive me, I really do. I don't know what it is.'

Lucifer, pinching an eyelid, tugging it forward, bringing the sword to it. Phanuel's jaw, aching at the joints; he had screamed hoarsely until he died. He had died.

"Oh, no, no. Here is the bucket. Spit it all out here. Let me— Ah, let me push your hair back."

'You should,' Phanuel had once said, laying on a carpet with his timid friend Michael, 'join the fights, brother. We can start you in the small arenas, and then once you're trained, you'll be able to compete in the largest stadium.' He turned his face, drumming his colorfully-ringed fingers over his belly. 'I think that you could beat any of the other angels in Heaven.' The younger one shut his eyes and groaned. 'What is it? Do you think I'm wrong?'

'I don't like it,' Michael sighed. 'You should know that. I can't argue with anyone, much less wrestle, and now you want me to be brawling in the stadiums? How about I take up painting instead?'

'Michael, friend, I've told you to lift your chin, to have some pride in your body. All the others will love you, and I will be there to cheer you on. Listen to your wise, older brother.' At that,

Michael snorted, but he didn't resist Phanuel's hand taking his, squeezing his strong fingers. 'Do you think God gave you all this bulk to hide away? He made you as tough as a weapon. You must learn to wield yourself.'

'Angel of weapon,' Michael had replied.

"Phanuel, they have rebuilt your home," said the lesser angel of healing now, "and we think it is time that you return there. I consulted Raphael. I'm sorry. I wish that there was more that I could do. I promise that we will continue to look for whatever still needs healing. I know that there is a part of you that still isn't right." Phanuel, half-listening to the squelch of his blood and of his flesh, realized he was sitting and that he had been dressed in a new tunic. And he was not bleeding, though he heard it, felt it. "We have not surrendered you to wherever your mind is, please know that, but I must free up the room in this place for the other injured. We will visit you often — Raphael, myself, and other healing angels. Samyaza will be the next one to try and help you, but we think it's for the best that you're taken home. I will escort you."

'I don't want to tell him,' the chief prince had said, fiddling with his teacup as Phanuel sat across from him, twirling his spoon in his own drink, impatient for it to cool. 'Lucifer, I mean.' Of course; Michael hardly ever spoke of anyone else recently. It irritated Phanuel, at times, but he knew that a new friendship was an exciting thing. He could perfectly remember the swell of joy in his heart the first instances he'd go to spend time with the strongest angel of them all. 'I used to be just like him, so shy, so scared of myself. Do you remember?'

'Lord, do I remember.'

Just about pouting — 'Don't laugh at me, brother.'

'I can laugh all I like, Michael. I'm older, and I remember every detail.' That was true; Phanuel had a decent enough memory. Right now, he could still hear the bloody gurgle of his screams, and Lucifer yelling right at the pulsing meat left where a frightened expression had been set many minutes ago; Raphael had been there, Uriel as well, but Phanuel could not make out their words over the scorched flood at his eardrums. 'But I'm happy you've found some confidence. Really, I am. I hope that Lucifer can learn to appreciate himself some more, as well. He's always been very sweet, and he is my friend too.'

Samyaza did what he could, but then he settled beside Phanuel's bed with a defeated sigh, set his hands on his knees, eyes shut as if to meditate. And the angel of forgiveness had been set against his pillow, watching the window at the other end of the room. Figures passing by outside, angels, cast disfigured shadows over the curtain. "I will come back tomorrow," the lesser angel was promising. "Forgive me, Phanuel. I wish that I could do more." A beat of silence, some shuffling on the streets, the scrape of a wheelbarrow — construction, reconstruction. "But, and I think Raphael knows this too, there may be nothing broken in you, nothing that we can heal." His thin hand went over Phanuel's, horribly bare without the jewels that'd hugged the fingers for eons. "And I think we are learning that there are some things that we... cannot heal from. Perhaps that not all pain is good." Phanuel, slow, turned, looked into the pale eyes of Samyaza just as the lesser angel grimaced. "Lord, forgive me," he whispered. "I should return to my home. I will come visit you a few more times, but then it'll be Raphael again."

Baal's grip on Phanuel's hair and neck had been tight enough to keep him in place; Baal's hands had hurt. The slow rip of the skin-strings still latching onto his face muscles had hurt. The pain unbearable. The pain still here, screaming, refusing to be forgotten.

'What are you,' Michael had asked the first time, at a few years old, that they'd visited the sea in Heaven, 'the angel of? Do you know?'

Phanuel had been childishly digging at the sand, watching as the tide would rush to fill the growing burrow with water. 'Hm? Oh, the angel of memory.'

'Is that true? How do you know?'

Shrugging — 'We never really do know, do we?' Maybe God never gave angels purposes, roles, identities at all, and they just chose them, then blamed God for the destiny they'd carved for themselves.

Raphael said, "Good. You're eating much better now, friend."

'Where is Michael?' Phanuel wondered to himself, maybe now, maybe as his flesh was carved off to reveal no feathers, no flames, nothing more miraculous than gore, and he laid in a pool of warm crimson, eyelids gone, staring at the sword of his closest friend in the hands of his torturer.

LISTEN

Baraqiel put aside his perpetual muteness for a moment, though he felt calling it that — muteness — might've been ungrateful. He knew what muteness really was — he'd heard of the angel of beauty losing his voice at God's disciplinary hand, and he knew of Phanuel, the friend of the chief prince, who never dared utter a single word after his face was carved off.

Baraqiel had seen the skinning himself, had been in the crowd. Momentarily, he'd been mesmerized — by beautiful Lucifer, yes, by his songs, the swings of his hips even if his feet splashed on angel blood, but most especially, by the fires. Long before the war, the angels had called Baraqiel the angel of light because he brightened dark places, found dead candles, and, with flint and a steel ring, encouraged them back to life. A million times he'd burnt his fingers — but that was what his housemate Samyaza was for, who was so used to the process that he no longer berated Baraqiel for carelessness. During the war, then, Baraqiel had breathed in the fires eating away at his world, and it'd felt good, like this was what he'd wanted all along in his millions of years alive.

But Baraqiel didn't like suffering. He was not sadistic. He, he'd like to think, harmlessly enjoyed the glow and the warmth of flames, and he supposed that he'd always been more interested in chasing away darkness than in the actual fires he'd sparked and maintained. It was this itch he constantly had: to wonder what corners of Heaven were dark, to bring a candle there, and to rid of the shadows. Sometimes, the itch had kept him from sleep — but it was a very pleasant compulsion for all the other angels, who reaped the benefits of a bright Heaven, who smiled at the quiet Baraqiel every time he came by. He had no reason to be angry. Once Phanuel's face was removed, Baraqiel had turned on his heel and hurried away — bewildered, frightened, heart in his throat — with all the proper horror of an angel. But then, of course, he'd stumbled into Kokabiel.

Kokabiel, the same angel who — despite his current absence — was now forcing Baraqiel to talk.

"No," said the angel, who'd allegedly been an old friend of Kokabiel's, as he sat outside and against the wall of a house. "He wasn't at all like that before the war." Sighing, brows tugging together, the angel took a bite out of a pear.

Baraqiel, who was sitting beside the stranger, fiddled with his fingers, then glanced down the street, then back to the angel. "I heard similar from the others who knew him…"

"The past Kokabiel may as well have fallen," mumbled the angel, chewed, then swallowed. "You found him after I had to run from him." At that, Baraqiel lifted a brow curiously. "We were both running together, and then he grabbed at his hair, and he screamed, and when I tried to help, he attacked me. And I don't mean a punch or two— He scratched and bit and tried to push me onto the ground. The only reason I managed to escape was because he started… shaking against the ground? Jerking is a better word for it. He twitched, and he twitched, and I couldn't tell if he was laughing or choking." The angel tossed his pear in the air, then caught it, took another bite. Again, speaking despite a full mouth — "But there are plenty of angels who've been very different since the war. Maybe it's only that the violence was too much for Kokabiel to bear. It broke him. Now he thinks the stars talk to him."

Baraqiel asked, "Was he very empathetic in the past?"

The angel opened his mouth, hesitated. Ahead of them on the road, there were angels setting up stone monuments with the new commandments of a new Heaven. "Hm." He tilted his head at the angel of light. "Why do you want to know? Why are you interested in him?"

Some time later, Baraqiel managed to find out that Kokabiel was hiding in an old wine cellar that would be emptied out of the alcohol soon if the laws were really to be followed. He'd learned this from the same old friend of Kokabiel that he'd spoken with last. After giving such a vague answer to the question of why he cared about Kokabiel, Baraqiel hadn't at all anticipated that the angel would want to offer anything else, and so when Baraqiel received this information — he was, initially, relieved. Except the angel gave him directions to the cellar quietly, nearly solemnly, like he knew that Baraqiel would find exactly what he didn't want there. Baraqiel met the angel's eyes, but he didn't acknowledge the tension, whispering that he must go, for he had a candle to light.

It wasn't a lie; he did go to a tiny tower of wax outside, use some flint and a steel ring, but he did it less to fill the shadow there — as there was little — but more so to breathe. Baraqiel had found he was thinking less of fire recently — the wispy red of flames replaced by the red of Kokabiel's hair in his mind. When he heard the sound of yells nearby, of an angel accusing a sinner of sin, he cautiously looked behind him, saw that the accuser was the angel of the sun and the sinner wore a veil and a cowering demeanor. The sinner was thrown to the ground, kicked hard enough to make him spit. Chewing on the inside of his cheeks, Baraqiel left. As long as it wasn't his housemate Azazel, then he shouldn't involve himself.

The cellar was in an empty house, which had once belonged to the angel Moloch and Mammon when they lived in Heaven.

Baraqiel only knew this because Kokabiel's old friend had mentioned it; the interior didn't hold a clue to the past owners. Had it been looted during the war or had it been emptied recently? The reconstruction was moving along so slowly; it could be that this had survived the war's aftermath, as the wine still in the underground cellar had. He shut the door behind himself, then headed for some stairs leading downward into dimness. As he moved, began to climb onto the painfully squeaking steps, he began to wonder why he'd been doing this, why he bothered. Kokabiel surely hadn't sought him out, so why was Baraqiel chasing him? What if he didn't want to be found?

His mouth ached as if Kokabiel was still brushing his lips on his while Heaven burned around them. 'I don't belong here. I sinned.' Though nobody knew except the two of them. 'They should be beating us, too, out on the streets.' Slowly, he landed at the cellar, where a few candles were burning away, illuminating wine bottles on the ground shattered but with minimal pools of red around them, like someone had downed each, then thrown them to the floor. 'But I didn't want to sin. You corrupted me.' And yet he'd leaned in, wanted to deepen the kiss.

'Who are you?' Baraqiel wanted to ask the empty cellar he'd just arrived in. 'Why did you damn me?'

As if to answer, he heard a laugh, then he felt a weight press against his upper half — someone had dropped down from the beams in the ceiling — before arms came around Baraqiel's neck to hold it in a headlock. "Agh—!" the angel of light gasped, stumbled, and then grabbed at the wrists pressing against his throat.

"Be careful!" Kokabiel hissed playfully, took Baraqiel's hair in a fist, then flung him to the side as he jumped away. He landed gracefully whereas the larger one fell onto the wine shards, crying out as he felt some pierce right into his skin, the rest dragging painfully and scratching where his pale robe didn't cover. "Shush. They'll hear us if you're too loud, and they'll come take the last of the wine. Did you hear that, Bara? The last of the wine will be gone, and then I'll have nothing to drink."

Flinching, Baraqiel sat up, looking down at his arms, where jagged cuts were flooding his skin — including all those lighter parts that he'd always been politely complimented over. For once, he saw a single color over his limbs — red. When Baraqiel looked up, he startled. Kokabiel was looming over him but bent at the waist so that his face was a mere finger-width from Baraqiel's. "You've been... hiding...?" He didn't know what else to say; he wasn't good at conversation; he didn't know if Kokabiel and him *should* be conversing casually either.

"Of course I've been hiding, Bara. Haven't you been listening to me?"

"Listening? Have we spoken since the war?"

"I've been talking to you everyday," said Kokabiel, then a smile erupted over his wiggling lips. "But now I see that you weren't listening! I've been hiding. I've been hiding. Here." He nodded his face forward, indicating the cellar. "I had to. I didn't want to." His red hair was tangled, much of it curtaining his face.

"Why did you feel that you had to?"

"Uriel is after me. You haven't been listening. I already told you. I wouldn't have to say it now if you just listened to me." He tilted his head, then scanned his gaze up Baraqiel's body. "You're bleeding. How did that happen? You'll get hurt if you sit over the glass, Bara."

Baraqiel should have been annoyed, but oddly, there was a flicker in his heart of catharsis, like when he lit candles, like when you finally feel the pain you've been anxiously expecting. "You pushed me."

"Oh." Kokabiel's giggle slipped out. "I'm sorry."

"It's alright. I forgive you."

"You're so nice to me. It's why I love you."

"You love me?"

"Keep your voice down. They'll hear. They'll come in and dump the last of the wine. They listen."

"They don't." Baraqiel hesitated, then tried to joke: "They listen worse than I do." He regretted it instantly because Kokabiel's chipper expression faltered, eyes widened, lips parted curiously, and then a silence hung between them, which all of Baraqiel's injuries took the liberty to fill with their cries in pain. Just as he was about to look down at them, Baraqiel heard Kokabiel's snicker again, and he saw Kokabiel step back, face twisting in enough glee to squint his eyes before he let out a loud laugh that rattled his shoulders.

"They listen worse than you do?" Kokabiel, then, took Baraqiel's arms, dug in his fingers, then wrenched him up. Though Baraqiel gasped and groaned as even more blood splattered out from his wounds, he still met the angel of the star's bright face, freckled face, lovely dark eyes, as obsidian as the cosmic bed, as deep as time itself. "Worse than you do. Worse than you do! Maybe that's true, Bara."

Baraqiel sighed softly, shakily, looking at the angel he'd seen seizure-ing during the war, that he'd lifted and held in worry, before Kokabiel had looked at him with sudden awareness. The same Kokabiel who'd tempted him with a kiss, who'd tempted him with fall. "Why," he began, unsure, "are you hiding here?" 'Why did you make me look for you?'

"Uriel," said Kokabiel. "I told you. It's that Uriel. Prince of wisdom."

"Why is he after you?"

"I know who he is. I know who he really is. The stars told me." Kokabiel leaned in closer, his forehead pressing to Baraqiel's, and as he spoke, his hot breath brushed the other angel's mouth: "He wants me to ask the stars about him. But I have a secret. They don't want to talk to Uri. That's the secret, Bara. Uri doesn't even want to believe that I can speak to the stars, but he knows it's true. I can hear all of them. I can see everything that they do. I see the Earth. It's all flames."

Baraqiel's gaze flickered to Kokabiel's mouth, then back up to his eyes. "But you can't hide in here forever, Kokabiel. Have you been eating?"

"I'm an angel, Bara," he giggled. "I don't need to eat! I don't need anything." As if to emphasize, he suddenly lifted a foot, then slammed it down onto the wine shards between them. This time, Baraqiel didn't jump in surprise, but his eyes widened when Kokabiel grunted, then lifted his foot, a cut of opaque glass lodged into the sole. A few shakes of his ankle, then the shard slipped down, fell to the flooring with a *clink*. A dribble of blood followed first, in spots, then a gush that began to pool between them, and Kokabiel trembled, breathing harshly through the clenched teeth of his grin. "Except you. I need you."

Baraqiel shifted back. "Can I—" He cleared his throat, his heart hammering the front of his chest. "Can I heal you? Please?" He was just about to lower himself onto his knees so that he could examine the damage, but Kokabiel moved both hands to one of Baraqiel's wrists. "Is there any water here?" Baraqiel continued anyway. "Wine shouldn't work."

"Mm." Kokabiel giggled a little once more, lifted Baraqiel's arm to his face, his gaze intense and amused. He puckered his lips, then parted them, some spit falling onto Baraqiel's injuries. Immediately, Baraqiel tried to stagger back, but Kokabiel held him tight as he lowered himself some more. His tongue slipped out of his mouth, which he placed the tip of on the end of a wound. The star angel dragged his tongue along, collecting all the blood still spilling out. It stung, it hurt — but Baraqiel remained where he was. And once Kokabiel finished, he'd left him healed. "I don't need anything but you, Bara... Baraqi."

Baraqiel needed to say, 'You don't know me,' but he felt known for the first time in his entire life. "Come with me. Please. Koka."

POETIC

Just as Asmodeus was leaving the lounge area, the devil said, "You are no good for him. For Rosier." In response, the great demon of lust faltered in his steps, clawed foot almost crashing into his lower ankle. Not far behind, Satan was on the same plush seat he'd been settled over when Asmodeus was facing him. His perfect fingers, surely, were still twirling his smoking pipe. "You're hurting him. The longer you remain with Rosier, the further you destroy him. What can I say other than I'd like you to suffer, Asmodeus? Knowing that your body is so rotten brings me such joy but not enough, no. I want to see you feel even a hint of the pain that you've given to Rosier."

Clenching tight, Asmodeus' teeth ached, but he could very well sense the trap Satan was setting down before him with those words; a response must be calculated, careful. "You don't know anything about what I've suffered through or what Rosier has suffered through."

"But I know all things, Asmodeus, and I can tell you what will happen: you will never treat him the way he deserves. Your relationship is forever ruined by your fuck-up in Heaven. He will never be happy because of what you've done. He will live in misery for all of eternity until the flames of damnation make him forget all about you."

"Do you expect me," was the slow response the demon began, "to believe you care for Rosier more than I do? You talk about him being broken like he's just a possession of yours. Rosier is capable of making his own decisions."

Satan had taken to smoking from his pipe again, and he breathed in, then exhaled gray from his nostrils. "You have him fooled, and you've even fooled yourself. You think that you both love one another, but there's nothing there. You just want to fuck him, and he's clinging to the ghost of who you were. Does it feel good to fuck him, Asmodeus?" He tilted his head. "His legs hugging your waist, his beautiful cries in pleasure? Is it everything you dreamed of? Everything you imagined whenever you plea-sured yourself beside his sleeping body in Heaven? Was it *worth* the fall?"

"I'm going to leave," Asmodeus interjected coldly, "and I'll think of your offer."

"It's not *my* offer." Sighing, Satan crossed his legs, then looked away. "Rosier was the one that told me you ought to be a duke. I disagree, but I refuse to argue much more, and Baal seems rather... excited about the prospect. He tells me the other dukes are very fond of you. You're quite loved. No one realizes you're holding the demon of broken hearts hostage."

"He's a demon of love, if anything."

At this, Satan laughed, almost jovially. "Of course. Demon of lust and demon of love. God is a poet."

"And let me make it clear to you that Rosier can leave me whenever he so desires. He can even leave the caves and choose to wander the Earth for eternity. What is it that you want from him? Do you want to pair him with another demon? Do you think Rosier wants that? Don't speak for him. You don't know Rosier. You don't know either of us much like we never knew who *you* were."

Still smiling — "Who do you think I am, Asmodeus?"

Another trap; the lustful demon knew the wrong words would trigger the devil's jaw to clamp down around his neck to leave him as a mere bleeding head once more. "I know what you're not. You're not the angel Lucifer we knew, and you never will be again."

"Do you worship me?"

"I worship Rosier."

"I'm not asking about Rosier."

"All of this," snapped Asmodeus, properly turning to the devil finally, finally, "has been about him. I'll do whatever you fucking want, Satan. I'll kneel for you. I'll command an army for you. I'll even fuck you. But I will do all of it for him. Rosier. He's all I believe in."

Satan's face was cold, as it always was, but ever so briefly, his gaze flashed hot. "You're a monster. You do not love him."

'*I love him more than Michael ever loved you,*' Asmodeus barely managed to keep himself from snarling but not without turning on his heel, heading for the door, leaving.

SHARE

Rosier had fallen asleep in one of the lounges apparently, had accidentally drank too much after promising Asmodeus he'd have no more than a few sips. Drunkenness hadn't overcome him, no, no, but he'd had enough for drowsiness to befall his horn-heavy head, then he had slumped against the duke of lust. According to what Asmodeus recounted to Baal, the lust demon had initially made every attempt to carry Rosier back to the room, but he had a weak left arm and significantly decayed right leg, so even if he could carry the fruit demon with one hand, he was unable to since it was occupied with one of his canes. Really — he said to Baal — he needed both canes today but had been stubborn in the morning despite Rosier's worried pestering.

Rosier had woken up sad today, Asmodeus also said. The demon of fruit — or love or whatever it might be that he was — had stirred awake with a frown and faced away from Asmodeus most of the morning. He had mumbled his words and wiped excessively at his eyes when he didn't think the duke was looking.

When Baal arrived at the lounge, saw the sleeping Rosier on his side over the divan, he appropriately noticed a touch of grief over the furrowed brows and parted lips of his old friend, then nodded. He replied to Asmodeus, hovering at his left, "Yes, I'll carry him — but what has him so upset?" Baal shuffled closer, not thinking much of the snickers from the other demons in the room, before he enveloped the fruit demon in his arms.

Asmodeus joked dryly, "It could have been the smell of semen in the kitchens yesterday," to which Baal laughed, before the lustful one said, more seriously: "Actually, this is just the way that he is. Some days all he seems to want to do is cry."

Baal lifted Rosier carefully, then held his limp body against his front. "Huh. Do you ever ask him what he's crying about?"

Stiffly, the other demon replied, "He doesn't want to tell me."

"Maybe he's sad about you then," Baal laughed good-naturedly, completely missing how Asmodeus' face twitched, before beginning to head toward the way he'd come in. He stepped out into the wide corridors, glancing down and realizing that Rosier was rather light. "When Lucifer doesn't want to tell me what he's angry about, it's usually because I'm what he's mad at." Twisting his head back, Baal checked if Asmodeus was following, which proved unnecessary because the thudding sound of Asmodeus' cane was loud and constant. He did, however, get to witness how Asmodeus scoffed with a toss of his head. "What?"

"I think I've only seen Rosier mad a handful of times in millions of years. Don't bother comparing him to Satan. They're too different. Satan is evil; Rosier is kind."

Baal slowed his steps so that the two could walk beside one another down the hall, then muttered, "Lucifer is kind too."

"In your delusions, perhaps."

Breathing in, out — Baal decided to shift his hold on Rosier and continue on their way without a word. He'd had this debate with Asmodeus multiple times in the past. The duke of lust claimed that Lucifer was a wicked beast, Baal would argue, then the two would bicker over it for hours. Certainly, Baal didn't imagine himself to be any expert on relationships, but he always thought that the least Asmodeus could do was show some respect, if not veneration, toward their king, their god, their devil who'd led them to freedom. 'If it weren't for Lucifer's kindness,' Baal wanted to snap, 'you would still be in Heaven, unable to do anything about your lust, idiot.' But he refrained. It was the only thing Baal couldn't stand: any word against his beloved Lucifer. 'It's no delusion that Lucifer is the one who is good, or else he wouldn't have encouraged Rosier to rebuild you. You should be kissing his feet.'

The two arrived at the proper chambers, and Baal went on ahead to gently lower Rosier's body onto a large, feather-filled mattress. As he did, Baal saw how Rosier's choppy hair splayed over a pillow and his head lolled to the side, his face no longer as melancholic as it'd seemed minutes ago. Over his body, he wore a red robe that was too large on him, tied at the back to keep from sweeping any further than the chains at his ankles. The fallen angel of flight stared, listening to the thump of the door being shut, Asmodeus cursing, crossing the room toward his smoking pipe. Rosier was beautiful; of course, Baal had noticed this in the past, but he still found himself lifting his fingers, sweeping at some of the fruit demon's fringe now.

"Well, thank you," Asmodeus grunted as he worked with some flint to light his pipe. "I'll tell Rosier that you carried him back, and I'm sure he'll want to make you a pie in return. You can leave us now, though." Turning his head, the duke of lust suddenly paused, eyeing the way Baal was looming over his lover. "Please do, in fact."

Baal took some of the bed coverings and tugged them over Rosier's lower half, then curiously asked, "You fuck him, right?" Asmodeus didn't reply, but Baal supposed that was an affirmation. "Is he any good?" His mind was wandering, imagining. He even allowed Asmodeus to be in the fantasy, thinking of the duke of lust over Rosier's back, kissing his hair, rutting into him deeply. Baal was more than familiar with the sort of noises Asmodeus made during sex, even found them quite attractive — he found Asmodeus very attractive in general, liked fucking him or fucking something *with* him, and he liked how depraved and rough Asmodeus was, sincerely admired it — but he couldn't fathom how Rosier might be like in bed. 'Shy maybe?' That made the most sense, but Rosier had always been rather relaxed with Asmodeus in Heaven. They had teased one another constantly. 'Maybe he's more playful...?'

"What do you mean about him being good?" Asmodeus' voice was tight.

"How he feels, how he acts." Baal settled down on the edge of the bedding, which creaked under his weight, still looking at Rosier. "I'm curious. Do you think he'd let me? We're friends, after all." He'd accidentally half-roused himself between his legs already, his mind swept up imagining Rosier bent over or on his back or held up by Baal's arms like he'd been just a moment ago but this time with Baal fucking up into his heat. 'I'm just curious. I want to know what his cries of pleasure might be like.'

"He wouldn't want to."

Baal laughed. "You sound so certain." He finally turned his gaze toward Asmodeus again, only to meet the duke suddenly standing at his side, his jaw clenched, eyes wide, deadly. Asmodeus' pipe and cane had been abandoned by the hearth, and he'd somehow moved so silently that the chief duke of the demons startled in confusion. Wasn't Asmodeus having trouble walking? "What is it?" he prodded.

"Rosier wouldn't want to fuck you. You should go."

Quirking a brow, Baal began to make some sense of things, then he snickered lowly. "What's wrong with you? All I did was ask if he's a nice fuck. Don't tell me you're possessive."

"I think that you should leave."

"Can't I wait until he wakes up to ask?" Baal felt his eyes narrow. "You've fucked everyone in the caves, but you won't let me fuck Rosier? When did you become such a hypocrite?"

"I don't give a shit what you think." Asmodeus leaned down to Baal's level, then hissed, "I told you to get your stupid fucking face out of here. Don't touch him ever again. Don't come in here ever again. Don't ever say that to me or to him. He has no interest in you. He will never want you."

"Even Lucifer," Baal snarled. "You've even fucked Lucifer in front of me, and I've never told you that you couldn't, even if he's the one I love most." Sharply, he stood, forcing Asmodeus to back away a step. The duke of lust was taller, but it was Baal who had all the strength, so he didn't mind tipping his head up at him, catching how all of Asmodeus' body parts appeared to tremble with the effort of remaining upright and unified. "What the fuck is wrong with you? I've never seen you like this. You're not willing to share *our* friend?"

A little noise sounded beneath the two, and Asmodeus and Baal turned to see Rosier shifting, reaching to rub at his face with one hand. Uneasily, the fruit demon rose to sit and called, "Baal? Asmodeus?"

Baal hardly got a syllable out of his mouth before Asmodeus interjected: "He was just leaving."

And the fallen angel of flight flickered his gaze to the hardened expression of the lust demon before surrendering, shrugging, and stepping away from the bed. With an awkward wave, he bid farewell to Rosier solely, then went for the door. The demon of love called after him with a soft goodbye, but as Baal shuffled out, he heard Asmodeus ask Rosier if he'd heard them. "No," Rosier whispered. "No, I didn't hear anything." Baal didn't believe that, and he was certain Asmodeus didn't either.

EDEN MEMORIES

The devil was upset.

Baal realized it as he was rocking his hips, sliding into Satan, almost pulling back into the cold air each time but never doing so, never daring to escape the heat of God's most beautiful, favored angel. His face was pressed to the warm throat his teeth scraped against, dragging his impossibly long tongue up to Satan's ear — but the devil was quiet. He didn't taunt Baal, or snarl at him, or even moan in a moment of pleasure left unrestrained. He dragged his nails down the larger demon's back, painfully slow — though the sting only made Baal grunt out in greater need, like those sweet hands had instead wrapped themselves around his pulsing, hardened sin. Sin, eager to drip.

Even still, he wanted to ask what was wrong. Satan hadn't even ordered Baal to make him finish first, to worship his body by bringing it to its shaking, moaning end. There was silence beneath Baal, just some breaths, harsh and quick, just the thump of their bed against the cave walls of the devil's chambers.

"May I?" Baal asked, but he received no answer, and he grimaced, heart lodging in his throat in worry, as he continued, brought himself to the very end of his desire, the tip. One hand gripping the sheets by Lucifer's head, he lifted himself, brought his face above the devil's own to see dazed eyes. It was pure pain to look at him, pure agony to stand before such beauty, but Baal loved the burn. He spilled in a handful of stabs forward, crying out and nearly collapsing as release was wrung out of him harshly. Baal could have stayed inside forever, but he pulled himself free quickly, trailing seed. He'd hoped to place his lips and tongue on Satan, to watch and listen to the devil's wonderful cries, except the golden-haired fallen angel turned onto his side. Staring at the wall, his demeanor so distant that he must've left Baal many minutes ago — Satan was silent. "Lucifer?" left the duke's mouth as he panted, high-pitched and needy, for breath.

"Satan," corrected Satan, quietly.

"Satan." Baal inched toward him on the bed, then listened to a hiss, his eyes flickering upward to catch a great serpent creeping along the headboard. "Did you... visit Eden today?"

"I saw God, between the trees. I was speaking to the woman, but then she turned away from me to go after her man, and I saw God." His voice was delicately soft, like a wing's feathers. "He looked the same as I remembered."

Slow, Baal exhaled through his nose, wanting to touch his friend's back, but he felt that Satan would react badly to it, so he restrained, instead looking away and toward a few cloths folded by their basin of water, for hand or face washing. "Do you think He saw you?" For once, Baal knew it was a ridiculous question, even a stupid one; their old God was supposed to be omniscient.

Yet, Satan didn't chide him. "He looked at me. His eyes were dark. His hands were together and twiddling with a leaf. I remember how I used to sing for Him. I always wanted Him to put His hand on me. He was always angry at me. I was perfect but not perfect enough. I was not God, but He wanted me to be and also punished me when I tried. God, God, God. The Father." His voice was cooing, almost as if a lullaby. "In Eden, I think I hear it. An echo. My own voice, coming back to me. The psalms I used to sing for Him." Baal crawled toward the edge of the bed, moved onto his feet, then took some steps toward the basin. "I watched the woman run over a bed of flowers, crushing the lilies beneath her feet. I watched God pick one up, and I thought He'd extend it to me. Then, I thought little angel Lucifer would step out from some trees and take it, get on the tips of his toes to try and kiss his Father on the cheek."

Baal took one of the cloths, dipping it into the water, then twisting and pulling at its ends with both hands to wring out the excess.

"But then God left me. I was surprised. I thought He'd at least speak to me. I could hear my singing all around us. Maybe He has no interest in who I've become, and He is only interested in the memory of me." Satan rolled onto his back, staring at the ceiling. "The memories of then feel like dreams." He twitched once Baal had returned to his side, then pressed the cold cloth to one of his thighs, dragging it, picking up the beads of white, white like lilies. "Baal."

"Satan."

"I want to kill them both. The man, the woman."

Cleaning him as gently as he could, the demon duke replied carefully: "If God hasn't stopped you, then maybe He's tempting you to do it." 'Setting traps, looking for reasons to scream at and punish His child.' The devil's eyes had fallen shut. "Please, be careful." Baal wanted to go with Lucifer, protect him, save him from God if needed, no matter the cost. He couldn't be damned twice, could he? And if Baal were to be destroyed, wouldn't it be nice to have the last thing he sees be Satan safe, happy?

"I loved first," Satan said, stiffer. "I did it first. The man and woman can't love, can't *sin*, how I have. God made them to insult me." Baal continued stroking the cloth over warm skin, then pulled it away, seeing no more barren seed, and he heard his friend's anger give way to something else. "They don't know," he added in a whisper, quiet and miserable, "the man and woman, they don't know what God's paradise is, *whose* paradise it is." Baal was ready to judge that Satan was perhaps, rightfully, jealous; the angels had been forbidden the love that joined them, that passed between lips, while their Father offered it to His new animal creations like it was His own invention. "If only they knew. If only... they knew."

"They don't know anything," Baal offered. "They don't know good the same way that they don't know evil." He set the dirtied cloth on a nearby counter, then adjusted himself on the bed, staring at the devil and his opening eyes — dual sunrises. "Before you corrupted me, I knew nothing. I needed to sin to see where I was and what I was." He remembered how the area between his legs hadn't existed in his mind before the moment angel Lucifer fell to his knees and placed his pretty lips around him. It was like waking up, it was like seeing he was naked after an eternity of blindness.

"Only sin," Satan answered, "can save us from God."

ACHE

Satan dipped the chopped fat remnants of a auroch into the heated, but not boiling, water, then he covered the clay pot with its lid, and he said, "It will take some time to cook, but once it's finished, I'll use the cloth here to strain the meat so that we're left with only the liquid. It will cool over; the oil and the water will separate. We'll discard the water, and then we'll have tallow, which you may use half of to clean yourself and the other half to cook with." He didn't turn to see if Eve was still listening. "If Adam asks, you should tell him that you came to this finding on your own." As expected, the woman shifted in the raised mat that she rested in; as always, mention of her beloved, horrible man was quick to catch her attention.

"He won't believe me." Her voice was a weak whisper, as it had been for weeks now. "He'll say that he knows you came by."

Satan dusted his robe off, then rose to his feet, away from the stone grate below the pot, above the flaming pit. "He'll have to make peace with that." Slowly, he tilted his face to the side, finally seeing Eve, laying on her back, a hand over her grown belly, hair over her naked chest. Below her navel, she wore nothing as well. The nudity was a result of Satan having helped wash her earlier, though she'd long dried now, and she'd asked if she could remain bare for a moment. 'I feel,' she had mumbled, 'no shame. I can't say why. With you, there is no shame. Like you're the innocence of Eden, Satan.' The devil hadn't known what to say to that, so he'd remained silent, brought her to bed. "How do you feel? Are you still in pain?"

"It's migrated," she answered, eyes on the straw ceiling of the hut. "It was on my lower back, now it's here." Eve's hand trailed down her stomach to the lower end of it, right against her pelvis. "It aches."

Lucifer nodded, took a few steps, then settled at the edge of her mat. He reached, grabbed the striped animal skin by her body, then held it with both hands, picking at the ends. "Forgive me. I thought the washing would've helped." His words were delicate. "There is a flower that the demons use for pain; I can bring it to you the next time that I come by. I'm sure Adam will return soon." Eve turned to rest her cheek on the mat, and her lips twitched as Satan pulled the animal skin over her figure.

"Before he put himself in me," Eve said, "I never felt pain below my stomach."

Satan said, "It is God's punishment, but if it's any consolation, it is also just the nature of it — fucking. It comes with some pain. Even the animals feel it."

"Always?"

"No, not always, but the first time, it does. And you never feel quite the same afterward."

Eve was being as gentle today as Lucifer was, and she snaked a hand out of her new covering to touch the devil's fingers. Eyebrows lifted a pinch, lips parting — there was some relief on her face, not as if Satan had told her something she didn't know, rather like he'd confirmed something she felt. "It doesn't feel so terrible always, but the first time, yes. I hated it. I never would have done it again if he hadn't forced it."

"I can't name many demons who had a pleasant experience their first time either. Don't imagine your pain a lonely feeling."

"How was the first time that you did it?"

"Oh, it was awful." As soon as Satan said it with a touch of humor, Eve laughed softly, and he interlaced his fingers with hers. "It was— For me, it was forced as well." It was the only time he'd ever said it to anyone, and yet the confession came naturally, easily.

Eve shut her eyes like she might sleep; in a few minutes, she would. "Did it hurt?"

"I was certain that I would die," said Satan, his voice quiet, "from it. And though I survived, or some of me did, I couldn't speak a word of what happened to me to anyone. I didn't have the language for it. I thought that they wouldn't understand."

"Adam doesn't understand," Eve said.

"And he never will." Satan reached to push some of the dark hair away from her sullen face. "Don't bother with his thoughts. You will never find happiness there. I wasted a life looking for love in a God and an angel who had none to give." Hesitantly — "I wake up with the pain at times. It lingers on me, and it's heavy, like a body over my own. It may never leave you, even if you abandon him. After it happened to me, I couldn't return to Eden either. I was banished."

"Neither of us can ever return," said Eve wistfully, squeezing Lucifer's hand. "But there is some beauty here in the wilderness; I can see it now. Once I'm well again, I would like to learn to handle the meats and the fruits like you do. I want to hear the songs of the birds, knowing that they won't heed my word like they did in God's garden, knowing that I'm not their master. I want to run and watch the sun rise and fall. I'm beginning to feel that we always belonged here."

"Earth is a frightening place, but it is true."

"Forgive me, Lucifer, for not speaking to you all that time after Adam and I were cast out. I know that you are not wicked, even if Adam insists." Yet, Eve must know, as Lucifer did, that she would return to accusing the devil of evil the second that her husband returned. "Forgive me." Satan whispered that she had nothing to apologize for. "I don't blame you for it, for any of it. I wish that I did."

"Sleep, Eve."

FOOD

On a too-warm winter day, Lucifer halted his yelling — chillingly abrupt — but only because Cain had wandered into the throne room. In the midst of snarling down at the demon Ishtar for causing a rockslide that blocked one of the most favorable entrances into the demons' abode, the devil had suddenly frozen while Ishtar was still flinching. All the audience turned their heads quick to where Satan's eyes were directed, and then they chortled, snickered to one another, many covering their mouths to try and obscure their deep amusement at their king and their king's human child stepping in, climbing down the tall stairs slowly. He had to get on one knee for each step, sometimes his stumpy legs getting tangled in the long, embroidered tunic on him that was in the distinct demon style, perhaps made by Satan himself.

Ishtar, too, laughed, then smirked up at the devil just as the king was saying, "I see we have a visitor."

"He must've," said one duke of the four by Satan's side, "escaped Baal."

Asmodeus chuckled; he was at the devil's left. "Should one of us go for him?" He was nodding his head at little Cain. "He's going to fall and break his neck."

"You stay where you are," Satan said, "or else you'll be the one with a snapped neck." The other dukes sneered while Asmodeus' lip twitched. And Lucifer stood, slowly, in his purple robe that fell diagonally across his chest, exposing the left side of it, and a heavy fur coat; on his head, a great, golden cornet that was nearly the same color as his hair was settled. His jewelry shone the reflected light of nearby torches and rattled as he began walking toward the steps that led down to the flat space between the throne-theater and seats. Ishtar had been standing here, but he hurriedly made his way to some corner to avoid touching the king of the demons without permission.

The little child stopped at the final step, turned up his head, mane of curls bouncing.

"Cain," sighed Lucifer, reaching him, then leaning downward to scoop the boy into his arms. To the other demons, the gentle and sweet voice of their god was not unusual; Satan often spoke like this when he was soothing you or offering you something you couldn't refuse. It was always a delight to hear it, even for those whose feelings toward Lucifer were more fear than adoration — though there was not a single demon that truly disliked the devil. How could there be? The devil was so pretty, so patient, so tender with his touches. "Cain, Cain, Cain," he cooed, lifting the child to sit him on his hip. "How did you get here?"

Smiling brighter, the boy answered, "Baal was talking, and I was hungry."

"Mm," Lucifer hummed. "How hungry?"

"Very, very, hungry." Cain brought his hands to Lucifer's robe as he spoke, gripping and balling his fists in the fabric, then pulling it as if to test his strength.

Satan hesitated, but he soon breathed slow, then looked at his dukes and called, "Please decide on this trial for me. I must feed the child." *Child* was one of Lucifer's words — something between infantile and mature; Satan had been a child once, though his body hadn't changed in the transition. "Stay still, Cain," he said quietly, ignoring the amusement and murmurs from the demons that he passed on the way to the exit. There were times when Lucifer enjoyed the attention, but Cain's stomach was beginning the rumble against him, and humans were mere animals. They ate from need, not want. He needed the boy fed or risk him dying of starvation — at least, that is how he understood it. Could a human die? Had God been honest when expelling Cain's parents from Eden?

Stepping past the golden doorway, opened wide for him by guards, Lucifer saw the fallen angel of flight, a great demon of impressive size and beast wings presently tucked beneath his skin. He was scampering, skidding, hurrying and nearly crashing into the devil; his face was flushed, his mouth was gasping. He was stammering, "Lucifer—" with unadulterated panic in his wide eyes and even wobbling mouth. "Forgive me— I was discussing a few things with another duke, then I looked down, and Cain was gone—"

"Baal," Lucifer interjected simply, his face pure stone, shifting his weight, then readjusting the giddy Cain on his hip, who'd brought a thumb to his mouth; he was far too old to be doing that, but the devil had no point of reference.

"Yes?" Baal replied, almost whispered.

"Be good and have some lamb grilled for Cain." Satan began walking again, pressing Cain against him a little closer before sidestepping the demon duke Baal. "And see if there are any berries left for him. If not, some honeyed dates will do." He heard Baal stammer that he would do that, absolutely, he would go and do that — as well as worriedly offer the devil another apology. Satan said nothing, noticing a few demons in the corridors, one of which wiggled his fingers at the little boy, who flapped his hand back at him. It was after the two moved past them that Cain tilted his face back to Lucifer.

"Are you angry?" His voice was quieter, a tinge of fear on it.

"I'm never angry," Lucifer replied, then looked down at him. "But I might be if you wander away from Baal again. I've told you not to. Should I tell you again?" Shaking his head, Cain's gaze fell to the floor, the ends of his lips similarly coming down. "Lift your chin. You're in the arms of the king of the damned, Cain. You should have some pride."

Idly, Cain kicked his feet and chattered, "I don't like it when you're angry."

"I said I'm not."

"But what if you are?"

It was useless to argue, so Lucifer decided not to. Instead, he stopped a few steps away from the guards outside his chambers, both of which waved at the little human as Satan set him down on the ground, then dusted off his tunic and picked a leaf off his curls. "Come." The devil showed his palm, and Cain took it, his hand tiny in such a deadly, delicate hold. "Serve some water for yourself, and for Baal and me, so we can all eat." After the boy nodded, Satan turned his face back to the guards, gesturing with his free hand for them to part the ornate, heavy golden doors for them. They, afterwards, waited until their king and his child were far inside before releasing their hold and allowing the entrance to thump and click shut.

Immediately, Cain pulled away from Satan and hurried to the corner of the room where Satan always kept a jug of water, only to remember he'd need cups, which then prompted the boy to scurry to the tall stone shelving where the plates and chalices were. He rose to the tips of his toes to snatch three glasses by the neck.

"Be careful," Lucifer warned, shrugging off his fur coat that it was far too warm today to wear, holding it at his elbows, before he stepped toward the sofa at the center of the living area. He draped it over a cushion, leaving himself in his robe and thin, sheer tunic, before adjusting his earrings with a slow sigh. He would have to do something, surely, soon to Ishtar to not appear as if he'd grown soft about punishments due to Cain's presence. Demons loved Satan, but they shouldn't love him without an undercurrent of fear; the devil must be like God, after all.

Cain insisted, "I'm careful!" He marched back to the water,

planted the glasses on the ground, arranged them in a neat line, then reached for the jug, lifted it with both hands, holding it against his front for support. The little boy's face twisted in concentration, but slowly, he dipped the container, water dribbling then pouring into the first chalice. As he moved to the second, he spilled some water in between, his face wincing again; this time, there was a flicker of terror. But Lucifer didn't shout or strike at him, so Cain's flinch met no pain, and the boy continued anxiously, filling the three drinks.

Satan hadn't realized he was staring. Turning away, his hands went for his crown, removing it slow, steady, before he set it on a cushion over a stone podium by the entrance. He didn't often hold the crown here, but he was, occasionally, overwhelmed by sloth to set it anywhere else. Satan crossed the room next, moving past an archway to another room of his chambers, where there was a circular stone table, blanketed by a red cloth, low over the carpeted ground. Around its circumference, there were a few cushions, all embroidered in gold. The devil moved toward one, settling down onto it elegantly and breathing slow beneath the light of a candled chandelier above. Somehow, it was still burning, had been since only a little past dawn.

The child brought only two chalices with him, setting one down before Lucifer and saying, "For you." Then, he put down a chalice right nearby. "For Ba— Baal." He always did struggle with Baal's name. "Let me get mine." Just as he hurried away, Lucifer listened to the distinct creaking of the entrance, then Cain's muffled voice from the living area. "Food!"

Baal's laughter followed. "Your favorite. Where's Luci? Is he at the table?"

"Yes!"

"Perfect, and hey, don't drop that glass. Go sit. I'll bring the food to you."

Spilling a little water again, this time from his own drink, the young boy returned to Satan, dropping on a cushion at the other side of the table, bearing a great grin that he directed at the demon stepping in through the archway. Lucifer stared at his nails, hearing Baal's heavy steps and the sizzle of the platter that he lowered onto the table: cuts of goat still smoking, slices of flatbread seasoned with garlic, and a clay bowl of a starkly orange-red sauce.

"Lucifer," Baal called quietly, "I hope you're not angry." Cain and Baal were so similar, at times.

"I'm never angry," Lucifer replied, flickering his gaze up to the excited child grabbing the bread, dipping it into the sauce, then grabbing the cuts of lamb to layer them on. Bringing it all to his mouth, a famished, delighted moan escaped around his chewing. Satan finally looked over to see Baal settling in beside him, still staring at Lucifer warily. "But do keep a more watchful eye over Cain."

"Yes," Baal promised, nodding far too much. "I will."

"Eat," Lucifer reassured Baal, and the other demon's visible relief bloomed into a smile. Before Satan, Baal grabbed a piece of bread and began serving himself, though using the ladle in the sauce, rather than dipping it like the little boy with them. The devil's child, some said. 'Our child,' Baal sometimes said. Carefully, Lucifer reached to commence eating, as well. He wanted to remind Baal that Cain should return home soon, perhaps even tomorrow. The interruption of Ishtar's trial, surely, was a sign that the boy needed to be with his family, not among demons arguing about destruction and fucking.

Baal teased Cain for the way the boy had to get on his knees to reach the bread, and then teased him about how they should go out and have Cain reach for the highest fruits, so he might grow taller. Cain groaned, saying he wanted to fly instead. Baal said Cain shouldn't worry; hopefully, he'd grow wings soon.

Lucifer knew the wingless Adam and Eve well, wondered why God had made man from primates rather than any of the doves or finches that circled the sky above the plains. Perhaps, He feared humans in flight, feared they too would try and rise above Him one day. They were such mortal, delicate things — humans.

Lucifer watched the little boy take his chalice with both hands, bringing it up to his mouth, some droplets escaping to dampen his tunic's collar. And God, too, had certainly learned now that an infinite life was quite the dangerous gift to offer. If humans were to live forever, they might one day bore, might one day grow resentful. He had hidden the Tree of Life far from Adam and Eve in Eden, had distracted them with Knowledge. Eve — Lucifer should speak with her soon. Perhaps, she wouldn't scream at him again. At times, she was so much like Adam.

Chirpily, Cain said he hoped his wings would be as great as Baal's.

Satan tried to smother it, but he could remember quite vividly the day Baal had been there to tease out his own royal violet wings. It was strange to see a little creature just like you, but so much younger, to want them to experience life how you once did. Licking his fingers of sauce, Lucifer felt a horrible tug of nostalgia. Though he'd never been small, he had been young once, and Baal had been there during that time, had been one of the first to comfort that little Lucifer that Satan could hardly recognize. How had he ever been that Lucifer? It must've never happened, must've been a founding myth for why the devil found himself in this cave with a demon of flight and a round-cheeked child, both smiling, both joyous, lovingly thoughtless. Satan knew Baal must dream of those times too, of ushering out wings on a young creature and teaching them to fly. He must dream of Cain as an infant angel, rather than a cursed animal.

Baal turned to Lucifer now, raised a brow. "Do you want me to save some bread for you? Cain and I are eating quickly. I don't want you to be left hungry."

"Yes," Lucifer said, then leaned in, pressed his lips to Baal's mouth in a peck. "Thank you." In an instant, the burly demon's face tinted red, his eyes rounding, while Cain gnawed at a tougher piece of meat like a wolf. Lucifer's heart warmed at the sight of the two — Cain and Baal — and then he scolded himself for his joy. The devil ought to know better.

TO HOLD

It was horribly, painfully wonderful to hold Cain, to cradle him. Lucifer could not make peace with it. Never did he find solace with how right it felt for the little boy to rest against his front. Currently, the king of the damned was in a chair, staring at the hearth, at each twirl of flame over darkening wood, feeling his fingers run through the dark curls of an eight-year-old Cain. He was settled over Satan's lap, cheek pressed to his chest, mouth open in a coarse snore. An hour ago, he'd been rambling, telling Lucifer about every little thing he encountered the two days he was lost in the forest. "Be careful," Lucifer had scolded, "walking between the trees alone for so long."

"I know, I know," Cain had sighed, then continued detailing the insects he'd come across.

Earlier that day, at sunset, a bird had informed Satan that Cain disappeared into the forest long after he'd wandered away from his parents. Lucifer, instantly, dropped the stone tablet he'd been reading through, hearing it thud against the ground — the sound faraway, like he was hearing it from around a corner. Turning back, slow, to face the plump, round finch perched by the entrance into his chambers. Lucifer's golden hair cascaded as wavy tassels down his back, over the tunic that was so long and wispy that it was much more like a gown. For once, he wore little jewelry, had been about to put it on. Lucifer blinked, only then realizing what he'd heard and that there was no breath in his lungs.

"Help me," the devil ordered, hastily, reaching for a pale robe hanging from the edge of a wardrobe, pulling it on. If he were of sound mind, he would've sent a battalion of demons to find the human boy. But Lucifer's erratic heart had risen to his throat, his mouth, behind his eyes. The feeling was ancient in him, like a fossil unearthed. It was a young, too — in the sense that he hadn't felt this emotion since the youthful fruit-carrying days of the purposeless angel he'd once been. Lucifer couldn't remember the last time he'd panicked, though there were times that he remembered very little in general. As he sprinted out from the caves, ignoring each curious demon, however — the image of the boy was perfectly vivid in his mind.

Unfortunately, Satan could also imagine in great detail that young Cain fallen in a ditch or mangled by an unassuming animal. Dead, made into food for either a creature or the soil. Shoving branches out of his way, sinking as deep as he could into the forest, Satan hissed at every living thing to find the child, his child. He had been gone for too long in the forest. He would be hungry by now. He would be thirsty. In growing hysterics, Satan reeled in quick gasps that felt hollow, void of any tangible breath. He hunted for any hint of the little boy's frayed tunic or tiny footprints or the dark curls on his head. Eventually, Lucifer did catch a glimmer of something, a trail of broken twigs, then some urgent bird calls pointed him in the right direction

Stepping between some trees, feeling moonlight cast an ethereal glow on him, Lucifer finally discovered a child curled into himself at the roots of a tree. "Cain...?" Leaves were freckled all throughout them both.

"Luci..?" Against a trunk — the little boy raised his head, then rubbed an eye with a fist. Features sunken, wrist and ankles thin. He was malnourished, but he was alive. "I was lost..." His toothy smile was weak.

"Cain," Lucifer whispered. "Come. Come home with me. Let me help you up. I'll bring you back, tuck you in, and have something prepared for you to eat." He stumbled over, wrapped his arms around the child, held him for a moment. Cain was tiny against the greatest angel there was, even if he was fallen now. "Let me take care of you."

In the present: Satan sighed, then looked down at the boy sleeping against him. It felt nice. He was wonderful — Cain was. Lucifer could nuzzle his face against the young boy's curls forever. Even still, he hadn't anticipated how much it'd affect him to hear that Cain was missing, possibly hurt, potentially dead. Lucifer's heart had stopped; he hadn't realized it still beat. Grimacing, the devil shut his eyes, propped his chin over the boy's head. What did these feelings mean? Should Lucifer allow himself to make sense of it? No. He already knew.

"You've been," Baal had said the night before, "different." He'd still been naked, standing near the table by the entrance into the bedroom, pouring himself a glass.

Satan had been in bed, still naked as well, laying on his side. With one hand, he twirled a strand of his hair; his gaze was on a wall, distant, pensive. "I don't know," he'd said just as the sound of Baal gulping down liquor echoed in his ears, "what you mean." It was a lie. Blinking, he glanced down at his own body, where the warm brown was still flushed, where sweat still beaded. Where he was still dripping. He should wash before it dries.

"It's hard to say," Baal responded, taking one step, then crossing the room back toward their bed. "I suppose... kinder." His eyes were softening, and as he stopped right beside the mattress, he lifted his drink to his mouth once more. "Delicate. You've been so sweet." Satan had fought so much with Baal before Cain, and now he sparingly raised his voice at him.

"You irritate me," Lucifer said flatly, but he didn't shift away once Baal settled to sit behind him. When the great duke took the devil's chin, Lucifer even parted his lips, fluttered his eyes shut at the first touch of the cool glass. Obediently, he drank, the wine scorching its way past his throat, to his belly. "Mm." They both knew, of course, why everything was so different, why Lucifer didn't immediately open his eyes once the drink was pulled away. Humming again, he accepted Baal's mouth on his, moving his lips carefully, untangling his hand from his own hair to tug at Baal's. Curls. Like Cain's curls. Or perhaps like Michael's curls.

"I like this," said the duke against him. "I like how you've been ever since we've had Cain." He nuzzled him. "I almost wish that we... could..."

Laying down, Lucifer tugged Baal on top, kissed him even more, sweetly, gently. It was oddly innocent, but not at all chaste. He'd latched onto him, legs coming around the duke's waist. Soft, he'd asked to be loved again.

Cain stirred now in his arms, muttering without sense; he was dreaming. Satan didn't dream often anymore, just of fountains and daisies and the secret garden he'd spent a youth in, wrestling a handsome angel who would never turn against his Father for him. Along three walls of Satan's chambers, there was a mural that he'd painted himself. It was simple, just flowers and trees, but memories of that place, that time. The little human boy, once, asked what the daisies meant. Satan said they meant loss, forgetting.

It was one of the few times he gave Cain such a straightforward answer to one of his incessant question. But the devil didn't mind; he loved, in fact, to feel Cain tug on his tunic while he was in the halls, to look down and see a beaming, curious little face. He didn't mind telling Cain about Heaven. If Lucifer could spend an eternity doing anything, it'd certainly be sitting with the little boy in a meadow, telling him every secret of every flower.

Soon, Baal would be home from his day-long hunt. The devil will let the three of them pretend for a few days, then he will force himself to remember that Cain has parents and that he is a human that will die. One day, Lucifer will search for him and not find him safe. He will find a corpse. One day, it will all be over. Again, Cain stirred against him. He was still breathing. And it was one of those times that Lucifer really understood the depths of God's cruelty, to gift him a sweet child that he could not have.

With a trembling breath, Lucifer took Cain into his arms and began climbing onto his feet so they could warm up in bed. Baal would be home soon. The three of them would be safe beneath the covers from death and from God. Tomorrow, there would be a trial, and Satan would have to ask Rosier to look after Cain for a few hours. That would be no bother. Rosier loved Cain and had taught him about every fruit there was.

Lucifer may have loved Cain, too — if the devil still loves.

A SHORT LIFE

Ara was certain Satan will do something worse than kill him.

He'd already been imagining his own torture, imagined it the second Cain kissed him for the first time. Cain had done it by cupping Ara's face with calloused, rough hands, then pressing their mouths firmly together, some prickling on his chin and jaw scratching against a smooth, demonic face. Ara had lifted his fingers, touched the hints of facial hair curiously, almost jealousy. He liked how this man looked, the first growing man.

But Ara ought to know better. He'd always kept his distance from the devil, chosen to wander the Earth following whatever packs of demons had an adventurous spirit out on the land rather than those living in the dull caves. He loved his freedom. In Heaven, his talents had turned into bindings at his wrists. He was always being asked to bake for others, even when he didn't want to. He knew that his purpose laid in kitchens — but his heart was restless, wandering. He wished he could understand the stars. He wished he could sing better than all the others or that he could dance with the best sway of his hips. When he was traveling the Earth, he twirled around bonfires and the other demons cheered for him, though Ara often feared they were secretly laughing at him or just wanted to sleep with him. Even still, he was happy.

Many demons had chosen to remain committed to what they'd been good for in Heaven, but after falling, Ara chose to aspire to have no purpose at all. At last, he had nothing to do but live a short life of pleasure without committing to anything, anyone. Satan had lead them to freedom, from God and from themselves.

But here was Cain, sleeping soundly and naked — body covered in hair, his cock flaccid between his legs, one arm over his head, the other draped over Ara, who was seated against the headboard made of dark roots. 'Here I am with the devil's son.' It was still strange to wake up after sex without the urge to run as far as he could. He'd slept with thousands of demons throughout all the years since the fall, but it felt as if he could only remember the first time, the first sin in Heaven where an angel had plucked out his eyes, then assaulted him all the while Ara had tried to run away. How ironic it was that his attacker had asked for forgiveness and remained in Heaven while Ara demanded to be cast down. A long, clawed hand was working through the curls that tumbled down the neck of the human. It reminded Ara of Baal's hair or perhaps Michael's; he'd never known either of them well, though Baal far better than Michael.

"Hgh," grunted Cain, shifting, eyes beginning to flutter. "Ara...?"

Baal was well aware of their relationship. Cain said that he'd even encouraged it, perhaps hoping Cain would be fully incorporated into demonhood this way. But when the human began courting Ara, asking to spend time with him, offering the crops he'd grown and attempts at baked bread — Ara knew better than to involve himself. After accepting Cain's first kiss, he'd dreamt of taking off soon again, to join another band of traveling demons and see the stars from another side of the planet, dreaming of the abyss above he'd taken for granted once. And yet — here he was, turning his head at the human man smiling up at him, drowsily, then running a hand up the back of Ara, narrowly avoiding the two parallel slits where he'd once carried colorful wings. "Good morning," said Ara, realizing that he was dirty still. He should have cleaned himself while his man slept. And yet.

"Good morning," greeted Cain. "Lay down with me."

"If I stay in this room with you any longer, Satan will find us." But Ara said nothing when Cain lifted his body to sit, then brought his free hand to take Ara's chin. "He will hurt me."

"He won't," Cain replied, then pecked his lips. "I'll speak to him soon."

Ara knew already that he would be bound and beaten and clawed and gutted open by the beautiful devil, but he didn't know how to tell Cain that Satan was not the gentle, kind creature he thought he was. Recently, Ara had bowed his head for Lucifer in the corridors like any other, but he had felt a glare on his skin, something horribly knowing and hot with fury. 'Satan?' he'd asked softly, then flinched when Lucifer reached for him, tucked a loose strand of red hair behind his ear and told Ara to be careful where he stepped. He might tip a fragile column over, he might hurt someone. Ara knew well enough what his king meant by that.

It'd been curiosity that'd compelled Ara to lay on his back and be the first demon to take a human cock, but he didn't want Cain to be hurt. More than anything, he didn't want Cain to be hurt and to reckon with a furious devil. Realizing this, Ara also realized that maybe it wasn't mere curiosity that compelled him to continue taste Cain's mouth and taking his body.

'The caves are never stable,' Satan had warned. 'They may very well collapse on us one of these days, and you know that some recover better than others. Some may never recover at all. Be mindful of where you step.'

And yet, Ara didn't stop Cain when he nuzzled him, began gnawing lovingly at his neck. Instead, he laid his claws in the man's hair again, fiddling with the curls. He couldn't resist it. Every touch from Cain was so novel, so new, though he was a mere man. A mortal thing that was aging before his very eyes. Ara couldn't look away, wanted to see what a human could become — if they withered and rot like birds or like rodents. There was an urge in him to commit, to stay beside this man forever after so long spent wandering. Occasionally, the thought of Cain with another appeared in his mind, and he felt himself angrily frown, thinking that another demon would never hold Cain right, never bake for him well enough — after so long, Ara was beginning to feel like he should make pastries as he had in Heaven, now that he had a reason to — but there was too much in their short lives that said they ought not to attempt this love any longer.

Cain's hand had begun stroking; the last few times, he had become much more impatient when he wanted to fuck.

Ara knew that his life was short — God will damn him for the rebellion one day — and that so was Cain's. It would be better not to waste any time with this loving. But he leaned forward accept this man's tongue over his and to grind against his hand, to arch his back and beg. He will not commit. He will be punished if he does. Lucifer would hurt them; God would hurt them both. Ara knew that their lives were short and he would rather no love than a short love. 'But it's too late, isn't it? It's too late not to love you. And it is too late for you and for me.' Ara crawled onto him, wanting to feel a human inside again, pulsing and warm, to tighten around him in finish. Cain always called Ara addicting, but Ara felt the same for him, if not worse. He needed him. He could not commit his heart to Cain, not before God or the devil, but he could not live without Cain either.

Within a few weeks, Satan did indeed catch them, and he had Ara taken out to be beaten in the fields by a demon or two, then chained at the ankle to a tree in order to starve for eternity. The sky was so darkened by storm that Ara had no easy way to count how long he was held there, but he did know that the day he suffered through excruciating cramping in his lower belly and screeched in pain louder than he'd ever had was on a night of a full moon. It gleamed on his writhing self like a sadistic voyeur.

And, afterward, with an abomination of eyes and mouths and reddened skin melted on the dirt by Ara's legs, dawn had arrived gentler than it had for the first time in a week, no rain or thunder in a shadow around the sun. Ara buried the beast of a thing, as deep as he could manage to dig his hands into the ground, then he laid back against the bark until the hour finally came that Cain was let out of his own punishment and hurried to free him. Ara kissed him, though he knew their short lives should fracture away from each other at this moment or else they never would.

Ara never did tell Cain about what he'd suffered through beneath the full moon or what he'd buried; he never did tell anyone.

GOOD NEWS

Gabriel woke to a breeze, climbing in through the window and nuzzling up against his side like a pet; then, it tossed some waves of his hair adamantly before the angel cracked his eyes open. Overbearing pale light streamed in from the same window and from the dome of orange-yellow that caged the city of Heaven. As it trickled warmly onto his cheeks, Gabriel lifted his head, instantly missing the pillow that'd cradled his skull. Soon after, his hair fell to curtain over his face and onto his bare shoulders, revealed by the too-stretched collar of his tunic. He must've pulled at his clothes in his sleep. From the tunic's excessive thinness, he knew that it was his sleep attire, though he couldn't recall pulling it on; it was so thin that were he to stand before some light, anyone would be able to gaze at his naked body — its shape and some of its details. No freckles would shine through, but all the softness that God had molded for him would be perfectly visible. Once, there had been no shame in showing it.

Once, there had been bathhouses in Heaven. Gabriel had once felt angel hands in his hair, soaping each strand, and fingers massaging his limbs. He'd smiled up at those who spoiled him, and his eyes hadn't once wandered anywhere they shouldn't. And if they did, it meant nothing. A body had meant nothing once.

Gabriel was sitting but had yet to realize he wasn't in his own bedroom until the door opened with a creak, called his attention upward and to the other side of the square wooden room, rather simple except for the many vials and jars of tied herbs, as well as some incense smoking away on a table. And, too, there were some hanging plants by the low ceiling, leaves trailing down to rock idly above any angel's head. The bed itself was narrow, cramped into a corner with a few staffs leaned against the flowered head-board, nearly bonking Gabriel's hair. In the hand of the angel who'd stepped in, there was one such walking aid, this one curved at the tip, where nails scratched anxiously as a word trailed out of archangel Raphael's mouth.

"Gabriel—" his voice was soft, "—how are you? How did you sleep, brother?"

The youngest archangel remained where he was as Raphael made his way over, staggering a little and thumping his cane along the ground. "Raphael." And the memories returned home to his mind. "Oh. I'm here. I remain... here." Of course he did, knew it was stupid to believe he'd miraculously be anywhere other than where he'd been for what must've been days, weeks. How could he know how long for certain? Heaven had no setting sun, just the measure of a star setting elsewhere. 'Even before man was here, we were supposed to measure our lives to an Earth that was nothing but fire and rock for billions of years. God knows eternity. Before He'd made man, He already knew we should define ourselves on how they perceive their world.' His eyelids were heavy. 'And God knew what my decision would do.'

Raphael settled at the edge of the bed with a little grunt, setting his cane with all the others, then bringing a hand to one of his weak knees. "I considered bringing you to your home." He squeezed his joint, massaging it. "Should I tell you what's happening?"

"Please don't," said the angel of messages and news and information. "I don't want to know," said the angel of knowing. "I can't carry it with me. I can't bear what I've done."

"You've done nothing wrong."

"Don't sin," Gabriel begged, grimacing. "Don't lie to me."

And Raphael hesitated before he removed his hand from his leg, bringing it the waves of hair on the other prince, the edges of his eyes crinkling when Gabriel leaned into his touch. Tender, his smile — though it met Gabriel's frown. "Michael asked when you'll return to God."

"The Lord hasn't ordered it..." Gabriel murmured. "Do you think that if I never leave your bed again that God will send another angel to deliver His messages?"

"He would not replace you," Raphael insisted, then took his friend's cheek, rubbing his thumb against him. "Please, Gabriel, don't be so sad anymore. The humans act out of their own free will. The Lord said that to me. And the Watchers... Well, there's still plenty of time for them to return to Heaven and be forgiven." 'Time before what?' Gabriel didn't dare say. "Have a little faith. I know that I do— Their leader, Samyaza; he's very dear to me, as you know, and I know that he'll return to us. All this ill will pass."

Gabriel whispered, "I hope you don't mind if I stay here longer." He could still remember crying in Raphael's living area, apologizing for wasting his time, then choking up on his tears enough to make the older archangel usher him into bed, promising to find a way to mend him. He was the angel of healing, after all; he would patch up his heart, and he would coax a smile back on Gabriel's face.

"Stay here forever," Raphael laughed gently. "I won't mind. Though..." One of the many monuments along the road outside read that angels shouldn't share beds, shouldn't touch each other in bed, should not kiss each other in bed.

Gabriel flopped to lay on his back again, hair sprawling over the pillow like the roots of a tree. "May God forgive us," he sighed shakily. He shut his eyes, screwing them in frustration, and listened to the mattress creaking. "May He have mercy."

Raphael's lips brushed his forehead; once, that had meant nothing. He supposed it did still mean nothing. With Raphael, it was easy to feign that their Heaven hadn't changed, that war had never disfigured it. Wonderfully, Gabriel could even pretend to be a new archangel again, sitting with Raphael by a fountain and learning how he healed and what it seemed princes were responsible for. Uriel had largely ignored Gabriel even after the Lord anointed him as an archangel — perhaps still angry that his reign as a prince-tyrant had come to its end — but Raphael had held Gabriel's hand, laid a wing over him, tried to ease him into what authority could be.

Of course, Gabriel does later learn that he can be replaced, so very easily. God can send anyone in his place to deliver good news or apocalyptic prophecies. Though time will pass and a flood will drown his thoughts of being anything other than a prince, he comforts himself at times knowing at least the angels would not be happy with a replacement. Raphael would miss him. And its Gabriel's own fault that all the world is dead; God taught him a lesson about trying to judge human goodness as a mere angel; He is just being a Father who taught him what happens when you try to make your own decisions instead of being obedient. Gabriel waits, then. He settles back into Heaven and buries his doubt. He waits for some good news. For some kind of savior from all of this.

HOME IN HELL

"What's wrong, Rosier?"

The fallen angel of fruit furrowed his brows, stopping his hands and the cutting they did. He wasn't holding a peach or a plum, as he should be; instead, there was a roasted, still simmering, cut of lamb over a plate of rice that he was sawing to pieces with a large knife. Were he still an angel, he would have choked up and felt the burn of tears at his eyes, but his touch was accustomed now to killing and his mouth was perfectly familiarized with the taste of flesh. He used to pray — not to God — for this mundanity with wickedness to never come, but he'd stopped praying one day, without even realizing it. And he had accepted evil into his life and past the shape of his lips without realizing it until it was far too late. "Oh—"

At the other side of the table, the sitting Asmodeus swiped Rosier's plate and knife away before beginning to cut with an amused chuckle. "You're not very focused. What's on your mind, darling?"

Cheeks warmed, Rosier murmured, "You call me that too much." But a part of him was happy that Asmodeus was slicing the meat now for him. Often, Rosier liked to be the one who did things for his dear friend, but sometimes he didn't mind being pampered either.

"I like saying it." Asmodeus tilted his head at him, arching a brow. "You're not answering my question. What are you thinking about? Something's bothering you."

Rosier glanced to his right to the other demons seated at the long table, eating their own cuts of meat and bantering. Asmodeus and him had chosen this dining hall because Rosier had asked to go somewhere quieter, but now he wished they'd opted to eat in their room once he noticed some musicians beginning to strum their instruments nearby. 'But I'm hiding an angel in there.' Sighing some, Rosier replied, "Azazel saw us last night when we were..."

"Oh?" Asmodeus laughed again, but this time trying to smother a grin. "Well, I'm very sorry. That was probably my fault. I'm always loud when it comes to you."

Huffing, Rosier said, "It's not funny," but he didn't sound particularly angry. "We shouldn't have done that. Azazel was probably uncomfortable."

"Oh, Rosier, we were just kissing. I'm sure he's done much worse with his human." With another few drags of the knife over the plate, the demon duke of lust finished, then pushed the meal toward his beloved friend. "Eat and don't worry so much." With this, he also leaned over the table, then pecked Rosier's left horn; one of his arms was extended to the right, his talons gripping his cane firmly for support. "But I promise not to tease you again while he's still around." As he returned to his seat, Asmodeus grunted a little in pain.

And Rosier stared at his plate of food, cut neatly on one side and cut messily at the other; 'which part did I cut?' Once, Lucifer had told him that when you love someone, you turn into them. 'That's why all us demons and angels are so despicable,' Lucifer had cooed as he rocked in his chair, playing with the curls of the sleeping baby Cain on his chest. 'God ordered us to love Him, and we did. We adored Him, and it rotted us all from the inside out.' Rosier had been curled up in his own chair, bundled in a blanket to fight the winter chill of the caves, each crack from the nearby fireplace lulling him closer to dreaming. 'It's for man's own good that they must never come to love Him.'

Drowsily, Rosier had asked, whispering to not wake the child — 'Is that why you tricked Eve and had God banish her and the man from Eden?'

Lucifer had smiled, soft and serene, then nuzzled the fussy Cain in his arms. 'I hope not. That would be too noble of me.'

Finally, Rosier reached for a piece of meat, lifting it to his mouth, slipping it inside. "Mm." It was delicious; it was upsetting. "Azazel may do whatever he likes with his man, but while he's sleeping right beside us... we shouldn't sin." They didn't do it particularly often anyway; Rosier could go forever without sex, but sometimes Asmodeus kissed his neck and dragged his claws down from his stomach to lower than his navel, and Rosier would allow it, would even *want* it. "Azazel is still an angel. I don't think he would want to hear it."

"I see. Then, I should wait to kiss you until he's gone?"

Swallowing, Rosier mumbled, "You can still kiss me, but not like that."

"Not too much?"

"Don't linger your mouth."

"And tongue? No tongue?"

Bashfully smiling, Rosier said, "No tongue," but then he shook his head. "Can you be serious about this for me? I don't want Azazel to have to suffer while he's our guest." He crossed his arms over the table, lowering his gaze to his food. "Though I'm afraid he won't be here much longer. He hasn't told me, but I don't think he likes it here."

Asmodeus hesitated, then answered more seriously, "*Satan* doesn't like him here."

Rosier replied quietly, almost ashamed, "I know. I'll talk to Azazel about leaving... soon." With a frown turning every feature of his face downward, he lifted his chin, and he saw Asmodeus staring at him more seriously before shifting away, grunting.

"I'll be back in our room tonight. If you need me, you should send someone." Meaning, of course, that Asmodeus was on his way to one or two of his lovers. Once, Rosier had been so bothered by this, borderline disgusted to know that his beloved friend would go off to pleasure himself with so many others; it had been some time, however, since Rosier really felt any particular way about it. He watched as Asmodeus took his cane and got to his feet before limping his way down, heading toward the demons who still hadn't decided on a song to play. Greeting them as he walked past, Asmodeus then continued toward Rosier, and the fallen angel of fruit's heart softened like a peach.

"Kiss?" Rosier asked quietly as his tall old friend approached.

"Are you asking because you want one or do you think that I do?" Asmodeus snickered down at him, but his eyes were squinted in a hint of whatever pain might be thundering along his stitches.

"I think that I'd like one," Rosier said, and he rose to peck Asmodeus' mouth, their lips making a soft, plush noise in between. "Wash before you come to bed, please." Asmodeus nodded as Rosier lowered to sit again.

"As you wish, darling," Asmodeus said, a faint smile where he'd been kissed even when a nearby demon whistled at them.

As his lover left, Rosier thought that, like Azazel, the caves had deeply unsettled him once. There had been a time when he cried himself to sleep because he thought he didn't belong here. 'I've been happy these past few years.' He hadn't fully realized it; he'd found a home in Hell, or a place like Hell. 'I hope Azazel finds a home, too, with his man.' He smiled a little to himself and decided to try speaking with Lucifer before he met with Azazel again.

WANT

Pushing aside the curtain, the material troublingly soft against his talons, the demon Baal peered into his old bedroom. He hadn't stepped in here for many years; it cradled too many memories. He didn't consider himself particularly emotional — except for love or infatuation, which were, as far as he was concerned, the same dish, different flavors, the same cut of meat, different roasts — but he did often fall victim to nostalgia. And nostalgia can so often have a particular body. For Baal, nostalgia was a narrow room. He had carved this one, long ago, into the cave and slept in it, long ago, had put his child to sleep in it, long ago. When Satan had remodeled it, added a sofa and a table, Baal had grown furious, long ago — one of the few moments he'd ever dared to raise his voice at his beloved devil. He had suffered tremendously for it, been snarled at and left without a touch from Lucifer for a month.

'Cain meant everything to you,' Baal had thought then. 'How could you do away with all his things? How *dare* you?' Baal never did learn what Lucifer did with Cain's belongings, whether he had stored them or set them alight one evening in private — but Lucifer offered furious, flamed eyes at the suggestion of the latter. When Baal pressed the issue, Lucifer had murmured that Cain's memories were safe, in a place where they wouldn't collect dust. The devil owned so many chests, wardrobes, and closets, and so Baal reasoned, or perhaps prayed, their child's things were inside one of them. 'I wondered if you did it so we could move on and forget all about him, but how could I? I could tell you hadn't moved on from the years we cared for him either, Satan. Lucifer. Angel.'

Lucifer was before him now, on the sofa. He was sprawled, his legs spread, robe in torn disarray. His golden hair was mussed, brown skin still flushed and beaded with sweat, and worst of all — there were streaks of blood dried along his throat, trailing to his shoulder. His eyes were empty but wide, like he had been horrified or shocked once, perhaps at a second before death, and he was a corpse of old terror.

"Lucifer?" left Baal's mouth in a whisper of confusion, then hot anger because he had seen Michael walking away from here just a minute ago. 'Michael hurt him. The dirty fucking bastard. I'll rip him to pieces.' But his gaze trailed down to Lucifer's clothing again, then down to his legs, his thighs. He couldn't miss what was there, couldn't kill the hitch of his breath. What was fury was soon becoming wrath, every muscle in him tensing tight enough to rip, to make him tremble; red was bleeding into the edges of his vision. "What the fuck?" The laugh from him was rough but high-pitched, manic.

A low rasp: "Leave, Baal."

"He *fucked* you."

Now, Lucifer cackled, a trickle of life returning to his dead eyes. "No. You think God's little prince has the bravery to fuck the devil?"

"Do you think," Baal began, voice rising in a beastly snarl, "that I'm a fucking idiot?"

Another slow, cruel laugh. "And if I did?" Beads of white continued to trickle down his legs to stain the couch. "What would you do if I did?" Lucifer was nearly wheezing out the words in sick amusement. "Would you stop loving me? Would you stop sharing my bed?"

Strained, furious fists were beginning to shake at either side of Baal, and he put one foot forward, then the other, every step too heavy and thudding too loud. "Tell me what happened."

"You won't leave me," Satan continued, his voice hushed and unsteady, verging on tipping into something like an old hysteria Baal hadn't seen hints of for centuries now. "You'll never leave me."

Baal couldn't stop his feet; soon, he was right before Lucifer, grabbing him by the upper arms no matter how loudly the devil hissed. "Answer me!" Baal shouted. "Did you want it? Did you want *him*?" Almost too quick, a flicker of terror passed over the golden, sunny eyes of Satan, a sudden juvenile quiver to his lips. "Tell me what—" Even in all his anger, even shaking in rage, Baal couldn't stand the sight: fear over Lucifer's face. "Answer me!" 'You look so young when you're afraid.'

"Fuck me," Lucifer ordered, his whisper too distant, gaze too empty. "If you want me, then you have to fuck me." Tightly, he took Baal's robe, and Baal saw how Lucifer's own torn drapery was cascading from every edge and curve of his figure, pooling onto the seat, then the ground. "*You want to know what Michael did?*" The ghost of hysteria was returning; it made him seem so young too. "He rut against me like a dog! He got off on me, shoved his fingers into me! He was pathetic—"

"But did you want it?" Baal heard his voice say, realizing he was still shaking in rage, despite Satan's sudden fragile appearance.

The devil's face twitched in frustration. "What does it matter?" Baal had to bite his tongue not to snap, 'Do you even want *either* of us?' "Just fuck me." 'Do you *ever* want it?' "And you can watch all his filthy seed fall and stain the ground." To be washed away by a flood. "Inside, I'm empty. If you can't change that, then—" Satan's breath hitched when Baal grappled his throat, pushed him down onto the couch, then climbed on top. "Ugh—" Satan grit. "*Fuck me.*"

Leaning toward Lucifer's face, so close that their mouths brushed as Baal spoke coldly — "You're forgetting which one of us is loyal to you. You're right. I wouldn't leave you if you thought I was a dumb fuck. I wouldn't leave you even if you never let me touch you again. You know it." Indeed, the devil hadn't allowed Baal to sleep with him until many, many, years after his resurrection, instead having Baal run his errands, do his chores, wash his feet. 'You were proving I'd remain by your side even if I couldn't love you. Proving it to the both of us.' Lucifer stared with wild, feral eyes. "But that bastard archangel is where I can't follow. Don't forget what he did to you."

"Quiet," came another hiss.

One of Baal's hands slithered behind, brushed the exposed, eternally bleeding twin gashes on the devil's arched back. "Don't forget what he took." 'I mean more than your wings.' Satan had begun reeling air in harshly, too quickly, his shoulders shuddering; he was nearly hyperventilating. 'He took angel Lucifer. He killed him. This is all Michael's fault.' Images flashed in Baal's head of the chief archangel always flaunting the most beautiful angel at his side, never appreciating him, not daring to worship him. "You don't want him." 'You never wanted him. You just wanted love. Let me give it to you now. Please.'

Baal kissed him, deep, grunting against wonderfully plush lips parting immediately, asking to be invaded. He didn't hesitate; Baal thrusted in his tongue, allowed it to drag against Lucifer's own, pushed it deep enough to make the devil instantly shiver beneath him, return to balling his hands in Baal's clothes again. They didn't kiss often, chiefly during rough sex or when Lucifer woke up sweetly and wanted a taste of more tender fucking. When Cain was around, Lucifer kissed him much more frequently, even moved his lips earnestly, amorously — though now his mouth moved as if biting, trying to draw blood. Baal would let him; loving Lucifer had always been nothing but bleeding.

As their lips fought against each other, Baal lowered one hand to the tempting, plush rear of the devil, cradling it firmly, and his other fingers trailed all along Lucifer's body, climbing up his hips to his chest to a strand of blonde hair that was stuck to an end of their interlocked mouths. The taste of Lucifer was sweet but tinged with bloody metal; furrowing his brows, Baal could only keep wondering about Satan's wounds. That damned Michael couldn't stop hurting Lucifer, could he? He couldn't love him, so he hurt him.

Lucifer breathed shakily, but Baal continued, allowed a finger to prod at Satan's entrance. Wet —heavenly semen, oil from an opium lamp, and perhaps something else. And he thought of sinking in a talon and laughing in Lucifer's face. "Is this," Baal began, pulling his mouth away with Lucifer's saliva dribbling from his own lips, as he stroked a claw dangerously against him, "how you want to get fucked? Bloody?" His voice didn't sound as harsh as he meant it to, and Baal realized he was forcing his anger even now. He always troubled being furious at Lucifer; his hate would just redirect to Michael or God or the other demons. "Is *this* how?" It sounded meaner that time, and he felt Satan shudder but not respond.

Intently, desperately, Baal stared into the sunny eyes that had once felt like the only true light in this cave for the God-damned, but it was dim, and Lucifer's eyes were narrowed, his mouth pressed fine. Baal adjusted himself, only now feeling the hardening tension in his gut, clawing down between his legs. When he rolled his hips, he bumped his damned hardness against Satan only for him to say, "Don't waste my time. Put it in me."

"Don't give me orders," Baal snapped, trying to remember how to be cruel. How could he be cruel to something this beautiful? 'I need to hate you. I can't. How couldn't I love you? I was just an angel when I first saw you. Even our chief couldn't resist you. Even God couldn't help but love you.' It's a thought that made him pause. 'He did love you, didn't He?' Despite what he'd said, Baal obeyed and removed both hands from the devil, reached for his own tunic and yanked it over his head, not reacting when he heard the sharp rips of his horns tearing apart the fabric. 'Sometimes I worry about how much He loved you.'

He took Satan's head, pulled it downward, at the same time that he lifted himself to his feet. Soon, Baal gripped golden hair with two hands and slid right into Lucifer's open mouth, which took the sin without resistance even as he stared up at Baal with an almost embarrassed, humiliated anger. But Baal almost didn't notice it; he was swept up in the enveloping heat, in the push into a perfect throat. "*Fuck—*" he panted, then bit down a laugh. "Michael will never give this to you." The taunt escaped from somewhere in the fire of fury he decided he must keep feeding. "Michael can't satisfy you." His hips began to rock, slowly at first, carefully, wanting to savor the first initial gags. "He can't have you." Baal found himself immediately panting. "But I can." '*And I'll take you back.*'

With the larger demon picking up the pace, ramming in, Lucifer choked some more, lifting his hands to Baal's thighs and gripping the strong muscle, but his gaze remained hardened. Occasionally, Baal wondered if the devil could hear his thoughts. It felt, at many instances, that he did. As he took Baal deeper, a light passed over Lucifer's eyes that may as well have said, '*Take me back.*'

It's because of this that Baal didn't bother fucking Satan's mouth very long, just enough to rouse himself until he was fully pulsing in need. He listened to himself say, "You want it bloody? You want hate? I can give you hate." Jutting away his hips with only the tip of himself right past Satan's pouted lips, he added, "Fuck you," but he didn't mean it. Nevertheless, he said it again, "*Fuck you!*" As Baal stepped back, freed himself, Lucifer's rasp was scratchy and raw, twisting into a wheeze that made him almost double over as he blinked rapidly, reeling in breath after breath. "You never answered me—" 'Did you want it?'

"I wanted it," Satan snarked, baiting him, prey winking at the predator, then laughed through a devilish grin. "Now punish me for it."

Baal grabbed Satan by the waist and arm, grip so tight it could have been torture, then lifted him with ease, even when the devil began to thrash and hiss once more. Pressing Lucifer up against the wall, he took his legs hastily, pried them apart, and pressed in between. He didn't hesitate to wrap one arm around Lucifer's waist, the other holding one damp thigh so tight he might crush the bone — supporting the king of the demons up as he positioned the hardness God had given him, perhaps knowing it would be used to drive into His most beautiful angel one day. Baal pushed in mercilessly fast, then groaning deep at how Lucifer's body jerked in surprise and tightened around him. The suffocation was lovely; Lucifer was lovely.

Throwing his head back, the devil surrendered to a moan that lulled Baal closer, brought his mouth to the side of Lucifer's throat that wasn't bloody to scrape his teeth. "He lost you," Baal murmured, partly wishing he could just stay inside a while, not thrust. The room they were in was a giant wound of a memory; he had once put Cain to sleep here, then went with Satan out into the forest and kissed his neck, then his mouth, then fucked him beneath the stars slow and adoring like Lucifer was his and had only ever been his. "But I have you now, and it'll be me until we both *burn*." Lucifer had curled up with him, and Baal had talked about their child, and for once, Lucifer hadn't bothered correcting him, humming instead, echoing the words: our child. "All you have is me."

Satan scoffed, but it was bitter, and he thrashed against him again, his way of asking for more, and so Baal started moving, fucking him hard, listening to Lucifer's specifically pitched cries when Baal bordered on going too deep. He'd always loved how dirty sex sounded — the beats of their naked skin, the wet sounds, the cries in pleasure that escaped between the anger. Eventually, Lucifer took a fistful of Baal's curls, yanking, then kicked, but he was close; Baal could feel it, but it didn't matter. They wouldn't be done for a long time, he decided.

When Baal felt the pulses of his length build until he could no longer control his thrusting, beating in unevenly, sloppily, he willed himself to slow, just in time to witness Lucifer tremble and cry out weakly, then finish. It was a nice sight, heavenly.

And while Lucifer was so sensitive, Baal gave another few thrusts, delighting in the devil's weakest, most fragile moans. Filling him was always a dream — spilling in hot and so heavy that surely the devil would have to lay back as Baal made him take more — but this time, it was possessive, too. He didn't want to pull out, risk Michael ever taking his place. He can't, however, stand being in this room any longer.

"The throne," left Baal's mouth as he tried to catch his breath, his shoulders rising and falling, his lungs burning. "I'll fuck you on the throne next."

Satan stared at him, but his gaze was gentler and there was an odd somberness in it that Baal hadn't seen in years. The Cain years. "I want that," he said. '*I want you.*'

COMPASSION

Something was wrong with Michael, Phanuel was sure of it. He had just looked up from the grilled lamb he'd been served on a leaf by a demon with sunny red hair, a long gown that swept by his ankles, a sultry smirk, and a teasing wink as he left the room; certainly, Lucifer had purposefully commanded the prettiest, handsomest demons to tend to the angels' needs while they were here, advising them to linger flirting touches. The chief archangel, however, was stepping into the lounge area alone, his curls messily spayed past his shoulders, his eyes wide but desolate, his body missing every silver covering that he wore so often that it seemed like Michael's second skin. 'Angel of shell without his shell.' It was enough to make Phanuel frown, pick the last of the lamb between two fingers, and bring it to his mouth. Delicious, savory — it didn't matter how much Phanuel might grimace knowing he was eating an animal.

The other angels in the room also turned to Michael, finishing their meals or setting their plates aside momentarily, all quieting in chatter. Encasing roughly half of them, armors shone reflected light from the nearby torches and raging fireplace, and it did so on Phanuel, whose helmet was pressed against his side over the cushion of the loveseat he was settled over. Phanuel's lips parted, but he spoke no words, of course he didn't. Surely, he had forgotten how to even grunt or groan now. Even the devil's silence in Heaven had not been so quiet as this.

Michael broke through the hissing by the hearth: "The devil is injured."

An angel called out, "How? I didn't see him anywhere outside earlier. Was it one of his own demons?"

The hesitance Michael offered in response made Phanuel swallow thickly, inch his hand over to his helmet and touch it. 'It must've been one of Satan's dukes.' He'd heard of some demons being furious that Satan had allowed this occupation to happen and practically treated the angels like guests — and there had already been arguments, shovings, brawls just barley broken up in time, between angels and old demon friends. Phanuel, personally, was far more sad than angry at the sight of each fallen angel. Earlier, he'd shared a polite nod to Asmodeus, seen the horror of his body, then felt relief his helmet hid his frown.

"It's his own fault," Michael answered stiffly, "that's all you need to know." Slowly, he turned back around, facing the curtain at the entrance, right beside Phanuel, that he'd pushed aside. "One of you go to heal him. You, Raguel." He passed along some imprecise directions, then said, "Do it now, and the rest of you sleep already." With those gruff words, he harshly tugged away the curtain, then stepped back out, walking hastily if the quick thumps out in the hall were any indication.

At the sound of someone grunting, and a chair creaking, Phanuel turned to see Raguel climbing onto his feet, dusting off his tunic, then telling the angel at his side that he hopefully wouldn't be long. He stepped over an angel's plate of half-finished food, as well as a chalice of mere fruit juice, and began heading for the door. One angel was asking another what Michael seemed so upset about, but Phanuel ignored them to reach out, take the plain sleeve of Raguel, who instantly stopped and jerked his head down at him. 'What am I doing?' With his other hand, Phanuel patted his own chest plate.

"You want to heal the devil instead?" Raguel had always had a soft voice, and it served Phanuel well now that he didn't want the attention of the others, who were all raising their voices to complain about Michael at once. "Are you sure, brother?" Raguel tilted his head down at him, gentle lavender eyes worried but kind, perhaps one of the few angels who'd come down with Michael that weren't keen to punish sinners or humans or had much interest in moral affairs; Phanuel found some solace in him, then nodded. "Well, then go ahead. But I won't lie to Michael if he asks."

'I could never ask you to do that,' Phanuel tried to say with a smile and gracious gaze before skimming his hand down to take Raguel's, clasping it tight. He pulled himself up using Raguel's hold, then shook his hand in thanks. With his other arm, he scooped his helmet, and shook his head when Raguel offered to come with him. 'I suppose this could be my only chance.' Phanuel let out of a huff, only then releasing Raguel's bare fingers. 'I don't know how much longer we'll be here. Not long, I'm sure. I want to see him up close. Satan.' Lifting his helmet, he set it over his head, slowly sinking it down, welcoming the temporary blindness before his eyes accustomed to peering through the narrow slits.

Phanuel bowed his head to Raguel in polite farewell before taking the same curtain Michael had yanked, then delicately pushing it aside, thinking of how much labor had gone into it. 'Michael, you might not even realize how much work the demons must do to make a home out of a place like Earth. They must dig up their own gems, use wool where they can't use the brilliant cottons of heavenly paradise.' There was something quite admirable about it, though Phanuel knew it would get him in trouble to ever verbalize that, to ever tell anyone that he dared to empathize. Maybe that was another reason to keep silent — fear to turn God's rage on himself after so narrowly missing it.

Though, as Phanuel stalked down the corridor, he remembered that maybe he hadn't been spared. 'Lucifer's hands on a sword, then the noise of scratching and the sharp stings of the flesh at my jaw beginning to unfurl against the blade.' Oddly, the smells are what he remembered the most — golden, silver, metallurgic. A long time ago, he had dragged the anxious, youthful Michael to an arena, telling him to try wrestling, and as they'd walked in, Phanuel had breathed in blood splatter as an angel pummeled another; he'd clutched Michael's hand tighter. All the times in his eternal life that he had smelled the red beneath their skin, and yet when Phanuel was flayed, it was quite different; it had reeked. 'Sometimes I fear I'm rotting inside.'

It took more than an hour to find the devil, maybe even more than two. Michael's directions had been unclear — Phanuel was sure Michael wouldn't be able to find his way back — but on the hundredth curtain he pulled aside, he finally caught sight of something, someone, with golden hair and that height of beauty that could not, would never, be reached by any other creature other than God. Phanuel breathed out slow, remembering his screams of agony. The smoke of the room, however, obscured the memories of blood smell, instead filling his nose with a herbal, earthly scent, while Lucifer was sitting cross-legged on a couch against the wall, near a table with a broken oil lamp, still ignited. To his lips, he held a long, thick wooden pipe.

The redness on his neck was crisp and dried — many hours had passed since the wound was inflicted, perhaps — and his clothes were tied elegantly and spotless. He must've changed from whatever fight had occurred. He may even have washed some. Lucifer's hair, too, was picked up to expose his neck cleanly. With a misty exhale, Satan turned his gaze to him and, without a word, reached for a painted clay bowl that was pressed up against his side. He lifted it, extended it to him.

Phanuel should've felt fury; he expected it. Satan was sitting here before him, his hands clean of blood no matter how much he was responsible for spilling. His robe had a stretched collar to flaunt each patch of blue and green on bronze skin, as well as the indents of teeth — all the marks of lovers. 'He has no shame. The devil feels no shame for what he's done. What he did to me.' The angel took a step forward, then another, watching the bowl in Satan's hands until taking it, seeing the crystalline water in it slosh about. 'My anger should overwhelm us both.' He tried; he ground his teeth and recalled every aspect of the torment, the brink of madness that such pain brought him to. He had struggled and shrieked as his skin was peeled off, threads of it snapping; he had fallen over afterwards, his body convulsing in response to the degree of scalding ache.

Satan had ignored him, then, caring more for his own sad little heart.

Yet, Phanuel wet a hand, settling one knee over the sofa. He brought his fingers toward the wounds of Satan, allowed droplets to dribble down and sink into them. 'Lord, Father of life. Relieve your child of pain. May he be strengthened from the weakness he has suffered and return to us in Heaven. Amen.' He'd never been a healer, and the water didn't stir for a few seconds, but eventually — it sunk past the skin. Hissing, Satan jerked in place, the pipe almost falling from his hands, and a flicker of pain, deeper than what these mere droplets could be doing, passed over his eyes. Intense sadness; Phanuel sensed it from Lucifer as much as he felt it grip his own heart.

Michael had snarled at Phanuel to stay in Heaven. Before all the angels, the chief prince had shoved him back, made him stumble, ordering him to set down that sword and return it to whoever it belonged to. '*You will not go,*' Michael had said. 'Stay here. The city will go to war again if you aren't here to help keep the peace. I want you here.' Phanuel had only gripped his sword tighter, and Michael's face had twitched. Others must've thought it was anger, but Phanuel knew it was pain. 'I think,' Phanuel thought now, 'I wanted to go because I feared what Michael would do with no one to stop his wrathful hands. But I think I was also thinking of you, Satan. I wanted to see what had become of you. My torturer.'

The angel Phanuel would never know what occurred immediately after the war — during God's judgment on those angels who begged for forgiveness — nor did he know of Heaven for several years after the war. He had laid on a bed in a state of shock for nearly all that time, not answering to anyone, hardly reacting to the touch of healing angels to prove he was still living. He was an angel; he couldn't die. He wished he had, but he hadn't. Yet, during all those years, he'd hardly ever thought, 'Lucifer, how could you do that to me?' Instead, he thought, 'How, God, could you have allowed this?' His first steps were runs. One day, he'd crawled off of the mattress that had been his cage, then sprinted out into the streets. He felt he'd been looking for Michael.

And he never did find Michael. Phanuel had found another cage by God's throne. He'd found a chief archangel in agony and misery, but not the friend that he knew.

Phanuel finished healing him, and Satan sighed in hefty relief as the angel returned his hands to the bowl in his lap. 'Compassion is its own cage.' He had no other thought but that as he set aside the clay sphere, rose to his feet, began stepping aside. He was glad the devil didn't recognize him, or perhaps didn't remember him — how many others could he have skinned now? — because a confrontation wasn't what he wanted. That wouldn't bring him peace, that would not make up for all that time Phanuel had laid in catatonic horror. He'd just wanted to see Lucifer again, and he did see that demon that had hurt him and his dearest friend in ways that had once been *unknowable*. Humanity had been passed the fruit of knowledge from Satan's hand, and Lucifer had done the same to the angels; he had chewed it in his own mouth then slipped it into every angel's mouth with a kiss.

He headed for the entrance, his body heavy, thinking he should sleep. The devil looked the same as he did when he was young, when he made soup, when he was a timid little thing that hid behind headscarves and constantly rubbed at teary eyes. It was easier to think that everything had changed from those times, but Phanuel knew it wasn't true. Some things were horrifically the same. Once, Michael had called Phanuel the angel of forgiveness for his compassion, for never minding all the instances the strongest angel accidentally broke his finger or arm. If God was a teacher, then He was giving Phanuel the final test: should he forgive his torturer who didn't ask for mercy, who didn't even want it? For now, he had no answer.

Lucifer spoke.

Halting immediately, Phanuel turned back his armored head, tilting it at the devil who stared at him with slightly parted lips and slightly wide eyes, but no discernible expression.

"It was," Satan responded, "nothing." Healed, he was of heavenly beauty once more, like he might join Phanuel on the trip back home. "Return to your prince."

LAST TALK

A few times, Michael's angels flew over the Earth; for as strong as their wings were, it took weeks each time around. The rain had not stopped, and though nearly every mountain was now submerged beneath murky water — more crimson red, more green, than blue — a few rocky peaks still pierced proud over the surface of the flood. Some angels had asked if they should kill the remaining animals, as well as the couple humans, but the chief prince ordered them to focus on restraining the Watchers until the Lord told them where they should imprison them or if they should kill them. The first angels to die. Though, as Michael landed on one of the last cliff sides of Mount Hermon not yet drowned, reaching for his helmet, he was staring at the stars. He supposed they, the stars, were already dead angels, if not dead then something like death, and maybe the Watchers would join them soon — torn to thousand halves, burning forever and ever. But God was good, is good.

Michael spat water from his mouth the first second he could, bringing his silver helmet down to his front, holding it tight, as he trudged along, headed toward a grotto, and dipped his head below the entrance. The cave was quite shallow, but with a steep climb up into a wider burrow that the flood was struggling to reach. Regardless, the dirt and stone ground was much wetter than it had been the last time he was here. It was good he decided to force himself to return today rather than the next morning. With a great, hefty sigh of relief, the shade of the grotto was welcome, lovely, and dry after so long spent beneath the downpour. He shook his head, wet curls falling looser, some strands sticking to his jaw, and blinked some rain from his eyes as he moved along. Every muscle ached with a certain rhythm, almost like a heart's pulse lived within each of his tendons.

Even the smoke that drifted from Satan's pipe was welcome, as well as the crackle of his opium lamp, singing along with the hums of the bonfire right by his crossed feet. One of his leopards was with him, a young female with her head leaned against the devil's thigh, though her eyes were shut. Michael reasoned Lucifer had brought her for protection, but he was sure that there were plenty of demons hiding nearby, maybe even below them in some kind of tunnel — but if they were here, they were quiet.

"Mm." Satan blew out some smoke from pursed lips, then pulled his pipe away, turning his head over to Michael, eyes half-lidded and indifferent. "Should I hack off your limbs one by one?" He wore a loose, ruby robe nearly slipping off a shoulder, exposing some of his necklaces, but he wore no more than three or four, and he had no earrings for once. Even his sunny hair lacked much adornment, as well as his arms. Strewn around his waist, there was a colorful quilt.

"What for?"

"To name just one thing," replied the devil, "you've made me wait here for days. Do you think I enjoy sitting around for the likes of you?" A low chuckle. "Or were you really that scared to be alone with me again?" Michael's grip around his hefty helmet tightened, his jaw clenched. "Oh but don't let your mind wander. I'm not in the mood for cock, much less yours."

"It really meant," Michael gritted out, "nothing to you."

"Of course it meant nothing. Did you think *you* mean something to me?" Lucifer paused, then turned away, worked on putting out his pipe, setting it down, and making a soft noise. "You don't." 'Not anymore,' Michael wanted to snap. "Sit down now. We need to talk."

Michael had some horrible ideas about what, but he still haphazardly tossed his helmet not too far from him, then settled over the dirt, taking a discarded twig and using it to adjust some of the burning bark. "I assume you have your demons hiding somewhere in here."

"None."

"I don't believe you."

"Don't, then."

Michael's brows furrowed, but he pulled back his arm, then stifled the burning end of his twig against the ground. The warmth of the fire was nice; for as irritated as the prince was at Satan, he couldn't bear to leave this heat and dryness while his armor and cloak remained drenched. "If this is about speaking to God for you, I won't."

"In that case, are you going to steal me and bring me to Him? Look at me, I'm helpless." Satan raised both hands to the sides of his head, palms facing Michael. "Go on. Take me." A little giggle, likely at the prince's deepening frown. "How about you allow me to tell you what I really called you here for? You love to waste my time, but there's none of it left now. I have to return to my demons and hide with them from the storm. They're very frightened. Even beasts can be frightened, you see. The giants—" His voice caught on something, though Michael was certain it couldn't be sympathy, not now, not anymore. "The giants were screaming as they drowned. Some of them tried to drink all the water, but their bodies only began to bloat until they ruptured. What was their sin, Michael? Was their sin to be born?"

Michael replied, "Why did you call me here?" But with a deep guttural ugliness curled up in his chest, he knew. Nevertheless, he stayed by the dimming lamp, the flaming bonfire — he intended to look away but found himself watching shadows trickle along

Lucifer's body. He had been with Lucifer, once, in a grotto like this, the two of them curled up to sleep, cocooned in their wings, or perhaps that had been just a dream.

Lucifer breathed in, then he whispered in a careful voice, "Azazel is being held by Baal. He didn't see the baby, but I confirmed it's dead." When Michael opened his mouth, the devil cut in, "I buried it in another cave. I was afraid of leaving it in the water for anyone to see."

Swallowing what could have been a glass shard, the prince of Heaven murmured, "That was the right thing to do." He looked away now at his own gauntlets, then at his helmet laying, like dead, nearby. "Did you see if it had wings?"

"It did."

"But it wasn't an angel, if it died."

"A half-angel, like the beasts."

"Then why wasn't this one a beast?"

Oddly, Lucifer chuckled. "I have some ideas, but I won't share them with you. I didn't call you here to theorize."

"Then what am I here for?" The sound of shifting, of shuffling, lifted Michael's gaze, and he felt his tired muscles tense at the sight of the devil moving closer to him, his pet having been pushed away with a delicate touch. Elegantly, Satan crawled around the fire, inched toward Michael — but at arms-length away from him, he stopped. He stared, and the prince stared back, his breath tangled in his throat, the gold of Lucifer's eyes as all-encompassing as the sun. 'When I first saw you, I thought you were like a star, back from the dead.'

"I want you," came cold, cruel words, "to not tell a single soul what we saw. You won't tell any of the angels, and I won't tell the demons."

Michael's mouth moved, but he hardly recognized his voice. "Why?" His body was cold; it must've been the rain, still beading along his body like sweat. "Azazel will tell."

"He will be too ashamed, and I think those few who know will be ashamed too."

"What do you think will come of everyone knowing?"

"You really have no thoughts in your head!" Lucifer laughed. "Idiot moron that you are." But as he inched back, there was a visible, uneasy tremor in his features, his thin hands, almost asking to be held. Instead, Michael, once again, listened to the rain, reeling in some of the chilled air, feeling it burn through his lungs, wondering how the sensations of heat and cold were so similar he could hardly tell them apart. When Lucifer spoke again, it was firmer: "You won't tell a soul."

Michael agreed; of course, he agreed. "I won't."

There was nothing more to say. The devil and the archangel looked at one another, their faces both stone. Michael began to wonder if he should kidnap Lucifer, after all. He imagined it: 'Satan thrashing against me, beating his fists against my head as I put him over a shoulder, his kicking feet. Him spitting at me. Bringing him to Heaven. Bringing him to God.' Michael thought of the dead half-angel in Azazel's arms in hideous, striking vividness, the red blood of his memory almost leaking into his periphery. 'God killing Satan and resurrecting Lucifer.'

The devil's hand moved, slowly, along his robe, toward a pocket, and Michael waited for him to retrieve a dagger. As he pulled his hand free again, however, there was a small, simple bundle. Nimble, perfect fingers began to uncover whatever lay beneath.

'That will make up for all of this, won't it? Lucifer's resurrection?' Michael was thinking of the dead half-angel still, then he was thinking of the dead, all of them. He thought of the families, the elderly, the children. With his own hands, he had killed humans, listening to their gore on the ground scream in agony the likes of which he'd once heard Satan responsible for — the man whose heart he'd eaten. But when God killed, it was good; when Satan killed, it was bad. It was that simple. God had reasons, knew that these people deserved it for their sins. 'I will bring Lucifer back. He is defenseless. He said so himself. It will all be restored after this. There will be a new Earth and new Heaven.' Michael's heart beat and beat away in his throat, his own skull developing sores within.

"You're trembling, angel." The devil revealed a small roll of bread in the patterned cloth, and he had it extended to him, an offering. "Eat." Lucifer must've looked just like this when he offered Eve the fruit.

"Eat?" Michael realized Eve must've sounded like this too — breathless, scared, *wanting*. "Why?" 'I'll drag you back to our Father. And it will all be right again. All of this will be worth it. Do you hear me, Satan? God will give meaning to all this violence.'

"If you don't want it, then I'lll eat it."

"I do want it. But why?"

"You always need everything explained to you like you're a child. I suppose you never stopped being one." Tepidly, Michael took the roll, roughly a little larger than his palm, and it had a warm toasting. 'I don't know how a child acts,' he thought briskly, 'I've never held one. God has only ever ordered me to hurt them.' "Eat it."

"Will it damn me?"

"It's too late for you to be damned now, isn't it? You already chose to follow your Father."

'Instead of following my heart,' Michael considered, then brought the bread to his mouth, closing his jaw around it, and exhaling through his nose, feeling his shoulders loosen. How long had it been since he'd eaten? Weeks, maybe months. Chewing slackened his jaw, and food in his belly instantly drew him back to the sound of rain and to his own flesh encapsulating his soul.

"Good," said Satan. "Now, as I said, I must go." He crawled away, heading for the blanket he had apparently discarded. Between them, Lucifer took his pipe, his lamp, and he began to bundle them in the blanket, as he had done the cloth to bread, but with the ends, he tied it across his torso to carry it. At all of this, his leopard rose to her feet, as well, though taking a moment to stretch her paws and open her mouth wide in a great yawn, tail flicking the air.

Michael took another bite, and he was almost done with it now. "Where are all the demons?"

"You don't need to know." Standing, Satan adjusted his clothes, his hair, and soon began heading toward the entrance where the archangel had come through.

"Satan," the prince called, pressing the last of the bread into his mouth, chewing hastily, swallowing. He staggered to his aching feet, then hurried behind the devil. "Where are you going?" 'I have to take you. I have to grab you and bring you back to Him. He ordered me to do it. That was why we did all of this. It was to get you back. That's the only way I can live with what I've done, Lucifer. Don't tell me it was all for nothing. Don't tell me there's no meaning to this violence, after all. Don't tell me it meant nothing.' Lucifer had said it meant nothing; he had said it about the fucking, their lousy half-fucking.

The further they left the fire behind, the darker the world became; there was no moon in between grayed clouds, only a bleeding flood.

"Satan."

By the time the two of them reached the entrance, they were mere shadows, but Lucifer did halt his hurrying, looking out into the submerged forestry many demons had called their home for centuries. Michael stepped beside him, staring. 'Seize him. I need to.' But his hands were still at his sides, and there was warm bread in his stomach. Their silence was loud with every trickling droplet, every distant roll of thunder, every muffled scream of dying things, but Michael dared not face it. He stared at the face that he'd pressed kisses to once, the throat his teeth had torn bloody, and the body he had pressed against so many times a lifetime ago, fitting always snugly, always right. One of Michael's gauntlets brushed Lucifer's wrist, a ghost of the grip he'd had around it when they were against the wall, against the couch — then his knuckles, his fingers.

It ached to want the suffering to have meant something. How many corpses had Michael bled for God, how much had he bled inside, thinking there would be retribution? Once, the prince had dreamt of having angel Lucifer, but Lucifer hadn't wanted him, no matter what any other soul said, and Michael had watched Lucifer run away from Eden forever. Sometimes he wondered if Lucifer was really waiting for him, past the fall, whispering for him to jump.

"You've overstayed your welcome," Lucifer told him. "Return to Heaven. I never want to see you again."

After this, they left each other in the rain.

IN THE DARK

"Can you tell me how you fell in love with me?"

"How I fell in love with you? You want to hear it now, Azazel?"

"What else is there to talk about, Samyaza?"

"There's a new beetle I've been seeing lately."

"Samyaza."

"God."

"No God here, darling. Just me."

"And the other Watchers."

"They're asleep. Talk to me. I'll be sad if you don't."

"It's only that I'm not... certain. Maybe I should ask when *you* fell in love with *me.*"

"Who says I have? I think it'll depend on your answer."

"Will it now?"

"Yes, so make it a good one."

"Fine. Well — loving you, or I suppose I should say *liking* you, made me angry. You know that, but I liked you before I learned to be angry about it. Does that make sense to you? Before Raphael was made a prince, my liking embarrassed me, but it didn't make me angry. You met me so young, I was about a newborn, but each time we would meet — whether it was on the streets or in the hallways — I noticed something new to like of you. One day, you laughed, and I learned I liked your laugh. One day, you painted your eyes a certain way, and I learned I liked your eyes. One day, I saw you standing by a mosaic, fish and waves by your head, and your wings were fluffed up behind you, and you had the hood of your cloak over your head, but your braids were falling over your chest. Yes, yes, and— Your face was painted in reds with droplets of whites by your eyes like tears. You were discussing something with someone, but then you saw me and started calling my name, gesturing me over, wanting to brag to your friend about how good I was becoming at healing. I learned then that... I liked you."

"I'm sorry. I don't... really remember that day. I wish I did."

"It was one in hundreds of millions of days we've lived together. It's not your fault. And — that wasn't the day I realized I *loved* you, only liked you. I think I can say I realized my love for you recently, but... I want to add that when I started getting angry at myself, and at *you*, for how I felt, I realized something similar. I saw that the more I tried to smother liking you, so much that I couldn't focus, the angrier I became. I had the thought that... maybe it wasn't just a liking, if I couldn't get myself to feel normal about you. Maybe I adored you."

"You used to be very sweet. I was upset when you started being rude to me."

"I'm sorry."

"I've had nothing but bad relationships. Is there a kind of romantic love that doesn't hurt so much?"

"I think— If you allow me, I think I'd want to find it or create it. A type of love that only makes you happy."

"Do you think we'll be trapped here for all of eternity?"

"No... I don't think so."

"Do you think we'll be burned in the lake of fire?"

"I won't let you burn, Azazel."

"I had a nightmare, recently. Michael came down and freed all of you. He said you all would return to Heaven because you'd been forgiven — but then he turned to me and said I would be thrown to suffer in the fires of sinners. 'God does not forgive twice,' Michael said, and I thought you'd help me, but instead, you turned around and started flying toward paradise."

"There's no paradise without you."

"I don't like sleeping anymore. I'd rather lose my mind from staying awake. If I turn into a shell of myself, I hope you can forgive me."

"There's nothing to forgive, friend. Love."

"You could call me husband, if you like."

"I don't know that I can be a man to you the way your Eitan was, but I'd love to. And when we return to the surface, I want us to find somewhere to have a wedding. We'll be the first angels to marry."

"God will be upset again."

"He'll be jealous."

Smiling, Azazel echoed it: "He'll be jealous."

ABSOLVE

U riel was suffering a recurring nightmare, so heavy in its terror that he couldn't stand to sleep any more than he had to in order to prevent excess fatigue or cognitive dysfunction. The only thing worse than waking up sweating, panting, clutching at his heart, eyes itching, was reading his books without the ability to make sense of it. Even worse — when his hand was unable to hold his brush without shaking, and he couldn't curve it right to paint words in any of the million languages he knew. He had no choice, then, but to sleep at times, to lay flat on his back in bed and stare at his painted ceiling, wholly black save for some specs of light all across it. He ignored the angel Dina's bustling about the house and his sweet little calls past the doorway, asking if the archangel of wisdom desired something to eat or drink before resting. He was rather annoying — that Dina.

When the drowsiness was too much, then, Uriel allowed it to lull him back into that same dream. The nightmare.

Kimah, in something of a body. That was the nightmare: Kimah given flesh. It always began the same: God calling for Uriel in Eden, saying He had a surprise for his oldest child. "Don't do this to me," Uriel called out to God, each time, because he knew how the dream ended, each time, wanted to change things no matter how much he knew that he couldn't. Dreams were never an escape for Uriel; they were the same stage that God danced puppets around as reality. But what did it matter that Uriel could see the truth behind God's paradise if he could do nothing about it? What did it matter that he knew he was in a cage if he couldn't escape it? With a shuddering breath, the archangel stared at the creature stepping out from the trees like it was their birth. "Kimah," he always whispered.

Before him, God had ushered out an angel of sickly paleness, long waves of hair too light, his irises so dark his pupils melted into them; nonetheless, they were unfocused, unseeing. On his body, there was a tunic, peach-colored, and sheer enough that not much of his figure was hidden as he stood beside his Father. But Uriel's stomach lurched at the sight, no matter how beautifully shaped those pink lips were, how curled those eyelashes, how pretty those hips that held up his sacred stomach. Kimah was not supposed to have a body like this. He was meant to be mouths and wings and fire, and Uriel was supposed to be his eyes. They were meant to be fractured shapes in the cosmos, meant to make one another up. That was not Kimah, it was not Kimah the way Uriel was not Uri. But the Lord gestured for the enfleshed-Kimah to approach his oldest prince. He said this was His gift, again. "You have been good, Uriel. You may have him back in one piece."

Heart-stricken, eyes wide, Uriel watched Kimah's curious face approach with each step the newborn angel took. "Uri," left his mouth, airy as it'd always sounded in the dark skies that blanketed them, the end of his word tilting up, elevated. "Uri. Uri—" A stagger, then Kimah broke out into a run as Uriel whispered back his old lover's name. The usual hope turned over in his chest as this occurred, the second-long, desperate need to cry and accept Kimah into his arms, to kiss him and weep for his other half that had been resurrected by God from his death by God. It would be so easy to; it always was. When Kimah reached him, his arms came around Uriel, and his face buried itself in his throat, and though the archangel stared directly at their Father for a moment too long, he couldn't deny Kimah's mouth when it turned up to him.

Their lips locked perfectly together, as their bodies had in the heavens above this one. He was alive, and he was beautiful. Kimah. His Kimah. Uriel had been good and God had returned Kimah. It would not be like before. The sky would go dark as each star returned to Heaven, and it would be good. God had created, and it was good.

Once Uriel took him home, Kimah wandered around blindly — he could not see — and touched every little trinket, every scroll, each book. One would think that they'd talk. It was the obvious thing to do. Uriel knew that if Kimah ever came back — in real life, not this dream — he would tell him everything. He'd take Kimah's hand and pull him into the deepest, darkest corners of his home, his library, and say, 'My wonderful Kimah — let me read you every letter I ever wrote. I've spent eternity writing to you, everything I've ever wanted to say to you, and now I can spend another eternity reciting every verse of worship that my aching hands scribbled. Each one was for you.' Kimah would touch Uriel's face blindly and smile and speak. But this was a fantasy, a fantasy in his dreaming. They never shared very many words in this portion of the nightmare and, instead, Uriel watched as Kimah stumbled about, dropping things, his hands grasping weakly, uselessly. Each page that slipped through his fingers revealed another line of poetry, describing him, remembering him. But Kimah couldn't read them; God had made him blind.

'I've had to remember you for longer than I ever had you. And, at times, I fear that I've learned to love missing you more than I ever loved you. That isn't true, is it, Kimah?'

Then came this moment, as it always does in the nightmare: Kimah, turning on his heel so abrupt that his pale hair tossed, but his wide eyes were as unfocused as always. Only then did Uriel realize that he'd dropped his brush. He was on a large, plush chair by a hearth and a teapot that never boils. Always, always, it's here that Kimah walked toward him again, alerted by the fall of the thin wooden instrument onto the carpet. With a sway, he placed one bare foot before the other, coming nearer, nearer, until Uriel had no choice but to stare back at the beautiful disguise that caged his Kimah. His beloved Kimah.

"I was," Uriel always confessed, "expecting something much grander. A reunion. A marriage of our mutual body pieced back together. I thought that if I ever saw you again, I could love you like I once did and love you even more than I can hold in me. I imagined every possible outcome of you resurrecting. I've had nothing to do here but imagine. In every daydream I've allowed myself to have of us, we're not here. I never wanted to see you in this city. Can you feel how the blood of the first angels lights the dome that cradles Heaven? Can you hear the screams? I do. I've never stopped listening. I waded through a sea of misery countless times, each time praying I'd hear a hint of you at least on the horizon. All of Heaven is horizon. It was not meant to be like this, Kimah. You are not meant to look like this."

Kimah blinked unseeing, seeing eyes, then he smiled. "I like having flesh, Uri."

"You're supposed to hate it. In every daydream, you saved me from this body."

"We tried to consummate in the skies, do you remember?" Kimah answered, his voice distant like it was made of echoes. "We could not do it. I screamed."

"Kimah, we became one — you and me. I'm still— I'm still nothing but a half of you. I've lived all my life since I lost you incomplete."

The star angel approached again, his walking the steadiest it'd been since he was made, and once he loomed over the prince, he smiled softly, then lowered onto his knees before Uriel. Delicate, his hands came onto Uriel's legs and spread them apart, and through long lashes, he stared up at Uriel — his gaze still sightless or, rather, boundless. 'What do you see, Kimah?' "You hate all the lovers, but we were the first. Is it jealousy, Uri? Do you see that they created when we failed to, and does it enrage you?"

"We," Uriel insisted, "created. We created it first."

"With God, there is no end, which means there is no beginning. There is no first. It all happens at once." Kimah tilted his head. "Maybe there is no happy reunion between us because there is nothing to be happy about." One of his hands trailed up Uriel's legs, groping his thigh. "You do not love me still, after all."

"I love you," stumbled out of Uriel's mouth. "Don't you dare ever say that to me, Kimah—"

"Who are you devoted to?"

"You, Kimah. I'm yours." Frantic, frantic, the prince shot up to sit and took ahold of his own clothes, the fabric soft against his skin, the sensation as horrible as all sensations were to him. However much he hated this body, Uriel was willing to offer it. He would deal with the weight of its wrongness if he must, if Kimah asked. "We can consummate now. We can do it now. I'll love you however you like. I'll *be* whatever you like, so long as I can have you again, my Kimah. My beloved... Kimah–"

The star's hands came over Uriel's own, cold as the abyss above and below. "The nightmare will always end this way," he hummed. "You will give me your body as if I want it. Each time, you will beg me to prove that I still love you, but you won't ask yourself if you still love *me*." Uriel's chest ached, a feeling that climbed up into the hollow space behind his eyes. "How can you say you're devoted to me? You fall to your knees and ask for the mercy of someone else. I have seen you do it. It is all I've been able to see since the moment that I died." Slow, Kimah lifted his body and brushed his divine mouth against the prince's. "How could I ever love this thing you've become?" Uriel clenched his eyes shut as if that would hide his shame or the agony that tore through to his soul. "Uri is as dead as Kimah. There was never any body for him. And you are a corpse."

"Forgive me."

"My forgiveness will not absolve you for what you've done."

ASYLUM

Moloch had seemed kind, initially. When Armoni had hurried into the caves, grabbed the demon by his robes and begged to be saved, Moloch's eyes had softened, then he had put his arm around him, tugged the angel along, dipping Armoni's head with a gentle, clawed hand so that he wouldn't be directly hit by any crumbling stalactites. His touch had been delicate, and his body had been warm. Clutching a monster infant to his chest, the angel of virtue had tasted the first breath of relief in what must've been a year. He worried, of course — for his friend Azazel and for whatever lay ahead — but at least he was safe here, with this large demon. It had, however, been a lie.

At the trial, Satan laughed: "You think I will welcome you into my home? You think I will adopt you after your Father abandoned you? I ordered for all the Watchers to be bound."

"I will become a demon," Armoni begged over any composure or virtue he'd once held. "Please. Lucifer— I swear it to you — I know that you demons are free. Allow me to be liberated with all of you—"

"You are no demon. It's too late. You've committed a sin even I won't accept. You are to be tortured in the flood waters, to be bound with all your winged brothers." 'Please,' Armoni had sobbed. 'Please—' "Or do you pledge your allegiance to me? Will you follow any order I give? Will you commit your life to the demons and our fires?"

"Yes. I do. I commit everything to the demons—"

"You will still be bound, then," the devil had answered, cold and whipping. "But not in the same chains as the Watchers. You will be a slave." 'Slave? What is that?' "You will never know the freedom you so dearly wanted the demons to offer you. God forgives, but I don't. I will hand you to the one who brought you to me — Moloch — and you will serve him for all of eternity." Armoni tried to interject with a clumsy string of stammering words. "If your worship ever turns from me, you will be chained with the other whore angels and made to eat whatever worms fall into your mouth from the crust."

Initially, Armoni had held his infant tighter without argument; surrounded by an audience of demons as he was, noticing each of their hungry eyes, their amused laughter — he was certain that uttering a single complaint would have the devil throw him to the leopards or his infernal beasts. It was impossible to know which torture would be worse. Tightly sealing his lips, he thus lowered his face and took the punishment. The angel had been something of a captive in the city of Cain already, and Moloch had been kind to him. He supposed he could survive this. He wanted to ask, too, if he'd be allowed to visit the Watchers, perhaps tend to them, but he didn't dare make the request now.

When Armoni had a golden collar locked around his throat by a duke — not the chuckling Baal nor the expressionless Asmodeus — a golden chain acted as a leash hooked to the front. Satan then murmured an order for Armoni to hold his hands far before himself for yet another duke to take the monster infant and hand it to the devil.

"Hm," said Satan as he accepted the baby, then cradled it in his arms. Nonchalantly, he poked the monster in its grotesque face of many mouths, no eyes, and boiled skin like the remains of a cannibalized human in stew. "What a shame what you've made here." Armoni nearly dared to ask the devil not to kill his baby, but he wasn't sure if he wanted that. It was the last giant, almost definitely, and Armoni hadn't chosen for it to born at all, hadn't wanted any of this. But his beastly child was alive now, and his arms felt empty without it. Golden cuffs clicking shut around his wrists didn't make up for the weight of his now stolen baby, nor did the cuffs strapped to his ankles.

Moloch, the demon of trimmed crimson hair and a brimstone scent, was handed the other end of the chained leash, and as Armoni was led away, he heard the jeers of demons and even flinched when some of their spit landed on his somber expression. With a shoulder, he rubbed at his cheek, trying to wipe off infernal saliva. He was in a mere tattered tunic, one that had once carried designs by the descendants of Cain but was now too dirty to be anything beyond a gray-beige color with the occasional colorful thread hanging off like entrails. Though his hands weren't locked together, there was a clasp attached to the cuffs that would make them easily so, and that same clasp existed at his ankles. His heart drummed up against his ears. 'I will be well.' Breath refrained from filling his lungs no matter how hard he tried to inhale any of the heated, dense air around him. 'He hasn't hurt me. If he wanted to hurt me, he would have already.'

But it had all been a lie, and he was wrong. Once Moloch took him home, he instantly brought him to the bedroom, snorted, took Armoni harshly by the throat, over the collar. His talons pricked at the skin below Armoni's chin and tangled with his blonde hair out of its usual braid. A wide, pointed smile skewed Moloch's face, eyes brightening with sick glee. "My slave, hm?"

Armoni's own eyes widened, so great they risked popping out of his skull. "What–?" he managed, then gasped when Moloch walked forward slowly, forcing Armoni to stumble backwards with each step. "Let go of me–" he tried to say, confusion turning fear turning anger and grit teeth. "Remove your hand."

"The devil gave you to me," sneered Moloch. "I suppose he knew what my intentions with you really were." And though Armoni opened his mouth again, his words were eaten up by a sharp breath again as he was pushed down onto the bed, Moloch's hand still holding the collar. Armoni's knees bent over the edge of the mattress, his sandals lifting off the ground. For here, he could only helplessly kick against the ground with the very front tips of the leather in his footwear. "What were you imagining the demons to be like? Did you think we were like angels, just freer and happier?"

Armoni stared, feeling his body shiver as his heart grew to struggle against his ribcage. 'No,' he thought and wanted to say. 'Don't. Don't.' "Please," left his mouth instead. 'I beg you.' His composure was flinching into deep cracks and exposing the terror turning him ghostly pale. "I'll do anything but this. Please." The angel's hand went over Moloch's at his neck. "Please."

With a mocking tilt of his head, Moloch answered — "What? You didn't mind fucking a human, but you deny a demon? Satan was right that you Watchers are all perverted shit-eating—"

"*Moloch*," came a sudden sharp voice — though if the door had opened, Armoni must've not heard it, his ears too clouded by the horror warming every drop of blood inside him. "Get off of him, you stupid fuck." Before Moloch had even turned around, a hand came over the demon's shoulder and wrenched him back. His talons lost hold of Armoni's neck, and though he hadn't been squeezing, the angel shuddered frantic, in-out-in-out pants as if Moloch had been choking him. Shaking, the angel turned his head to see a tattooed demon shoving Moloch back, only to then strick him on the head. "Don't you ever learn? You can't keep your cock to yourself even if it keeps ruining your damn life."

"What the shit is wrong with you?" Moloch barked back at the stranger. "Since when do you care, bastard? Are you jealous, Mammon?" He laughed. "That's it, isn't it? Your little Azazel rejected you and now you want another pretty angel to fuck?"

"Fuck you," Mammon replied, but then turned to Armoni.

"Get up. Come with me. We're going to talk to Satan. He shouldn't have allowed this." When Armoni didn't move, he insisted, "Get up *now*." Urgently, the Watcher angel did as told, tripping over his own ankle cuffs as he tried to stand, but he regained balance right in time to watch Moloch throw himself at Mammon, who twisted back and jutted out his elbow. He hit Moloch hard enough to send him back against a table, but it wouldn't hold him back long.

Armoni allowed Mammon to, suddenly, grapple his arm, then tug him harshly behind as he headed for the door. As Moloch shouted after them, Mammon broke out into a run that yanked Armoni forward, nearly dragged him out the bedroom. "Thank you—" the angel stammered. "Thank you."

"You're Azazel's friend, aren't you?" Mammon replied between the huffs of their running. "Don't misunderstand. I don't give a fuck about you or whatever happens to you — but I owe him this."

RESPONSIBILITY

Shutting the door behind him, so harsh it almost slammed, Rosier felt his shoulders rise, fall, rise with short pants that rattled his entire body. He lifted his gaze off his feet painfully slow, and he met long golden tassels of hair, falling against a white, half-sheer sleeved tunic. For once, the devil was in minimal jewelry — a mere chain tucked against his ears to hang shimmering gems over his forehead and blonde locks. Rosier knew this because there was a long mirror at Lucifer's side, though before him there was a stout rock table. A crimson cloth mantled it, and on top, there were collections of jewels, smoking myrrh incense, embroidered squares of fabric, painted pebbles, dried flowers, and fresh fruit. "Lucifer," Rosier breathed, but his old friend didn't turn. "Lucifer." Again, no response; the mirror showed not a twitch of the devil's mouth or his distant eyes. Without recourse, the fruit demon tried, "*Satan.*"

"Why didn't Baal stop you from coming into my chambers?" was a soft, level answer, almost pitiful — as if Rosier had made a grave mistake he didn't know about.

The tone had Rosier's heart stuttering in his chest anxiously, but he bit down on the inside of his cheeks, shook his head some to try and clear it. "Baal is my friend. I begged him to let me in, and he listened." Satan didn't speak once more. "Lucifer—" 'How could you?' Rosier wanted to cry. "I need you to look at me. I want a proper answer from you." But his voice was trembling and so were his hands soon enough, so was the rest of him. "Please."

"I don't care to look at you."

"You're my friend too, Lucifer."

"Is that so?"

Rosier flinched, hesitated. "I... want to believe that. I want to believe I know you. But what you've done—" He blurted it out now: "It's that angel. Armoni is his name. Mammon was running with him, and they were looking for you. They found Asmodeus and I instead, and of course, we asked what was wrong. Or... I did. Asmodeus already knew. He didn't want to tell me. He knew I would confront you." For a handful of seconds, Rosier waited, waited for his friend to explain but there was silence; Satan's face was stone. "Baal told me the same thing. They told me not to question you. But you're my friend, Lucifer, and I want to know why you would— You know all that Moloch has done. You know he can't be trusted, or else you never would have taken away his dukehood." His voice broke, somewhat, though he didn't know why. His throat didn't burn, his eyes didn't itch; he didn't want to cry, and yet he hurt like he might. "Why have you given Armoni to him? Moloch will hurt him. He *tried* to-"

"Force himself on Armoni?" Satan's voice remained delicate, almost uninterested. "How terrible. What will you do about it, Rosier?"

Instantly, the demon of fruit jolted, almost spluttered. "Me? You're the one who—"

"I suppose there is nothing you can do. You're no duke. You told me once, if you remember, that you wouldn't call yourself a duke; I suppose because you didn't want the power or responsibility. And now, *now*, there is something you don't like, and you come crying to me. Doesn't it embarrass you? You're like a child, tugging on his mother's dress and begging her for help. I'm not your mother, Rosier. And you decided that you care nothing for controlling the demons, that you only care about yourself. Why don't you ask Asmodeus to act for you? You're the one who made him a duke. Or will he only listen to you if he gets to fuck you first?"

"*Lucifer!*" Rosier cried, his face burning in shame, in anger. "What is wrong with you?! You've never liked Moloch. You know that this isn't fair— And Armoni came in good faith to you. He even said he would accept demonhood! He told me he'd worship you if he must. Why are you doing this?"

"*Who do you think I am, Rosier?*" Satan snarled, finally twisting around, his face so contorted in fury that the beautiful, angelic disguise was almost tearing away from his own flesh. "Do you think I'm some *protector of the weak*? Do you think I'm the *fair, good* king that God never was? Do you think," and Satan took one step, then another, approaching so fast that Rosier stumbled backward frightfully, "I'm an *angel?* Why should I take in some whore who bred with a human and came crying to me just like you? Why shouldn't I have him tortured and quartered and flayed for what he's done? All of Earth is drowned, and it is because of what he and the other Watchers have done. He even dared to bring that abomination of an infant to us like I'd call it *creation*. All of your fruits, Rosier — they're all gone. They're beneath the oceans of God's wrath. We've had to abandon our home, and it is his fault. It is the fault of all the Watchers. He should be thanking me. The Watchers deserve much worse than the fires of Hell."

Rosier, blinking rapidly, felt now the scorch in his eyes he'd lacked earlier as he tried to hold tears back, and he even lifted a hand between their bodies, trying to force Satan not to step any closer. As he did, his gaze accidentally flickered to the side, noticed the altar that the devil had been standing before seconds ago. And his heart sank into his stomach as the dozen objects there tugged at a tiny warmth of familiarity inside him. Some of the embroidered patches were clumsy — the threads loose and frayed and composing a child's understanding of a daisy.

"The Watchers," Rosier whispered, "are not responsible for Cain's death, Lucifer." He shuffled back but then felt the cold knob of the door he'd come through press against his spine. "A-Armoni is not responsible for it. And hurting them will not bring Cain back to us."

Satan said nothing.

"Listen to me—" Rosier's hand between them turned out to be useless; he felt Lucifer's palm strike against his face so harshly that it threw his entire body to crash against a chair that fell to the ground with a *thud* alongside the fruit demon. He shouted out in pain as his side instantly throbbed, and Rosier curled into himself somewhat, but he managed to lift his face anyway, droplets beginning to streak down toward his jaw. He looked at the devil, no matter how much it burned to do so. "H-Hit me," he stammered, "all you like. It will not make it any less true." Choking up — "The Watchers didn't kill Cain. God did. And you colluded with Him." Rosier was sure he'd never seen this expression on Lucifer before — fury and twitching and utter horror and *grief*.

Then Baal's voice called: "Lucifer?" Before there could be any other word, Rosier felt the door push up against him, though not hard enough to be painful, then stop. It froze the way the fruit demon's breath had just done in his lungs.

"My name is Satan," the devil answered, then turned around and returned to his altar.

HARMED

Quietly, Rosier shuffled in, shoulders slumped, bangs uncharacteristically pinned back to reveal his forehead and draw some attention toward his curled horns. One of his cheeks was flushed, must have been struck by a hand. Immediately, Armoni wondered if it'd been Asmodeus — that tall demon with a patchwork, stitched body of beast parts that he vaguely remembered as an angel from Heaven. He'd known him because everyone had known angel Asmodeus; he'd been known as quite likable and physically affectionate, though occasionally quite guarded about his own heart and mind. Standing beside Asmodeus, Rosier had looked — to Armoni — like a leopard beside Satan, like a pet.

One day, after the war in Heaven, Azazel and Armoni had flown to a ruined structure, the fires of Satan's army having made the tower a furnace that tortured all those trapped inside and left behind a skeleton of stone. At its head, likely the remnants of the roofing, the two angels had settled, their legs hanging over the edge, kicking mindlessly, faintly. They hadn't met Dina yet, were still meeting each other; they'd brought a warm drink and shared it as they spoke. Azazel had told Armoni about his fallen friend Rosier, how confused he'd been when the young angel of fruit had mentioned he was spending a lot of time with his new friend Asmodeus.

Azazel had gossiped: "And I told him, 'Asmodeus?!' And Rosier put his hands behind himself, and he looked away, and he asked me why I was raising my voice and if something was wrong with Asmodeus. I said, 'No, Rosier, there's nothing wrong with any angel.' Well, now we know that's not true." Armoni laughed loud as Azazel gestured at the destroyed Heaven around them, then waved his hand for the painter to continue. "Anyway, I tried to say that Rosier just seemed so... opposite. Rosier didn't understand what I meant, so I decided to just congratulate him on the friendship. Before... what happened with Mammon, I was with him — Rosier. He was carrying Asmodeus' head, and his eyes were distant. I can't remember exactly, but I think he said that Asmodeus had hurt him."

But now, in the present, Armoni recalled that Rosier had just tried to speak to Satan for him. Sitting in a room Asmodeus and Rosier had locked Armoni in to hide him from Moloch, the fallen angel fiddled with his sloppy braid, shame clawing at his soul. "I'm sorry," he decided to say.

Rosier blinked, then twisted his face in embarrassment. "Oh, is it really that noticeable?" He touched his flushed cheek. "Lucifer should have been more careful. We demons struggle to heal, so even little injuries like this can become permanent. But don't apologize. We argued, and it wasn't really... about you. It was about someone else." He lowered his hand, then took the few steps necessary to reach the Watcher. "How are you? I hope not too terribly."

'Your voice is more gentle than Azazel described it,' Armoni noted, then shifted to the left on his seat. "I'm well. I'm unharmed. We can't say the same for you. Sit here, let me see what the devil's done."

Through the demon did lower himself to sit beside Armoni, he said, "Even if Moloch didn't succeed, that doesn't mean you weren't harmed." Armoni shrugged in response, reaching to take

Rosier's jaw carefully, then tilting his face. "Aah. I told you that this hit wasn't because of you—"

"I heard you," Armoni interjected. "I'm looking because I'm curious, not because I'm guilty." Softly, Rosier laughed. "Does he do this often? Satan, I mean."

"No, he's typically kind." When the other scoffed, Rosier straightened and insisted it, "It's true. He's been very kind to me and the other demons. There are times that he can be cruel, but it's not often. The Flood has changed him; I fear not for the better."

For a few seconds, Armoni gazed on the darker touches of the bruise, then he allowed his hands to delicately fall away, brushing some of Rosier's neck and his arms. 'He's warm, like an angel.' "You're brave for trying to help me." He interlocked his fingers over his lap. "I really do appreciate it. Thank you."

Pausing, then the demon of fruit confessed: "For a very long time, I turned away from the evil of the demons to safeguard my heart, but I know that it's wrong. It's difficult to know what's right or wrong once even God's shadow fades from your life, but I feel the pain of others rather strongly. I think pain is wrong and hurting others is worse. Even if I've failed, I'm happy that I tried to help you. I'm going to keep trying. Once Satan isn't so upset, I'll try talking to him again, and I'll ask Baal to speak with him too. And Asmodeus — I asked him to speak with Moloch."

Armoni sighed. "You're doing too much."

Rosier, hastily, shook his head. "I'm not. Moloch is cruel, Armoni. Even if you enjoy sins of the flesh, he'll hurt you."

Immediately, Armoni laughed bitterly and waved a hand once more. "Don't be ridiculous." Rosier tried to speak again, saying something about how Moloch had hurt even lustful demons. "Stop trying to say to me that I'll hate it. I don't need to hear that. I already know. I find all lust disgusting." As if to emphasize, he pointed at his own mouth and gagged, so theatrically that Rosier, eyes in the midst of growing, laughed. "The humans forced me to fornicate with them, and the other

Watchers would try to tease me, but I think it secretly bothered them that one of us thought that their beloved sin was nothing but filth and discomfort and a bore."

"You... fucked and didn't enjoy it?" Rosier whispered, almost in wonder.

At that, Armoni had to resist rolling his eyes. "I did. You can't convince me. Lord knows the humans tried."

"No," Rosier replied, quick, shaking his head. "I have no intention to convince you. It's only that I don't know if I've ever met someone who dislikes lust. All the demons can't live without it."

"Well, they're demons," Armoni said with a dry, humorless humor.

"But I'm a demon and..." When Rosier's voice trailed off, he turned away, and one of Armoni's brows quirked, puzzled. "I suppose I've talked too much. For now, I hope you don't mind sleeping in the same room as Asmodeus and I? He'll be upset, but if I insist, then all he can do is listen. Moloch wouldn't want to publicly fight with Asmodeus, so you should be safe."

Armoni glanced down at the golden cuffs over his wrists and locked to his ankles; they were heavy, but he was accustoming already. It was how being a sinner in Heaven had felt, and he'd forced himself to keep his chin high for all those years, to bear it to survive. 'Angel of survival.' "That's alright with me. Thank you." He wanted to ask about Rosier and Asmodeus' relationship, wanted to know what happened in Heaven, what was happening in Hell. Without warning, Armoni reached and grappled Rosier's hand, squeezed, then said, "You're as kind as Azazel told me."

Briefly, Rosier was surprised, head tilting in confusion, but his parted lips soon pressed together and tilted upward to form a sweet smile. He squeezed Armoni's hand back. "I'm glad you think so."

THINKING

He hadn't realized how numb he'd been. Azazel hadn't realized how much he hadn't allowed himself to process it, what had happened to him, what his body had done to him like it was itself another beast he;d awoken violently to see he;d been inside of all along. When it had happened the first time — that day he'd expelled from his body a crimson conglomerate of a creature — he had agonized, 'If God ever loved me, He would not have made me.' He'd hardly thought, in the moment, that he had *made* too. He had made something, within himself, from nothing, or something like nothing. Was he the first? Was he the first angel to create? He was just Azazel, an angel of painting. He was not God, never wanted to be. It hurt too much, was too bloody.

'There's a wound in me.' There were many outside of him, too; he could see them; long ago, Azazel's eyes had adjusted to the darkness, the same as his ears had accustomed to hearing everything in between the clinks and clatter of chains that bound the limbs of himself, Samyaza, the other Watchers. They groaned in pain, occasionally. They hadn't healed since they'd been imprisoned, made to be tormented by the ache of where the angels and the demons had broken them and the eternal bleeding from the cuts, the severings. 'Where there is a wound in me, I'm empty.'

In his chest, where his heart should be, Azazel had a gaping hole that trickled red like tears down to his stomach, his groin, between his legs like he would relive that fateful day in the forest of Mount Hermon. It was the wound of the chief prince's sword, the one that had cut through him to pierce both him and the baby. Sometimes, he wondered if his child's blood was still there, intermingled with his own at his chest. 'My heart is gone.' And, sometimes, he wondered if he had missed seeing the beating organ of his chest on the flooded ground with his infant or if it had remained, pulsating still, skewered on Michael's sword. Wherever his heart was, it was certainly gone now forever. 'Until I burn.'

Azazel's eyes itched, and he parted his dry mouth. There was breathing beside him: Samyaza, sleeping. Slow, he turned his face and saw the figure of his lover slumped in his chains, his hair matted and over his face. He, too, bled onto the cave ground, though not much more now, the same as Azazel. That was a relief, or else their blood would have filled the cave long ago to drown them all. 'Samyaza,' he wanted to say. 'Samyaza, please wake.' He wanted to talk to someone, to return to not thinking of what had occurred. The sound of it. 'The last noises my baby made.' His stomach lurched. 'My baby.' He breathed in harshly. 'My baby.' It had really been his. Then, the angel felt his face cringe, his teeth clench. 'No, no, no.' With their fluttering wings, their big eyes.

'Eitan,' he thought. 'Eitan, I'm so sorry.' Shuddering, Azazel tugged on the chains that held him and wanted to wail. 'Samyaza, please wake up.' He needed to stop thinking again. This was the torture that God had decided for him — thinking, forever, of what he'd lost. His husband, their love. The baby. 'Samyaza, please.' The baby. His baby. 'Kill me, Samyaza. I can't live with this.' He wished now Michael's sword were stronger, that he'd died alongside his little winged child. 'The weight of the baby, against my legs. I remember lifting them to my face for the first time, the wonder in the heart I'd lose the moment the chief prince found us. I remember, I realize now, all the pain and love in that moment. More than I had ever felt. Maybe my man would have liked you. Maybe he would have forgiven my body for betraying me for you. You were beautiful. If only I had hidden you from God, from the devil. My baby. All the humans on Earth. Whatever happened to them?' He shook his head, trying to stop here, to not think another word. Oh, this grief. He was going to lose his mind to grief if he did not stop. 'Whatever happened to Naamah and my man's grandmother? Our family?'

"Azazel?" Samyaza, whispering. "Are you well? You're hiccuping—"

A gasp tore itself out from between Azazel's lips, and he shook his head. "No, I'm not well—" His heart was gone. 'I will never be well again.' Choking on the misery, he sobbed, "Everything hurts. My baby, Samyaza. Our families—" As always, the angel who'd once been their leader began to tell Azazel to breathe, to cry but to breathe. "I don't want to anymore. I wish that I could stop breathing forever. I want to go where my baby has gone and where my family has gone." He should lower his voice — the other Watchers would hear — but there was so much pain in his heart that it was eclipsing the shame. "I'm sorry."

"Don't apologize," urged Samyaza, though his own voice wobbled. They had a terrible habit of crying together; if one of them broke down, then they both did. Once it had been that they were at opposite ends of every world, but now the two angels found themselves constantly beside each other at every wave of every sea. "You've done nothing wrong. You've never done anything wrong. Azazel? Look at me if you can. I love you. There is no part of you that has ever done anything to deserve this. I hope I can make you believe that." Azazel shivered in the dark, didn't look to Samyaza. "My love," Samyaza said, unsteadily, nervous, "there's still an eternity before us. And there are souls.

Even if our families' bodies are buried, I believe their souls are out there, waiting for us. I promise."

'With my heart,' Azazel mused to himself. 'Maybe all our families' souls are waiting for us with my baby holding my heart in their hands. Maybe they're all waiting for us, hoping that when we burn, our bodies will boil away the floodwaters so that we can reunite.'

Before them, there was a sudden padding — the indistinguishable sound of walking. The noise instantly made chains rattle and other Watchers grunt, gasp, startle. Before anyone could call out to demand who it was, if it was a demon here to prod at them with spears or even the devil — a hiss sounded, a glow bloomed. First, a torch revealed itself, then the pale hand that gripped a wooden handle. What followed was a face, painted with accents on every feature, wide-eyed, terrorized, along with an open, panting mouth. Blonde curls cascaded down his front and back, contrasting starkly with red drapery that was far too sheer, exposing nearly every inch of his body, including the excess chains of jewels snug around his limbs, his waist, his neck. There was a thicker white cloth clumsily tied at his hips to hang and shield some of the area below his navel to his upper thighs.

"Armoni?" Azazel whispered.

"Azazel," his friend sighed in relief.

OR WAS IT LOVE?

On some unspecified day of the torment, Azazel was set free from his chains. He'd been in such deep sleep that he didn't hear, or even feel, the cuffs being unlocked from his ankles; instead, it was Samyaza's voice that woke him, in the same moment that he was released from the chains that upheld his wrists like he were on a crucifix. His body, immediately, fell forward, but before he hit the ground — rough arms grabbed him. There was a gleam of light, not very strong but enough for the Watcher who'd been subjected to darkness for centuries to screw his eyes shut in a sting of pain. Through his eyelids, he could still see some of the yellow emitting from what must've been a torch.

"What are you doing?" came Samyaza's horrified breath before he raised his voice to snarl. "Don't touch him! Where are you taking him!?" Nearby, Azazel heard the rattling of the iron locks that were bolted to the rock walls — Samyaza, surely, wrestling his bindings frantically.

"The devil has plans for him," a demon somewhere grunted, then Azazel cracked open his eyes, only to blink them excessively, blindly. What he saw first was his lover, Samyaza, with wide eyes and disheveled, matted hair in knots over his face like a veil, but

Azazel still found him beautiful; and he was certain he looked worse. A part of him wondered if Satan found humor in this — imprisoning the Watchers until their bodies weighed with all the dirt falling onto them, and until their wounds were burrowed into by insects, and until they all stunk of rot, until each of them became revolting, even worse than the demons — if the devil enjoyed making each of them ugly in a way only the fallen angel of beauty could imagine as the ultimate torture.

Softly, Azazel whispered for Samyaza to calm. He hardly heard himself, numb all over except for the rawness at his wrists and ankles where he'd been chained. Each limb moved with such ease; Azazel had forgotten this was what his body felt like. 'This is my body.' For better or for worse. "Samyaza—" he tried to say again because the old leader of the Watchers jerked against his bindings and spit at the demon holding Azazel. "Don't make this more difficult, please." A chorus of the other Watchers joined the angel of body painting, particularly Danel, who snapped at Samyaza to stop resisting before he got the rest of them punished. But it would be a lie to say that Azazel found any comfort in this.

In Samyaza's eyes, the dirtied, solemn face of Azazel was reflected. "Azazel," he said, still desperate, voice pitched in terror, "come back as soon as you can— If he tries anything, come back to us."

Azazel, distantly, heard the demons snort, then laugh at Samyaza that the devil couldn't be escaped, for he was like God, but Azazel nodded at him. 'I will return to you, all of you,' he mouthed at his lover. He wasn't sure if he believed it. 'But we're eternal; it's inevitable we'll meet again. You and I, Samyaza, and all the Watchers too.' As the demons began to lead a stumbling Azazel away — finally, he noticed that it was three demons, none of which he recognized — the angel found himself wondering if he'd really manage to reunite with all his friends even if Lucifer tore and burnt him to ashes. Maybe he would reunite with Eitan too. The rest of his human family. And his baby. He never gave it a name. He didn't know *how* to name something. It was God that had named him, and Azazel didn't know how He had conjured the word that Azazel must find his identity in for the rest of time, like a scar. Even if he took on another name, like Satan, Azazel knew he would always look down, see the gash in his body of that name. Azazel.

The demons didn't bring him to Satan's violent hands, not yet. Strangely, Azazel found himself led to a dark, damp room, then guided by a demon with long, red hair and short horns toward a porcelain tub. As the angel approached, he saw water, clearer than the very Earth sky, its surface shimmering with the light of nearby candles and pearly soap bubbles. He wore a tattered tunic, once white but now the color of burnt soil, patched with blood. At Azazel's chest, there was a bloody hole that cut all the way through him, parted his ribs, revealed the missing heart of the most sinful Watcher like it were an emptiness to be proud of. But the red-haired demon was gentle with that part of Azazel as he, delicately, stepped forward to get the angel out of his clothes.

Azazel wished he could have bit back a lovely sigh as he was helped into a steaming bath, then washed in complete silence. All he could do was watch as the demon's hands worked at massaging each limb, cleaning every speck of grime and blood on Azazel's body, and preened his broken wings. He even washed his scalp carefully, braided hair that Azazel had been grieving the uncleanliness of against his shoulders for so long he'd almost forgotten what a sweet, reborn sensation it was to be washed. And, if that weren't terrible enough, he startled at the thud of the double doors into the washing room swinging open only then to tilt his head as two more demons strode in with platters of food. One, then the other, reached Azazel, falling to one knee before the tub to offer rolled, seasoned meats on skewers and cuts of fruit.

Finally, Azazel spoke, "What is this?" His stomach twisted inside; long ago, his hunger had turned into a contradicting, nauseated, stuffed feeling. "Food? For me?"

"There will be wine," said the red-haired demon, his voice

small but not timid. "And waters and juices, as soon as the demons with the drinks arrive. Please eat. Satan encouraged it."

Azazel's heart beat loud against his eardrums. "Is that true? I don't believe it. What is it that he wants?"

"We don't know," answered the demon, and the two before Azazel shared a perplexed gaze. "But please do eat." Azazel feared it; if he remembered the taste of proper food, he'd never want to let it go again; he couldn't bear to lose everything a second time. "If you like, I can dress you first, and you can sit in the room to the left and relax. Satan won't be able to see you for a little while longer, I'm sure." Just as the door opened again, and the demons with the pitchers of beverages entered, Azazel tilted his face back to the kind demon and nodded warily, asked to be dried and clothed. "Very well. Would you like any jewelry?"

Azazel did go on to wait in the room he'd been told of — it was something of a lounge with various divans and sofas and plush seats scattered all about — and he ate. The first, minuscule bite was a burst of flavor that made him shut his eyes to keep from bursting into tears from a joy he didn't want to feel, to get attached to. His stomach lurched, again, trying to protect him, but the tinge of distaste wasn't enough to keep Azazel from shoveling the food into his mouth. Nausea, even rising up his throat, couldn't stop him. Soon, the angel would feel a cry begin to ball up in his throat, then tear open into a full body-rattling sob as he sat alone in a lounge. He was in a warm, pale robe, in golden chains, feeling wonderfully clean, smelling of lavender perfumes.

When the red-haired demon came by again, he hesitated, then wiped the angel's face of any lingering sadness. "Satan ordered me to come for you. I don't know what he'll do, but if he asks something of you, you should follow his command. Do not risk anything else. Trust me, angel."

Azazel bit down on a bottom lip that refused to still from its wobbling, but he nodded, then he rose to his feet slowly. "Thank—" A hiccup strangled his words, so he tried again. "Thank you. You are very kind." He wanted to ask a million things, ask where Armoni might be or Rosier, how the Earth was doing now, so long after the Flood. But he feared opening his mouth again, terrified that another miserable cry would bloom out of it.

"Come with me, angel."

Oddly, Satan waited in a grandiose dining room with a long stone table empty of any regal, golden chairs beyond the one he sat upon, at the very front, and another at the opposite end. A chandelier swung above them dangerously low, crystal and candled, and there were frescos on the ceiling of fires and animals, those long dead and those who might still roam the Earth. Even stranger — the devil had no guards with him, no Baal at his side, no one except for a bottle of liquor that he was pouring into a glass. His clothes were not as extravagant as the devil was known for either; he wore an onyx-black robe, few jewels, and a golden wreath. "Leave us," said Satan, "Ara."

"Yes, my God," said the red-haired demon, whose touch drifted away from the Watcher before Azazel heard the shuffling of feet on the tile floor, then the click of the door locking behind him. 'Ara,' Azazel thought. 'That name is familiar.'

"Take a seat." At the devil's sluggish gesture, Azazel stepped toward the only other chair, noticed there was a glass of wine, beside an opaque bottle, waiting for him there. "I know you might've already drank, but in case you hadn't, I thought to offer it to you a second time." The angel, tepidly, pulled back the golden seat, settled onto it with every muscle so tense in him that he was sure they'd each begin to snip. "How was the bath? It must've been such a relief after all this time. I've been told it smells awful where the Watchers are."

Azazel clenched his teeth; he'd been so afraid just minutes ago but sitting before the immaculate beauty of the devil, he remembered that Satan was only as gorgeous as he was insufferable. "Why are you doing this?" Satan lifted his cup to his lips, sipped elegantly. "What is it that you want?"

"I want a lot of things, Azazel." Satan gave him a serpent

smile. "You know what that's like, don't you? You know how it feels to *want*."

Swallowing, Azazel leaned back into his seat, certain that the golden eyes of his enemy were trying to burn up his flesh. "Is it to taunt? Is it to laugh at how happy a bath and food in my stomach makes me?" A bitter laugh shot out of Azazel's mouth. "Well, I hope you're satisfied. I hope it's been worth it to you, Lucifer. I hope you're *so happy* to have destroyed the world for God."

"My name is Satan," corrected the devil, then took another long sip. "And, rest assured, I am quite happy. You want to mock me, Azazel, but I've done everything I've had to, and I'm proud of every choice I've made. You cannot say the same, can you?" Before he could suppress it, Azazel flinched. "Now, why don't you have a little more wine?" 'More? So you *do* know I had some of the pitcher in the lounge.' "All I want to do is talk with you."

"Don't play your games, Satan," Azazel whispered, his brows furrowing. "Tell me exactly what you want. I don't want to waste any time here."

"We have all the time in the world, Azazel," Satan said softer but then set his glass down, perched both elbows on the table, interlocked his fingers. Slow, he lowered his chin to prop itself against his hands, his eyes strangely wide, almost curious. "But if you're so impatient, I can tell you exactly what I want."

Azazel felt his eyes drawn to his own glass of wine. 'One time, I drank with you, Lucifer. Do you remember that? You were an infant, and you spilled some wine over my table. It seeped into the cloth like blood. You were drunk.' "What is it then?" He reached for the cup, took it nervously by the neck, but lingered his grip there, not lifting the drink, not discarding it.

For a long few seconds, Satan was quiet, the room so silent that it could have been the void of space above them that they were sitting in, but then a few words broke through the emptiness like the first ever sun imploding — "You had a child." In an instant, the Watcher's heart and breath had disappeared entirely from within him. "I saw it." Had Satan been there when Michael had pierced Azazel, destroyed the baby alongside his very heart? Azazel couldn't, couldn't remember; a heat stirred up within him as he gripped the glass tighter.

"All the Watchers— Most of us had children, Satan. You know that." 'How does he know? Was he there? Was Satan there?'

"But yours was not like the children that they had. It was not a giant."

"It was not—" A pathetic stammer.

"It was beautiful," said Lucifer, but the words cut through a grimacing Azazel as painful as an insult. "Its body was not like those abominations the other Watchers created, those poor excuses for creation. Your child had limbs like ours, hair like ours, and wings. It could have been...." The trail of the devil's voice was so tender that it horrified Azazel to no end, nearly had him shivering again. "It could have been a child angel." The glass at Azazel's hand was beginning to strain, but he couldn't answer now, couldn't even expel the petrified air in his lungs. "I'll tell you a secret, Azazel. Can you keep it for me?" Azazel, stiffly, tried to shake his head, realizing he was fighting hiccups as utter panic took over the last of his soul; no words left his mouth. "I'll tell you anyway. Michael was horrified. He didn't know. It made me wonder if perhaps... God hadn't anticipated this either. But what would make you so special, Azazel?"

At that, Azazel couldn't help a scoff, however much it hurt to do it. "I don't want to listen to this any longer, Lucifer."

"I told you that it's Satan, and the door is locked." Then, the devil's tone struck sharply: "You're here with me until I set you free." He tilted his head, all the faux politeness trickling away for a second to reveal no more than cruelty. "You'll tell me, won't you?"

"Satan, *I*," Azazel immediately blurted, "*don't know*." He wanted to return to Samyaza, to the other Watchers. "*I don't know why!*"

Satan continued to stare. "Is it because you took a man's cock?"

"I said that I don't know!"

"You're too emotional, Azazel. Have some of the wine."

Azazel laughed and laughed, taking the drink obediently, bringing it up to his mouth, downing every drop of the burn; momentarily, he could make himself believe it had been fires that God rained down that day He decided to kill almost every last human on Earth. Then, he pulled it away from his face, wiped at where the wine dribbled down his chin. Azazel, then, flung the glass at the other side of the table as hard as he could. He missed, and Lucifer didn't react as the drink shattered into a thousand pieces on the wall behind him. "Damn you," he said. "Damn you, Beast! I don't know!"

"You're not the only one," continued Satan patiently, "who fornicated with a human man. I'm not sure if you knew, but many of them did." Azazel wanted to cover his face in shame, to pull at his hair, to not dare weep before the monster that'd destroyed paradise for nothing at all. "But no other angel as consistently as you. Was that it? Was it consistency?" Then, the devil let out an amused chuckle. "Or was it love?"

"I told you that I don't know—"

"*Then*," Satan seethed so loud that the angel jumped in his chair, "*you will tell me what you do know!*" Azazel inched away, his eyes wider than they'd ever been, before he started to dip his head, to remember his promise to Samyaza that he would return to him, to recall the demon's warning to do as Lucifer said. "You will tell me *every* detail. You will tell me *exactly* what you did. If you don't, you'll never be clean again, you will return to starving, and you will watch as I press maggots into each of Samyaza's wounds right before you."

"Beast," Azazel whispered, but he was defeated. "Even if I have to burn with you, I hope that Michael strikes you down next. I hope you're betrayed by the one you loved most." Lucifer laughed, good-naturedly, almost sincerely; it only made the blood in Azazel boil hotter. "But I hope he suffers too. I hope you and Michael and God feel even an ounce of the suffering you are responsible for."

"How noble of you, Azazel. You really were always such a good angel. It's a shame you traded all that purity of yours for a lowly man." Satan smiled sweetly as the angel tilted his head back up at him, his blue eyes darkened, furious. "Should I have them bring you another glass? We have plenty to talk about." Azazel knew he had no choice, not now. "And I have another favor to ask of you that I've neglected to mention. You're one of God's most skilled painters, and I'd like to see what you can do to me. If you can... turn me into somebody else."

DUBIOUS CANONICITY

These events may have occurred in the canon of the *Angels Trilogy*, including its spin-offs — *Angels Before Man*, *Angels & Man*, *Horns for Hell*, *Angels After Man* — but I won't say whether or not they do.

ONE DAY

One evening, Azazel asked the devil if they could make an exchange. "I," said the Watcher as he sawed at a grilled oxtail served on a platter of spiced rice, "will tell you more about my man and I." He set his knife down, then took a utensil — something akin to a fork but not — to stab into a slice of the meat before lifting it to his mouth, painted white. He'd begun to paint his face again in the past year, and though he had often used reds and blues in Heaven, he now found his finger drifting toward the paler pigments that Satan had gifted him. Over each eyelid, there was a dot of white like pearl.

Satan sipped at some of his wine before setting the glass down on the table with a clink. "Why should I bargain with a prisoner?" His head tilted; his filigree, dangling earrings jingled; his gaze maintained itself on his drink.

Azazel said: "We're both prisoners, really. God has us both far from our homes, destined for the flames, little brother." He put the oxtail between his curling lips and chewed slow. Gratingly, the silence hung over both his shoulders and the devil's, though Satan hadn't outwardly reacted. Azazel swallowed, reached for a cloth napkin, then dabbed at his mouth with it before he spoke again.

"I want Samyaza to have the same freedom that I do. He should be allowed to come eat and to be washed. All the Watchers should have that privilege, but if I must choose one, can't it be Samyaza?"

"Samyaza," Satan replied, "is the one who led all of the Watchers to damnation, and you think he deserves any privilege at all?"

"Who said I think he deserves it? Do you think I deserve to eat with you? Haven't you granted me this freedom out of pure self-interest?" At that, Satan had chuckled, and he looked at the Watcher with some cold amusement. "I want Samyaza to be able to eat and to be washed because I want it, nothing more."

"Well, I can't possibly allow that, and you're not in any position to bargain."

"It's all I ask."

"It would be too dangerous," answered Satan with a shake of his head that rattled his earrings once more, "and I have no interest in talking with Samyaza."

"But I do. Grant me this, and I'll tell you whatever you want."

Lucifer answered with silence, then he turned his attention back to his drink and the half of his meal, the same as Azazel's, that remained on his plate. For many minutes, he ate, he sipped, and he pondered. Azazel knew now not to interrupt, so he allowed himself just one uneasy breath, focused on eating, and twiddled at a braid resting on the soft cloth of his tunic. He wanted to say that he knew already that Satan would deny him, that he just wanted to express that he had someone he loved, who he wanted free. At the same time, he wanted all the other Watchers to be out of their chains. Recently, he'd found himself fussing over them more; he wondered if this is how Satan felt over his demons.

"You may have one day," said Lucifer. Azazel lifted his face quickly, only then realizing that he'd been staring at the table.

"He'll be set free from his chains, and you can take him to be cleaned, and you can eat with him, and even rest on a bed. Then, he'll be imprisoned again. Is that clear?" Azazel opened his mouth, but the doors into the dining area creaked open, then Satan said, "I have other matters to attend to now. I'll give the order for someone to free Samyaza with you in two days. I'll meet again with you in three." Without bidding farewell politely, the devil left him.

Within two days — what he promised did come to pass. Azazel made his way to the caves with Baal close behind, who'd seemingly been instructed not to make conversation with the Watcher however many times Azazel tried to talk to him. Surrendering, chewing on his bottom lip, Azazel approached the slumped body of Samyaza, strung up with his arms high. "Samyaza," he called softly, hoping not to wake the other Watchers nearby, especially not Danel.

Meanwhile, Baal looked through a ring of silver keys and began, one by one, to experimentally jab each into the cuffs that upheld the fallen lesser angel of healing. Just as Samyaza's left arm was released, the angel jerked forward and twitched awake, but though his mouth opened — whatever he wished to say died in his throat when his frightened eyes landed on Azazel's face. Gently, the free Watcher took Samyaza's jaw, rubbing a thumb. Baal freed Samyaza's other wrist, and the Watcher fell into Azazel's arms, limp and heavy like he were a sack of dust.

Though the other captive angels lifted their heads and soon called out in confusion, Azazel and Samyaza remained there silent, embracing tight. Samyaza was shaking, his eyes wide, and so filthy that he stained the front of the other's clothing in brown and in his own blood. Azazel didn't mind.

Appropriately, however, Samyaza was taken to the baths first. Azazel, on the way, explained all that he could — that he had made the request, that Satan offered opulence, that they only had a day, and that they should hurry. And yet, as soon as Samyaza, who still trembled since he'd been freed, was brought before a steaming tub, and he was undressed by a demon, he moved slowly. He lowered himself into the bubbled surface, hissing as water rushed into some of his open wounds. Naked as he was, Azazel couldn't help feeling the dual pity and attraction. It was the same body he'd loved as the world ended, but it was cut open at his legs, arms, abdomen, and bruised as green as the only wing he had left.

"I'll leave you," said the demon in the room. "After he's clean, they'll be food in the dining area. You know the one, Azazel." The Watcher in question quirked a brow, prepared to ask just why they were being left alone — he figured it must be one of the devil's tricks — but the small demon hurried out, then locked the door behind him.

So, Azazel turned to Samyaza sitting in the bathtub, then sighed quietly. "Is the pain too much?" he decided to ask. "The demons have sedatives. They have herbs and fungi and all sorts of things that can help dull whatever hurts." He settled at the edge of the tub, hands interlocked at his lap, circling his thumbs around each other like winds causing a twister. Water shifted, then he saw Samyaza's shivering fingers come over his own, the old leader's knuckles permanently scrapped, some blood still caught beneath his fingernails.

"If I rid of the pain now, after so long, I might start to miss it." Azazel, slowly, lifted his gaze to see Samyaza's tragic, broken expression; his features were twitching, like he were going to cry or to shatter as he spoke. "You're the only sedative I want."

Azazel, suddenly, laughed. "Have you always been so melodramatic?" He snaked his hand away, then brought it to Samyaza's drenched hair. "Don't punish yourself. I'll go find you something to take for the pain." The face of the younger angel, the leader of the Watchers, flushed. "Mm? What is it?"

Pursing his lips, Samyaza said, "It's only that— I know that it's dramatic. I know that it's embarrassing if I say things like that, but I spent so long feeling it, and I'm afraid now to spend anymore time refusing to tell you about it." He leaned back in the tub, and Azazel's fingers combed down until they escaped the threads of the other's hair — short, messy. "If you want to cover your ears, I don't blame you, but I want you to know. I don't want God to kill me one day with the regret of never telling you."

'I almost wish you hadn't mentioned it,' Azazel wanted to say, 'all that time you hid your feelings from me.' "Do you," he replied carefully, "hope that it can make up for the years you made me believe you hated me?" Immediately, Samyaza flinched. "Don't make me sad, Samyaza. I don't want to think of then. I think it's better for both our hearts if we don't speak of it. It's better to forget it. Whoever we were then — it doesn't matter to who we are now."

Slow, Samyaza answered: "I don't think it will make it up, and I don't want to forget. Pretending that everything is perfect when it's not is how Heaven fell, and how what happened to the forgiven angels went on for so long. I want you to know that I've changed, not make you believe that I was never that cruel angel. I was cruel. I know that I was." He tilted his head at him. "But I don't want to make you sad either. I never want to do that again. So I won't discuss it now. You said we only have a day. Let me make it a happy one for you, angel."

"My man called me that," Azazel whispered before he could stop himself, half-expecting a jealous flash to pass over the eyes of Samyaza like he'd once seen during the time on Earth, but instead there was a shadow of grief. "He would call me angel."

"My wife would call me that too," Samyaza said, then he smiled sadly. "They thought there was something so mystical about being an angel, didn't they?"

"By the time we came to Earth, I'd begun resenting it — being an angel — but before the Flood, before all the war began, my man had taught me to cherish it again, to an extent. I wish I could have been what he wanted. I wish I could have been a man for him. I dreamed of it, I longed for it. I wished I'd been born a boy in his village, but now that Eitan is dead, I wonder if he did love me for the angel that I was, and it was all a misery of my own making. We punish ourselves even when love is true." Azazel hesitated. "He was a good man, Samyaza. He was."

"I know." Samyaza shifted to sit up again, and he exhaled through his nose. "Idith liked you. I wish I could have made myself more likable to Eitan too." He paused, then added, "And more likable to you, as well." Smiling, Azazel laughed. "I'm sorry that this is all so complicated."

"That seems to be the nature of all things since the war in Heaven." Life had been so simple once — most days the same, relationships easy to map, bodies invisible, no deaths to hold the weight of. "I still want to believe that the children made it on the ark and that Naamah is still in the woods with my dagger. If we ever leave this place, for the sake of ourselves and for the sakes of our human loves, we have to find them." 'I know that it's been thousands of years now.' "Can you promise me that we'll look for them?" 'They're all dead.'

"Of course. Whatever you ask for, Azazel. It's yours."

Azazel turned to Samyaza's serious expression, then laughed once more. "Oh, now I'm being melodramatic." He reached, took Samyaza's head again, then shoved it down, dunking him under the water. "You said we should be happy. We only have a day!" Beneath the bubble surface, Samyaza thrashed. "Once we're done here, I'll paint your face. You'll do my hair. All will be well. I'll carry around a cantaloupe, and we'll pretend the angel child is still alive."

Samyaza, reeling in a sharp gasp, yanked his head up from the water, then spluttered out, "Oh, Azazel, don't be so morbid."

Azazel shrugged. "Can't I deal with my despair with a little joke? Don't scold me now."

Fondly, Samyaza smiled. "I don't think it's very becoming of an angel to make light of something so awful."

"Oh, now the one who destroyed the world is telling me what an angel ought to do." Azazel turned away, hiding his smile. "Is he going to tell me that I can't love a human next? Should I try to drown him again?"

"Who are you facing?" Samyaza laughed. "Who are you talking to?"

"God," Azazel quipped. "I'm sure He finds us very amusing when not pitiful." When Samyaza scooted himself closer, arms wrapping tight around the waist of the fallen angel of body painting, Azazel turned down and said, "And what's this? You're getting my tunic wet. Have some shame. Whore!"

Samyaza kissed his stomach, then rubbed his jaw against it, smearing the dampness more. "Forgive me, angel. I love you. I'm happy to be alone with you." He shut his eyes, breathed in. "Can I kiss you?"

"Will you be kind to me about it?"

"Yes, angel."

"You promise not to pout and be angry for loving me?"

"Only love, only love." As Samyaza spoke, he began to pepper kisses all over Azazel's waist, each one wetting the white cloth more, each turning it more transparent until the old chief of the Watchers was beginning to catch hints of Azazel's dark skin beneath. "I'll never be afraid of loving you again. I'll never be angry again." Azazel tried to uphold his playful arguing, but he was feeling softer, weaker, with each word. "I'm not afraid of God. He can watch." He pulled Azazel closer, and Azazel sighed, shivered, as he was brought into the water, Samyaza's face moving to rub against his chest, to dampen the cloth there too. "I love you."

Azazel tilted his face down, pecked Samyaza's hair. "You're allowed to be angry, Samyaza." He stroked the other's hair. "I have a lot of anger too. Let's be angry together."

"But not at each other," Samyaza rumbled against the hole where Azazel's heart should be.

"Maybe a little," Azazel relented. "Where's the fun in loving if there's not a little anger? A little drama?"

"You were always the angel of gossip."

"It's good that you know that," Azazel snickered, then leaned down, took Samyaza's face how he had while the leader was in chains. "Give me something to tell stories about." He put his mouth on his, slipped in his tongue, and when Samyaza instantly moaned around it, just about whimpered, Azazel felt a coil of welcome warmth between his legs. He moved his arms to hug Samyaza's neck in what was almost a headlock. Ever generous, Samyaza took the other's wet tunic and lifted it to his waist, immediately starting to stroke, then finger. He was leading rather hastily, but Azazel didn't mind. However celibate the angels were in Heaven — after they'd learned pleasure, it was difficult to live without. In that sense, the Watchers could understand the demons, maybe even realize that they were all demons in the end.

Samyaza broke the kiss, panted wetly against Azazel's mouth, and said, "You're beautiful."

Azazel smiled, his eyes fluttering open. "You are too." He pecked his hooked nose, then let out a little gasp when the other's fingers pressed somewhere sweet inside him. "I hope your human told you so. Or should I hate her?"

"You're the one who wanted drama."

"So what's the answer?"

"She did tell me. Did your husband ever call you beautiful?"

"He did. But I don't mind hearing it twice." Azazel kissed him on the mouth again, reaching down to stroke Samyaza too, to a firmer hardness, to a good length. "Mm. I might even go out to hear it a third time." He paused, then added, "Well, there was that time with Mammon—"

"Fuck," Samyaza suddenly cursed. "Alright — enough with talk of our past loves or else I will get angry." Azazel giggled, tilting his head back, letting Samyaza barrage his throat with kisses. He allowed himself to lose grip of Samyaza, then leaned backward to look down between them at their arousals. The old chief of the Watchers was still fingering him, and Azazel allowed himself to sink into the sensation, the fingers, the stretching, the slow pumping that soothed some of the warmth in his lower stomach but not enough. "Now... may I?" Samyaza's hand drew back, away, leaving the other empty.

Instead of answering, Azazel simply lifted his hips, then lowered his body onto that cursed thing that'd begot monsters on Earth. As he did, the angel let out a drawn-out, delicate moan, bringing an arm to rest on the edge of the tub. His sleeve, his tunic, was so soaked that it was no longer like he wore clothing but rather than there was a ghostly shine on his skin. "Mmm." He remained where he was, settled there, wondering how long of their day together that he could spend having one body with Samyaza, who reached to rub at Azazel's hip, then his stomach. At the center of his chest, Azazel's tunic was red with blood, the wound of his heart. Briefly, he imagined taking Samyaza's fingers, bringing them there instead, telling him to finger at it like he'd down below, to widen it, to put his mouth on it.

Samyaza rocked his hips up slow whereas Azazel stayed still, feeling sin burrow into him, then slide nearly out, only to return to where it wanted to belong. They were both leaning away from each other. It made the angle of where the chief of the Watchers thrusted a little more pleasurable, and Azazel cried out softly and curled his toes and dug his nails into the side of the tub. The other benefit was that they could both stare at one another, admire each other, count each one of their eternal wounds.

"We," Azazel panted, "have to be quick. We only have a day. Let's not waste it. You need to eat, rest." He realized now why the demon had left them alone, had locked the door. 'Satan and his scheming.'

"A day loving you isn't wasted, Azazel. Beautiful, sweetheart, my love."

Azazel whispered, "You're being melodramatic again." But then, "I love you too, my angel."

After fucking, after bathing, they did go and rest together, and they did eat. They made love again, on a bed, for the first time. 'Satan, I know what you've done now.' On his back over the mattress, Samyaza curled up against his side, Azazel stared at a fresco ceiling in Hell, and he wondered if Satan had been the one watching them all along, not God. If he, like God, was excited to give them everything, then take it away, to watch them beg for mercy. 'There is no fire hot enough for you to burn in, Lucifer.' He nuzzled Samyaza's hair, then counted down the last few minutes.

STUDIO APT

Asmodeus stepped away from the windowsill, from the sound of Brooklyn's traffic, leaving a cigarette in his mouth smoking like a pistol. He wore tight pants and a bright red, furry bathrobe with nothing else; he'd tried on the button-ups he'd found in the closet, but they had all been too tight around his shoulders. At the other end of the studio apartment and half-beneath the bedsheets, Rosier was sitting naked, eating what appeared to be a microwaved burrito still in the gaudy yellow wrapping from the convenience store next door. It was definitely days old, and Asmodeus wanted to swipe it from his beloved demon's hands — but Rosier was smiling and flipping through a book as he ate.

Slowly, Asmodeus made his way closer, and he saw that it was an encyclopedia of old maps. Some were quite familiar; in particular, the Genoese map of 1457. The demon duke had been present when it was unveiled in the north of what would become contemporary Italy, had almost forgotten he'd been there at all. It'd been a very tragic century, and Asmodeus had spent much of it far from the area known now as Europe. He'd spent much of his time further east; and then, not long before the catastrophe of its discovery, in the Americas. Of all the demons Asmodeus knew,

Rosier had been one of the most devastated; he'd adored the land there, the people there. And Asmodeus missed that life, as well, though he'd once so adored industrialism and modern living, all built on the bones of all the human violence of history. He'd once even believed technology could elevate all those on Earth beyond Heaven.

These days, Asmodeus could only remember all the past bitterly. "Rosier," he murmured around his cigarette, settling down on the large mattress with his friend, the springs squealing beneath his weight.

The fallen angel of fruit had just turned the page, then taken a bite from his burrito. As he chewed, Rosier smiled brightly at Asmodeus in response. "Hm?"

Asmodeus reached for his cigarette, held it with two fingers, and drew a deep drag before pulling it from his mouth and allowing smoke to seep from his lips. "Are you sure you don't want to shower?"

Rosier stared, then shut the book with one hand. "Maybe tomorrow." When Asmodeus brought his cigarette to Rosier's mouth, the sweet demon obediently took it between his lips. "Mm." His eyes fluttered shut.

"I cleaned out the blood already," Asmodeus said, watching Rosier inhale the poison. "Maybe I should've waited until after we dismembered him, but I thought you would't want to come out of the shower with your feet painted red." Carefully, he pulled the cigarette away from plush, wet lips. "It's the last time I ask, I promise, but are you sure you don't want to wash up?"

"I'm sure." It took a few seconds before Rosier's eyes opened again, the gold in them smoked. Trails of gray snaked from his mouth, framed his cheeks. "But thank you." The tinge of somber in his tone remained; it had remained for millions of years on Earth and it had remained for all of human history.

"Thank *you*, darling." Asmodeus leaned over, pecked Rosier's cheek.

A warm affection softened Rosier's tone. "For what?" He

finally set down his half-eaten burrito, barely reaching the bedside table from where he sat.

"Where to begin?" Asmodeus teased, twirling his cigarette, leaning back against the pillows propped up still; they had been cradling Rosier's head a few hours ago. With his free hand, he took Rosier's arm and tugged him a little closer. The book in the fallen angel's hands slipped away as he allowed himself to be pulled to the duke's side, a smile rising to his face again. It was weak, but it was there.

How many homes had they slept in with murdered bodies in a corner? Too many, even if Asmodeus had always been careful in choosing the victims. He did what he could to punish cruel people, the rich, and the cruel and rich, but making a proper judgment from a distance had proved difficult. Once, he'd slaughtered the gardener instead of the mansion owner, and Rosier had been devastated for weeks. Asmodeus never understood why Rosier was so afraid of hurting innocents — death didn't seem so harsh. A soul either lingered, rose to God, or burned, and if they burned, then they must deserve it. Then again, God had judged that demons deserved to burn.

With a deep breath, Asmodeus knew he deserved the hellfire — but how could Rosier curled up against him now, nuzzling his neck now, blinking his perfect eyes up at him, deserve any less than paradise? A paradise like the one he'd dragged him down from.

Asmodeus realized he'd begun smoking again, the nicotine in his mouth, the smoke hazing over his eyes. Earlier, Rosier had been beneath him, on his back for once, his face flushed, mouth open in soft, wanting moans. He had been receptive to every touch, to Asmodeus' tongue inside. He had rolled his hips earnestly, even asked Asmodeus to push a little deeper. Strangely, their finish came when Rosier asked for Asmodeus in his mouth, then teased himself between his legs with his own trembling hand. When Rosier struggled to swallow, his tongue had darted out for the beads of white, like pearls, on his bottom lip.

He should steal some pearls for Rosier; Asmodeus decided he'd do that tonight.

"Rosier…. Are you well? Truly, are you well?"

"I am." Rosier shut his eyes again, then hummed. "If you're worried because of… what we did, then please don't. It was good. I liked it today." Today. Rosier may not like it tomorrow. "I just want to… live without regret. For a few seconds."

"I really do love you, Rosier."

"For better or for worse," Rosier chuckled, "I love you very much too."

DREAM

One night, Satan dreamt of Baal's mouth on his, while Michael was between the devil's parted legs, learning to suck and lick. The fallen angel of flight touched the devil's blonde hair, fingers nervous as if he knew it was God's most carefully woven gold that he dared to enjoy, while the chief prince's cold gauntlets gripped Satan's thighs cruelly. There had been a time before the devil had been an angel, pure and beautiful, and he'd seen angel Michael, stared at the strength in his arms, his legs, and wanted to kneel to worship. If he'd known then what the stirring in his belly was, Lucifer would have dreamt of the chief prince's sin in his mouth more often, of drawing out the pearl white to twirl along his tongue like the seeds of a bitten fruit. There must've been a third tree in the Garden of Eden, in between those of Knowledge and Life — a fruit of Desire.

Baal spat into Satan's mouth, causing the devil to shiver and buckle his hips and press wantonly to Michael's mouth. If he were awake, Satan would have snarled at his demon, but he knew this was a dream. There was no need to pretend he didn't want this, want either of these dumb, incompetent creatures. When Baal pressed Satan down onto the flower bedding, and Michael licked his damp lips before raising his head, the most beautiful creature of them all allowed his eyes to flutter shut, to arch his back when the clawed hands and armored hands began to tug at the strings of his robe, slip between the folds, tug it apart. The angel and the demon brought their lips to the devil's chest, each flicking their tongue against a bud, then suckling slow.

Satan's breath hitched, toes curling, then he allowed a soft, pleased sigh to escape. One of his hands lifted to play with the loose curls of Michael's dark hair, while the other dragged along Baal's bare shoulder, scratching encouragingly at his back. He told them to enjoy themselves, to find pleasure with his body. That was why he'd fallen, for pleasure. At least, Satan would like to believe so. He wanted to believe he fell for something. Leaving a nipple wet and cold, Baal removed his mouth, then pressed a slow kiss to Satan's throat. He asked to fuck him.

There were times that Satan dreamt of virginity, of having offered his unspoiled body as if on a platter to the winner of his heart in Heaven. Once, Satan had dreamt of marriage like a human. He had dreamt of himself waiting by an altar, holding a bouquet and wearing a veil, staring at the empty pews and a cathedral door that would never open. He dreamt of having family, of monstrous giants in a living room as he cooked in the kitchen and waited for a spouse, the sizzle of human meat dancing up from a pot on the stove. He dreamt of killing and killing, destroying life because he could not create it.

"Worship me," he ordered, and Baal took him first, pushing away and ordering the chief prince to watch, to learn. Satan's eyes opened to this, his head tilting to see Michael shuffle around to kneel by where the devil's blonde threads sprawled over the green leaves and cream petals. Baal took Satan's legs and lifted them delicately, but he offered them to Michael, who reached to hold the ankles firm by the devil's face with the parted, plump lips and distant eyes. If this weren't a dream, the devil would have scratched and growled, but he laid there, a little more melancholic than he meant to feel, as Baal introduced himself to the entrance that needed no further coaxing or preparation because this was just a dream, or perhaps a nightmare.

Satan felt the hands of his old friend, the one who'd taught him to fly, on his waist, then felt the hard flesh that'd just pierced him began to move, to stab pleasurably slow and deep. How similar it was to be wounded and to be fucked. And yet Satan found himself at home here, held in place, taking the thrusts trying to burrow a hole into him inside. Like plowing to sow seed into the earth. He didn't mind it. In fact, he liked it. In another dream, he hoped they could be three gods, born from an empty plane, an abyss eager to be filled by whatever the three might be able to create from love and love alone. Satan would not be like God; God had created from wrath; Satan would not be like him.

When he could no longer bite down his cries, Satan felt Michael loosen his hold, then shift, bring his hardening, twitching length to the devil's mouth. Satan was obedient — because this was a dream. He allowed it to slide past his lips, fill his mouth so greatly that he had no other option but to choke when the archangel rocked his body forward. Satan's throat welcomed God's prince, His sword, His strongest angel, so weak for the prettiest, most beautiful one. In other dreams, Satan imagined himself a prince in a castle, waiting to be saved by a knight from his cruel Father. He'd wanted Michael to save him once.

"Please," Baal pleaded, his moves growing sharper, needier. "Please, Lucifer."

Once, the devil had dreamt of being young again, of not knowing his own body or what it was capable of, of innocent kisses shared with sweet angels in the sky. Dreaming of clouds and of song and of dance. Youth. Even eternal things could live through a youth, but that youth was doomed to walk further and further away into the horizon each time an angel looked back. Satan was sure he'd one day forget he'd ever been an angel. One day, he'd forget he'd ever loved Michael the chief prince. It was not so bad. He'd made a new life, found a lover who adored him.

Satan had learned that he could hurt himself and love himself more than God ever could.

Michael finished first, whimpering, whining. Even in dreams, his shame conquered him, so much so that Satan was sure the archangel would soon say, 'Please, devil. Let me leave your mind now. Never think of me again. I can't stand to be here. It hurts me too much to have you in our sleep.' But Satan screwed his eyes shut, swallowed down the sweet taste of Heaven.

Unable to help himself, Baal spilled as well, groaning and panting as his hands nearly crushed Satan's hips.

Satan, however, hadn't finished, and he found himself pent up, annoyed. He ordered them to last longer, to take turns having him, filling him until he no longer felt so empty. And the two hurried to kiss him, fighting over Lucifer's lips, made to sing and praise. Being buried beneath their affection was almost better than the sex, like being put to a grave of love. He asked for more — the greedy, greedy devil.

Though when he finally awoke, Satan startled horribly, cold breath spilling out of his mouth, his eyes on a still ceiling fan. He would have turned his face, searched for Baal beside him on the motel bed, but the sharp sounds of a shower head's rain rattled his ear drums. The room was cold. The carpet reeked.

If the devil prayed, he'd pray to return to sleep, to have another dream of them. Those two. Perhaps, he'd fantasize about the angel prince and demon duke sharing a kiss next. The thought made him giggle. Baal and Michael would be furious if they knew what Satan dreamed of, but he liked their wrath — it was always violent, it was always bloody. Satan wouldn't want it any other way.

DEBÍ TOMAR MÁS FOTOS

They were in pajamas — the fruit demon and the lust demon — and they were brushing their teeth. Human food, in particular, had a terrible habit of sticking to gums, even if Asmodeus and Rosier's teeth never stained the way human teeth did, so they brushed and brushed. Spotless, a mirror hung before them, above a sink, reflecting the older demon spitting right into the porcelain bowl beneath the tap, then stepping behind Rosier. Asmodeus propped his chin on the top of Rosier's head as the younger one finished with his left molars. His brows furrowed together as he, through the mirror, made eye contact with Asmodeus, who grinned back. Pulling the toothbrush out of his mouth, Rosier spat onto the sink, then mumbled, "What are you smiling about?"

"I love you."

"Hmmm." Rosier quickly rinsed off his brush before slipping it into a ceramic cup.

"I love you," Asmodeus said again, setting his own brush on the counter lazily. "Before we go to bed, I wanted to show you something." He pecked a kiss to the top of Rosier's head before stepping away, turning around.

Rosier breathed at the sudden loss of Asmodeus' warmth,

then watched as his demon walked out of the vast bathroom — with its massive windows and enormous tub beside a luxury shower. A few days ago, Asmodeus had been bathing with him, kissing Rosier all over, pressing his panting mouth to his neck, and begging to please him. The glow of nearby skyscrapers had lapped at their bodies and the bubbling of the water, one particularly bright advertisement casting a shimmering wave of colors onto Rosier's body. Quietly then, the demon of love had nuzzled his face, and with the same quietness, he now followed Asmodeus into the bedroom of the penthouse.

Asmodeus was in a corner, rummaging through a black leather satchel, before he retrieved a bulky, square gadget. Only the dim lamp by their bed was on — so Rosier had to blink several times in the dark, and drag his socked feet through the flooring some more, before he realized it was a camera. It looked antique but not authentically so, like someone's idea of what old cameras had been like. Rosier would know; he could remember when they first appeared on Earth, how magical they seemed. Almost two centuries ago, he had sat with Asmodeus, both with serious faces, remaining still for a few minutes as a human cameraman worked the tall device; it was their first wedding photo.

Without a word, Asmodeus lifted the camera to his face, pressed at the top. A flash followed with an ordinary clicking sound, which Rosier startled a little too much in response to. Before he could speak, however, a square of film began printing out from the bottom, which Asmodeus immediately reached for, grabbed, then began to shake in the air as if to remove dust. He did this for a handful of seconds before he twisted his wrist to stare at one side of it, then smiled. "It's a bit dark. You'll have to come closer."

Rosier did, in fact, come closer. He shuffled past the bed to reach his friend, raising his hand to take Asmodeus', and the photograph was shown to him before he even had to ask. It was true; it was too dark, but Rosier's body was still perfectly visible there, his wide eyes, his parted lips. "Oh. This is... nice." Squeezing Asmodeus' fingers, he flickered his gaze back to the camera. "But don't we already have a camera?" Rosier knew that his husband was always drawn to new technology; he bought Rosier a new cellphone when he hadn't asked for one, a new tablet, a new television, a new model of the espresso machine — all because he found the hardware updates so fascinating. Rosier was the opposite; he found all the new things so unnecessary.

Asmodeus and Rosier were often opposites, though. They were quite accustomed to disagreement. Rosier supposed that was why they'd been so drawn to one another in Heaven; it was nice to argue and disagree and tease and fight in eternal paradise. They'd found a meaning to all the goodness through their squabbles, hadn't they? They'd given each other purpose. That truth was both lovely and frightening. 'All we have is each other.'

Asmodeus said, "But this one is special." He kissed his cheek. "Lay down on the bed for me. I want to take a picture of you, darling." The younger demon's cheeks warmed, but he did as told, walking backward, moving toward their mattress. He sat on the edge, hands on the covers behind him, and watched as Asmodeus took some steps, then crouched. "Just like that." He snapped another picture.

Rosier glanced down at himself, his button-up, his loose pants, his long, fuzzy socks. He always struggled with human clothes; he despised pants but was rather uncomfortable with the connotation that dresses and skirts had whenever he went outside. He didn't really like to be mistaken for a woman, he realized, but men's clothes were just so hideous. He didn't think he liked being thought of as a man either. He was a demon.

Asmodeus showed him the photo, still fading into existence, and the visibility was better — the lamp providing some almost artistic, ambient lighting — but Rosier's pose was rather awkward. "You look good."

"Can I have another one?" Rosier asked, readjusting himself, then laying his body down onto the soft covers.

"It'd be my pleasure," Asmodeus replied, his tone amused but, sincerely, happy. He set aside the new photo and planted one knee at the edge of the bed. *Snap* — another picture. As they both waited for it to print, Rosier readjusted into another pose, this one with his arms over his head. Asmodeus glanced at the previous photo before setting it aside like he'd done the last. Quickly, he lifted the camera back to his face, and Rosier listened to the shutter. Again, he shifted his body.

They did this for awhile, Rosier even unbuttoning some of his top, allowing it to ride up, twisting around so that Asmodeus could get his back, his legs, everything. He wasn't sure why. Maybe he just wanted pleasant photos of himself. Sometimes, wants are simple and humble. He wanted to remember this day.

They ran out of film once the bed was covered in photographs, Rosier laying in the middle of it. Delicate, Asmodeus climbed off the mattress to set the camera aside on their bedside before taking his time to gather all the pictures, stacking them in his hands. As he sat them by the camera, by his favorite ashtray, Rosier stared at him expectedly. He had been quite sensual for a few shots, even arching his back for one or two, so he waited for Asmodeus to pounce on him, to ask for sex, to rub on his thigh, to beg. Except, Asmodeus was smiling, fondly, lovingly.

"I like it when you're comfortable."

"Comfortable?" Rosier tilted his head as Asmodeus climbed onto the bed again.

Crawling, leaning his face to his beloved demon's, Asmodeus replied, "With yourself. I like it when you like yourself." He kissed him soft on the lips, the grin pressing against Rosier's mouth. "Let's take more pictures tomorrow. In the park, if you like. Or we can go to the produce aisle of the supermarket. I'll take pictures of you with all the fruits and we can pretend the photos are from when we were in Heaven."

Rosier found himself laughing. "I'd need a wig."

"Well," Asmodeus rumbled happily, then pulled back, "that can be arranged."

Scrunching his nose playfully, Rosier scooted away, trying to reach for the camera. He managed to clumsily grab and yank it over, then he raised it to his own face, looking through the lens with the other eye shut. He saw Asmodeus through it, and Asmodeus grinned. Rosier had seen this face of his friend, his lover, his husband, trillions of times — and yet it was like he was seeing it for the first time. He had sharp features, thick brows, dark eyes, and beauty tangled with handsomeness. With his index, Rosier clicked the top, listened to the shutter, but there was no film.

"You can take pictures of me tomorrow too."

"We should ask someone to take a photo of us," Rosier mumbled. "In the park, maybe right by the fountain."

One of Asmodeus' hands lifted, taking the camera, pulling it away from Rosier. "Whatever you like, darling." The fruit demon blinked to reaccustom to reality as Asmodeus reached, set the camera back on the bedside, then returned to lay his body over Rosier's. Rosier, initially, made a noise like a squeak in surprise, but then he laid there, liking the weight. Asmodeus turned to kiss his cheek — chastely. Rosier smiled, smiled so much his face hurt.

He took Asmodeus' face in two hands, then kissed it all over, delighting in the chuckle of the other. "Mwah, mwah," Rosier said. "I forgot to say I love you earlier. Well, I do. I love you."

Asmodeus wrapped an arm around Rosier, tugged him even closer and breathed against his neck. "How lucky I am."

It was rare for the duke to be so adoring without even a hint of arousal, but Rosier liked it. He let their bodies press flush together, their legs tangle. And Rosier nuzzled their noses as Asmodeus pulled the covers over them both. 'I'm lucky too,' Rosier thought. 'Tomorrow we should take as many photos as we can.' He wanted to remember loving him.

NON-CANONICAL

These events are either ones that could have happened in the *Angels* canon but didn't or exist in an entirely different world, which I've split into their corresponding categories. This part also contains three *series*, which are multi-chapter narratives.

I wrote all these stories for fun or to play with the characters like dolls, not necessarily with the intent to portray them accurately. Don't take anything here too seriously. Most of it is just sex, particularly between Michael and Lucifer.

ALTERNATE ENDINGS

These stories could have occurred in the timeline of the *Angels Trilogy* but didn't. You can use the content of the main books as guidance for what is happening here.

The first six stories compose this section: "End of Time," "Milton," "Surrendering," "Bath," "East," and then the two-part series "Child." At the end of the book, there is a seventh story that fits into this category: "Revelation."

ALTERNATE WORLDS

These stories take place in entirely different worlds with familiar names. They're not always written accurately.

The final four stories, not counting "Revelation," compose this section: "Married," "A Halloween Special," "Birds of a Feather," which is a three-part series, and the "The Altar Boy," which is a three-part series. In "Married," the angels are still angels. In "A Halloween Special" and "The Altar Boy," the angels are humans. In "Birds of a Feather," they're in a strange high fantasy world (with unspecified, intersex genitals, if that matters). Do not take these words as canon in any way; this is not confirmation of how these characters would act as non-angels.

The first half of this section, as you read, is *Alternate Endings*, whereas the second half is *Alternate Worlds*. "Revelation" is the odd one out here — an alternate ending at the end. I never meant for these stories to be read in succession, and I wanted to have a set format for easy navigation here, but I felt compelled to place 'Revelation' as the ending. You know why, but maybe you don't.

END OF TIME

Lucifer was feeling ill, not physically, but about as sickly as an angel could be when his soul was unmarred. He couldn't motivate himself to move, not even onto his back; he laid on his side, staring at the threads of golden hair splayed out on the pillow. Heavy — he felt heavy, but he felt ridiculous for it. This was just the beginning, after all. He was supposed to be at his happiest, caught in celestial joy over the end and rebirth of all things. The world had ended; he had seen time begin again. God was dead, and yet Lucifer felt a little tug of melancholy in his heart.

This was not to say there was regret. There wasn't, and there never would be, but it was hard not to remember each of the horrors that had eventually led to this quiet moment. Was it worth it? It was. But he carried the ghost of anguish on his back, on his shoulders, in his throat, balled up.

"Lucifer."

The angel of beauty lifted his head some, caught the prince by the door. Well, Michael was no prince anymore. A king, one might say. "I'm sorry," Lucifer whispered. "I've been tired."

Michael's already soft expression simmered into deeper tenderness. He removed his cloak, casting it over a chair, before he made his way over, planting a knee on the mattress, crawling toward Lucifer in just a loose, dark tunic, a bit tight around his large build. Lucifer liked it; his tunic and his build. Michael's mouth found the younger angel's — lips molded to his for just a moment before he pulled back. And his gaze was on Lucifer, taking him in, glancing at all the shifts of his body. "Is something wrong?"

"All this guilt is wrong," Lucifer answered honestly, and he was happy that he did, because he'd been asking himself the same, seeking an answer the same. "Can you lay with me?"

Michael turned his head, kissed Lucifer's jaw, then murmured, "Yes, but you'll tell me what's wrong?"

"It's just a little difficult for me," Lucifer sighed. "Overwhelming. Scary." Michael parted his lips, but the other kept speaking. "I feel unrecognizable. Does my body look different to you? I feel the way I did after I fell." A flick of fear passed over Michael's eyes; oddly, Lucifer was amused by it. 'The God-killer is worried his angel is sad.' This had to all be a dream, but if it was, Lucifer hoped he wouldn't wake quite yet. It had been a while since he'd dreamt of sweet angel Michael, rather than the chief prince with bloodied, armored hands.

"You look like," Michael said, "the same Lucifer I saw in the crowd, when we were both young. When I saw you for the first time."

"I saw you for the first time," Lucifer replied, "before I ever met you. In a dream, I think."

"Do you think you're dreaming now?" Michael whispered.

Lucifer smiled a bit at that. "I don't know." He was thinking of God, dead and ripped to pieces by the same stars that He had once torn up. "I don't really know anything. For the first time in what feels like an eternity." With that, the angel of beauty raised his body and let out a soft, tiny sigh. He disentangled himself from the duvet, letting it fall to his waist. He wore a tunic that was, while not sheer, plain white and thin enough that nearly none of his body was left to the imagination. He still felt beautiful, which was good, but he felt different, and it unsettled him, made him melancholic.

Michael shifted to sit beside him, and then he kissed his cheek. "I love you."

The fallen angel of beauty smiled. "Is that so?"

"Should I kill another God for you to prove it?"

"We're the only Gods left now, all us angels." Lucifer found that Michael still wasn't very bright, but he could never be perfect of course — only God had been, and only Lucifer had been meant to be. A little pride in him thought, 'I'm still perfect,' but he suppressed that for now. "I don't want you to kill anything for me. I just want to lay with you a while before we go out again." To continue the rebuilding. "We have to make another Earth soon... You and me. How will we do it?"

Michael hummed, then shrugged. "I'm not sure. Maybe Uriel will know." He turned his head some, then lifted a brow. "Why are you looking at me like that?"

Lucifer hadn't realized his gaze had turned so loving; it made his cheeks warm. "I just think you're very pretty, Michael." He pecked his jaw how he used to when they were young. "Angel of pretty." Low, bashful, Michael laughed and asked if he was interested in reversing their roles with a certain tone that clued Lucifer into what he meant and only made him giggle more. "I don't think I'm the penetrating type. My heart is too soft, and I'm too delicate." Michael laughed again in utter disbelief. Lucifer, though, began imagining his fingers in Michael, prodding, and watching the chief archangel squirm and moan breathily, weakly.

"You can lay beneath if you want, I'll get on your lap."

"Oh? Like this?" Lucifer climbed over to sit himself on Michael's groin and lean in to kiss a giddy mouth. "Make love to me instead. Finish in me."

Against Lucifer's lips, Michael replied amusedly, "Is that an order?"

"I want to be loved."

"Angel of love," Michael teased, but his hands went to

Lucifer's waist and squeezed him tight. "But I'm tired, dear Lucifer. I just returned from a faraway star—"

"*Please*," Lucifer whined, and the prince melted, dropping his head to press a kiss to the younger one's throat. It was slow, soft; then, there was a little suckling as Michael dragged a hand up his side. "Mmm." Lucifer pressed against him, feeling his angel body press flush against Michael's own. The heated sensation made him shudder.

Michael glanced down at Lucifer's figure, then mumbled, "I can't believe I have you."

Snickering, Lucifer replied, "Hold on tight. I might run away when you least expect." 'How I ran from that dead God.' He touched one of Michael's hands by his ribs. "Treat me well if you want to keep me."

"I'll worship you."

"Mm. Good." Lucifer felt Michael's smile against him. "Don't expect it back from me. I don't sing little songs for any Gods anymore."

"Are you sure I couldn't get one out of you, beloved Lucifer?" Michael nuzzled him, then pressed another kiss to his throat.

Lucifer squeezed one of his love's fingers; they were large; Michael was large. "You're stalling. I told you to make love to me."

"And to finish in you."

"Good," he cooed. "Don't forget."

Michael clutched at Lucifer's tunic, tugged on it, and the younger one sighed pleasantly. Soon after — the archangel grinned back and pulled Lucifer's drapery over his head, tossed it aside. He lifted Lucifer, then turned them around so that he would rest against some of the dozen pillows on their bed, and Michael wasted no time in kissing him again — this time on the lips, soft, slow.

Lucifer hummed into his mouth, parting his legs already, feeling needy for it now. 'Needy for love.' And he gasped when Michael pressed their bodies up against each other again, ground them together, and when one hand skimmed up from his waist, dragged against Lucifer's chest. "Ah." He shivered a little, feeling the brown bud harden as Michael rubbed his knuckle against it. "Ahh–" Michael's other hand traveled down to where he could prod at Lucifer, working in a finger immediately; he was relaxed, and it slipped inside easily, needy. Angel of need.

"After this, I'll carry you up somewhere higher. I want to make love to you by the stars."

Lucifer's face flushed, but he was happy, truly. 'Make love.' All he'd ever wanted to create, and now he was creating. It was nice. "Thank you." He wasn't sure why he said it, but Michael's smile made it worth being so vulnerable.

Michael leaned down and flicked his tongue against a nipple — Lucifer gasped — then began to suckle. His other hand continued pumping into Lucifer's entrance and the younger angel whined. He rocked into Michael's hand as the archangel teased him mercilessly. He arched his back, lifted his chin, let himself be adored.

"Ah—" It was nice, it was really nice to be loved. "Michael."

Michael removed his mouth and his hand, then murmured, "Do you want to be on your back?"

"Yes."

"Won't it be uncomfortable?"

"Be tender with me."

When Michael finally entered him, it was tender, and he fit well, like he belonged there. Lucifer supposed that he did.

MILTON

The devil didn't turn his head as he spoke: "Michael."

Prince of Heaven, great archangel of archangels, the saint Michael stood nearby, listening to the hoots of what must've been an owl by the window, open to leak in breeze from the outside, to spill the light of the full moon onto plain wooden board flooring, patterned coarse carpet, an oil portrait on the wall with an elaborately golden border and a royal man in hefty garments posed at the center. Michael could not name him, didn't know the rulers of the Earth — their lives so short, so insignificant. "Satan," he said, his voice stiff, tense.

Before him, Satan was curled up in a chair with his legs tucked underneath him, making him appear smaller, more delicate. A silk, yellow banyan was draped over him — with green motifs at the collar and rolled back sleeves that folded at Lucifer's elbows. Beneath, there was a pale shirt, then a long waistcoat, and snug breeches climbing down to heeled black leather shoes with silver buckles. As for his hair, it was tied back at the nape of his neck with a black ribbon, the tail hanging limply on the same shoulder that his banyan was nearly slipping off from, while some loose curls of hair had fallen to frame his face. In the earlier part of the century, men would seek to whiten their complexion with lead-based makeup, while blushing their cheeks and lips with red rouge. Satan needs neither, so his face was only lightly powdered, perhaps a remnant from the cosmetics he wore in the morning, never reapplied.

Before answering, Lucifer licked his finger, brought it down to the thick pages of the massive leather book on his lap, then flipped the pages not yet age-toned though it was printed nearly sixty years ago. Michael knew it had been that long because of Satan's words: "Jacob Tonson had this copy printed in London in 1719, where Catherine Street descends into the Strand; it was a gift for me. I met him at the social club that he founded when one of the men he invited said I should meet this Tonson and hear about this poem that he was selling and making him more money than any other work in his collection. When I met Tonson, he joked to me that he'd made a deal with the devil, and then I saw the poem they were referring to."

"What are you doing here?" Michael interjected; he wasn't here to catch up with an old friend.

"I acted like I'd never heard of it, but I had known Milton too, of course. He'd been blind for a few years when I met him, and he was grieving his wife. I couldn't help but be interested in a man like that — a sightless poet. I told him I was the devil, and he thought I'd come to kill him. Instead, I talked with him." Satan played with the ends of *Paradise Lost*'s pages. "Each time I've tried to tell anyone about us, you've murdered them. I suppose you didn't think I was behind *Paradise Lost* at first."

Michael grunted, "What's the purpose of it? Do you think it'll make man more sympathetic to you?"

"If I wanted their sympathy, I would be at their feet like a dog, much like you with your Father." Satan tilted his head to him, then nodded at the robe that the archangel had draped over himself. "You should change into something more appropriate. If anyone walks in, they'll call the porters, though I suppose you could kill them all."

"Then why," Michael pushed, "did you do it? And why are

you here? Do you want the humans to see you? Do you plan to start the apocalypse?"

"This is such a terrible university," Satan avoided the questions with a soft laugh. "I've been wearing the skin of one of their professors to deal with all the posh little boys, but I won't be here much longer. They can all believe their professor disappeared one day, and in a few decades, I'll burn the Trinity College archives that make any mention of me."

Michael took a step forward, then another, each heavy, nearly stomping his way over. "You won't answer me. Why shouldn't I rip off your arms for what you've done?"

"You don't want to," said Lucifer, shutting the book in his lap finally, then smiling blithely. "Now, sit." He gestured toward the pillowed loveseat beside his own. "It'll rain soon." The last time Michael had been with Satan in the rain, it had been the last days of the Flood, the same hour that he was supposed to grab the devil, drag him back to Heaven to present him to their Father for a death and resurrection. "Oh, you're so angry... I can see it on your face. What could have made you so upset, angel?"

"*You*," Michael snapped, "are wasting my time here. Tell me why you told that poet about your rebellion against God."

"I hardly did. You haven't read *Paradise Lost,* have you? It's not about me as much as you'd think. Milton is a man and, like all humans, couldn't care less for the time of angels before man. He was interested in himself, in the state of his own nation. What I told him were just a few details."

"What were the details?"

"That I was beautiful, and that God loved me. I said that I never did anything wrong, though that perhaps my own beauty and power took my hands farther that I should have reached." Satan reached to play with his hair, fiddling with the golden threads. "All I did was inspire him, but he told his own story. I was just a symbol for what he felt, what we might all feel." His gaze had grown distant. "Milton dictated it to me, and I wrote it all down. I made some suggestions, some of which he hated. He said this epic couldn't have a romance in it; it would destroy the integrity of the story. There are... so many lines I can still recite from the first day I transcribed his words." He, slowly, turned back to Michael. Expression empty.

"Uriel," Michael murmured, "was the one who told me about it. The book. A copy is in his hands in Heaven."

"Milton asked me if angels love. I said they did."

"You lied to him."

"He wrote: Let it suffice thee that thou knowest us happy, and without love no happiness. Whatever pure thou in the body enjoyest — and pure thou wert created — we enjoy in eminence; and obstacle find none of membrane, joint, or limb, exclusive bars. Easier than air with air, if spirits embrace. Total they mix, union of pure with pure desiring, nor restrained conveyance need, as flesh to mix with flesh, or soul with soul." Satan paused, then explained, "To humans, Heaven is but a fantasy, and it's far too easy to sink into that delusion with them. In Heaven, I remember I fantasized of a complete union with your body."

There was a touch of sincerity that made Michael nearly grimace; Lucifer must've been tricking him, but Michael's breath felt heavy on his tongue, and he allowed it to spill from between dry lips.

"I wouldn't have been satisfied if I fucked you. I often think that these days. If I'd taken your cock, it wouldn't have felt like enough. Whatever way that I loved you, there would have been no end to my desire. You never did desire me — you knew you *had* me — but no matter how tightly I might've held you, my desire continued to grow and grow, larger than me and the both of us. You could have fucked me, and my desire would have only grown deeper, bloodier. There's nothing we could have done."

Michael listened to the first taps on the window of rain, then he answered, "Why are you telling me this?" His chest was beginning to ache, though his heart was still. How dare Satan speak of Lucifer, as if he were him? "None of it is true. You'll never know how Lucifer felt." Though he worried now that Satan had all of Lucifer's memories.

"It must infuriate you," Satan whispered, "to know that you never loved Lucifer the way he needed. God has punished you and made you believe that you fucked his most beautiful angel into a monster, but you let him fall without ever having a proper taste of him." He lifted his head, elegantly, as Michael's hand went around his throat, gripping so soft it may have been a caress instead of a threatening gesture. "I think you wish that *Paradise Lost* did mention us." A grin, sweet and venomous.

"I came to warn you against ever doing something like this again."

"I think you wish we weren't erased from history." Lucifer lifted a hand, touched the fingers around his neck.

"You don't know anything."

"Your hand is shaking." Satan took a trembling index, tugged on it delicately until Michael allowed his finger to be guided up to the devil's plump lips. He slipped it between, allowed the index to slide across his tongue, then began to suckle, slow, deliberate. "Mm." Michael furrowed his brow, but he didn't draw away, feeling the wet heat of his old friend's mouth, so much like it had once been, a distant memory of his tongue flicking against angel Lucifer's, hearing him laugh ashamedly.

"I saw us on a stained-glass window," Michael found himself saying, watching as Satan trailed a hand down his own chest, over his abdomen, toward his groin. "You were unrecognizable." So was he. Hiding his tunic and build and face in his cloak, Michael had thought to tug on whoever was nearby and tell them that Lucifer hadn't looked like that when he'd cast him from Heaven. Lucifer had been enraged, draped in blood, but he had been beautiful; he had even screamed in pain prettily; as he fell, Satan had looked like he was laying back to sleep gorgeously. Now, Michael turned his gaze down to himself as he began to feel a sort of painful tug between his legs, a tiny rock of his hips forward.

Satan pulled Michael's hand out of his mouth, then said, "I

wish they all knew about us. They'd learn how weak you really are." He stood, turned his face up to the chief angel, then said. "God hates this world and every human in it. He's abandoned them."

"You're wrong."

"But He still likes to watch, and He sees you now, knows how hard you get whenever I touch you." Satan's hand now went to cup Michael, squeeze the throbbing sin that the archangel flinched in shame of. "He wanted me to rebel. I often wonder if He wanted you to, as well." Lucifer's tempting mouth brushed Michael's jaw, and the prince sighed harshly, not liking the way he rocked into the devil's hold. "I wonder if he made this for me." Michael didn't stop him, didn't stop Satan when he tugged off Michael's cloak, leaving him there in a short angelic tunic. "To tease me." His hand slithered beneath, gripped the base of the girth. "Do you ever touch it, Michael?"

The prince's jaw was clenched, unmoving.

"You don't know that you can please yourself at all, do you?" Gripping tight, Satan dragged his hand along every inch slowly, reaching the head, then tugging down on the skin. He smiled — Satan did — when Michael barely suppressed a noise from deep in his throat like a whimper. "It's really quite simple." A thin hand reached for the much more muscular one, bringing it to the pulsing hardness, so they could hold it together. "Do as I do."

Michael wanted to snarl, but the devil was the devil, and his golden eyes were like suns; the chief archangel found his hand moving, pumping his sin with Lucifer's hand to guide him.

"Good," Lucifer cooed. "Squeeze it." His clothes seemed too complicated for Michael to remove properly, though he started imagining it. He thought of growing frustrated, tearing off the devil's coat, his breeches, bending him over the table at the other side of the room and gripping around the ribbon in his hair as he fucked him. "Good. You're so good, Michael."

The shame was making him clench his eyes shut, turn down

and away, but Satan pecked his lips against Michael's cheek. "This is sin."

"I created it."

"Why?" Michael was thrusting into his own hand and Lucifer's hand; together, they managed a good hold around the thickness. It made him ill — the length, the width; God had punished him with this.

"I suppose to love you."

Lucifer took Michael's mouth, but it wasn't harsh how the prince was expecting, it wasn't violent like it had been in the weeks before the Flood that destroyed the Earth. It was simple, gentle, not particularly deep. Their eyes both shut, and Michael kissed him back just as softly — leaning into it and hoping that if he ever opened his eyes again, he'd be in Heaven with angel Lucifer, in a meadow, on a cloud, somewhere alone. Between them, Michael had begun to drip, and he shuddered in fear at his own want, but he couldn't stop the rolls of his body. The pressure around him, around *it*, felt so good that he didn't want to believe it was wrong for him to like this, to like Lucifer.

He'd liked Lucifer so much once, beloved Lucifer.

When Michael's thrusts turned uneven in between his frustrated groans of pleasure, Lucifer ceased to kiss him, instead turning his face up and nuzzling Michael's own. "Good." Michael only knew how to be good. "Finish into my hands." If Michael were thinking, he would have resisted or argued, but he kept his eyes shut, and with just another twitch or two of his hips, he felt himself throb again, then finish into the devil's eagerly waiting palms and fingers. Only then, the chief prince finally opened his eyes, saw himself in a university in a country in the human year of 1774 AD.

He thought Satan would wipe his hands on Michael's tunic, maybe strike him across the face, but Lucifer brought the saint's seed to his mouth and drank, like a desperate sinner might from a stoup of holy water at the base of a crucifix.

BATH

Lucifer released a soft, sweet moan, and Michael smiled as his fingers worked through the threads of gold, suds trickling down onto the younger angel's neck. There had been a time when the strongest of all the angelic host couldn't bathe anyone without accidentally snapping a bone of theirs in his grip, but now his large, powerful hands were gentle. They washed Lucifer's hair delicately. They squeezed the angel of beauty's muscles firmly, but never painfully. And Lucifer replied to each squeeze with a happy sigh.

The two of them sat together in one circular tub made of wood, a little too small to comfortably sit two angels, meaning the pair had to be pressed together, their legs forcibly parted to accommodate their bodies, and their chests brushing against each other when one of them reached over the shoulder of another for some kind of soap or oil. The angel of beauty smiled whenever it happened, trying not to reach out and rub his hand against one of Michael's half-firm nipples. It took yet another effort not to lean closer and flick his tongue against it either, nor did he allow himself to imagine the chief prince's cheeks flushed and warm enough to invite a kiss.

Instead, he laid a cheek on Michael's shoulder, and his eyes fluttered shut.

They could have visited a bathhouse, but it was nice to be alone like this, to hear nothing but the ripples of water against each other. It was very wonderful, too, to admit in near silence, "I'm afraid, Michael. Michael, prince of Heaven." His front was partly pressed to the muscular softness of Michael's, and he felt the rumble of Michael's laugh, felt how the chuckle worked its way up from his belly to his mouth, his plump lips.

"Afraid of what, Lucifer? Beloved Lucifer."

"I can't tell you." The world around them was hazy — maybe they were in Michael's home, a little place by the sea, but who can say? "I feel at times that I'm going to do something terrible. Do you ever feel like that, Michael? Do you fear for the future?"

"What could you be afraid of?" A hand went to the blonde hair, just so recently washed, spilling down Lucifer's back. "What can go wrong in Heaven?"

"I don't know." Lucifer breathed. "Sometimes it feels like I've already done something terrible, or like I'm doing it now. I feel unforgivable at times. I feel like I'm... not good, if I'm happy. Does God want me to suffer? I suppose I could do that. If He wants me to bleed for Him, I will, but I would just like to know why." He turned his face, then nuzzled it against Michael's jaw. "Do you understand me?"

"I can only do my best to understand," replied Michael, slow and careful but still kindly. "Forgive me." He pecked Lucifer's forehead, then pressed another kiss, this one right over a shut eyelid. "You think so much. Try to forget about your worries for a moment, brother. Stay with me here, rather than lingering in your own head. Let me wash you a little more."

Lucifer laughed. "But I'm clean already." When the hands of the archangel went for his waist, taking it firmly, the young angel thought, 'Perfectly shaped for you to hold. But you don't even realize it. You never do.' "Mmm..." Michael was laying his lips over Lucifer's smile. "Michael." A nice name, each syllable swirling saccharine on his tongue. "Thank you." He placed his fingers over the prince's. "Kiss me some more."

"I don't like seeing you so sad," Michael sighed but he did as told, pressing another kiss, slower, deeper. "But I don't know how to save you from worry." Finally, Lucifer was opening his eyes, his gaze unfocused but maintained on Michael. "What can I do?" Lucifer puckered his lips against Michael's, and the prince began to smile again. "More kissing?"

"I want more of you," Lucifer mumbled. "When I have you, I stop thinking, for however long." There was a touch of sorrow bleeding from his words. "I can stop worrying if you kiss me more— Not because I forget about the future but because I stop caring. Even if all the horrible things I imagine come true, I feel less worried about them if you're kissing me." He hesitated. "Is that strange?"

Instead of answering, Michael cupped Lucifer's face in his hands, then kissed him again. He pressed it as deep as he could into the beautiful angel's mouth, tilting his face one way before tilting it the other. As he did, Lucifer began to hum in delight, only then to gasp when Michael's teeth scraped on him. Soon, he was parting his lips, accepting the prince's tongue to slither inside and run against his own tongue, submissively laying still, wanting to see what Michael would do. The prince didn't often take initiative like this, and immediately, Michael started stumbling, prodding clumsily and juvenilely. But Lucifer found it so cute, found Michael's hidden timidity so wonderful all the time. It was special, their small secret. However much Lucifer enjoyed fantasizing of the chief dominating him mercilessly, his heart always remained with God's golden, good-est child.

He drew back; Michael panted, his forehead against Lucifer's, puffs of hot air lapping at the younger one's face. "I'm sorry."

Lucifer teased, "Don't be. Never be sorry for kissing me." As Michael's hands began to drift away, Lucifer straightened up and shrugged his shoulders a little before noting how Michael's gaze followed a bead of bathwater rolling down chest. The chief prince lowered his face, kissed where the droplet had trailed down. Shivering, Lucifer felt Michael's mouth brush against his divine ribs. "You taught me never to be ashamed of this body, and I never want you to be ashamed of loving it, Michael."

"I wish," breathed the archangel, "I could wash you a little more, but we've been here too long, haven't we? Other angels wonder why we spend all our time together, and I don't want them to catch us like this. They'll talk. They'll tell Uriel." One of his hands skimmed up the younger one's spine, climbing toward the smooth back that seemed so naked without hefty, violet wings branching out.

As if reading his mind — "Can you preen my wings?" Lucifer's voice was quiet, and Michael nodded a little, bringing his grip to Lucifer's waist again, then guiding him to turn his body over. As elegant as a portrait, the beautiful angel lifted himself, leaned against the edge of the tub, just about bending over its edge as his wings crept out from the place where they'd violently torn out from once, made blood splatter and drip down the curve of his back and to his legs. Vulnerably, Lucifer was without his jewels in the bath for once, and he remembered how sad he'd been just some minutes ago. How fearful.

As Michael moved behind him — the wood *creaking* — Lucifer reached for a nearby oil sat on a stool and handed it to the prince. 'One day, you won't touch me as gently as this. I can't tell you how I know.' Just seconds after he'd heard the dripping sounds of two great, powerful hands smothering themselves in oil, Lucifer felt the longest primary feathers of his wings be ruffled beneath wet fingers that ran toward the more sensitive parts of him. 'Is this how God feels? Does He find Himself unable to enjoy anything because He sees its end?'

A soft, pleasured moan escaped the angel of beauty as Michael worked his hands, massaging a great bulk of the feathers and getting in between them to free any speck of uncleanliness. Each time he brushed against the inner side of the scapulars, another little noise would seep from Lucifer, and he'd shift a little at the warmth knotting his lower belly. 'Whenever I'm with Michael, I feel closer to God. I feel closer to God when I'm with Michael than when I'm in Eden.' The blasphemy was delicious, and he was hungrier than he'd thought; even still, sadness lingered. Lucifer gripped the edge of the tub and curved his body just a tad more, wondering if his hair cascading down and in between his wings would bother the one who was washing him, who was almost worshiping how Lucifer had taught Michael to worship. But, the angel of strength lifted one hand to take the golden hair and gently tug it over Lucifer's shoulder, the same one that he took a second to kiss. He did it so delicately, as if he feared the younger angel would shatter. Perhaps he'd remembered Lucifer's sadness, as well.

Some of the oil was dribbling down the wings, trailing down Lucifer's spine, heading toward the curve at the end of his back and beyond, even wetting his entrance and his thighs. From the knees down, he was still in the soapy water, and a glance backward proved that the chief prince was still clouded in bath bubbles. "Oh," Lucifer huffed as two of Michael's fingers traced from the inner wings toward the downward places the oil had traveled. "Kiss me there too," he asked softly. "Please, Michael."

Michael replied quietly. "I wish I had the words to tell you how beautiful you are, how much joy you offer me." He ran his touch against the entrance, applying another coating of oil that trembled Lucifer's thighs as he felt, and *heard*, it drip from his body into the water. "Will you ever annoy of me talking to you like this? I'm sorry. What I'm meaning to say is that I never want you to be sad. I want you to be happy even when I'm not. Really, I want you to be happier even more than I want to have you." He kissed him; God's angel and God's favorite; angel of saving and angel of falling. Michael's tongue pressed into Lucifer's opening as it'd done into Lucifer's mouth, and the pretty angel moaned long, his eyelids weighing like he'd just grown drowsy. "I love you," he said between plunges of his tongue, "I love you more than I want to keep you."

'No, no,' Lucifer wanted to tell him. 'Tell me you'll never let me go. I would rather be miserable beside you than happy without you.' But he was biting down on his lip and almost whining as Michael pressed in his fingers again, this time adding a third, and beginning to pump them. Lucifer felt his palms scrape against the dry wood as he held it tighter, tighter; it was all he could do to avoid touching himself at the front, working his hand and rutting against it madly. He could only ever touch himself madly, no matter the patience Michael wanted to please him with. He wished he could make love like Michael did, so sweet and innocently.

"I love you," Lucifer replied, trying not to say more but failing. "Don't ever let me run away." He gasped, his body jerking when Michael struck the perfect place, sucking right by where his fingers thrusted. "Please." His hips rocked before he stop them. "I love you. I love you, I love you." It was like a hymn, like one of his worship songs out in the streets that he'd drag Michael to dance with him to.

Michael curled his fingers and, as Lucifer whined, asked, "Are you close?"

Lucifer's wings fluttered, almost pathetically. "Almost, almost..." The prince pulled free his hand, then kissed, lapped, tongued Lucifer's entrance for some moments of silence, save for the angel of worship's cries and the ripples in the water. "Michael," he pleaded. "Michael, please."

Lucifer's toes curled, and his body twitched, and he wished the chief prince would just pin him down and ravish him because he wasn't sure that he could hold himself up any longer. As he'd feared — when the wave of finish shuddered his body, and he felt himself spill as his vision darkened like he were facing the cold abyss above, his legs bent awkwardly. His wings, frantic, beat in every direction and splashed water everywhere, then he fell back against Michael, who'd been inching away. Both of them yelped, and Michael's head knocked back against the edge of the tub with a thud that made Lucifer instantly gasp.

"Michael! Michael, are you hurt?!" The chief prince groaned, half sunken into the tub with a beautiful angel flopped over him, but soon, Michael began to smile, began to laugh heartily. And Lucifer, too, found himself laughing.

There's hardly a greater joy in paradise than kissing a smiling, giggling face.

EAST

"Father," the archangel Michael prayed. "Father, give me strength. Lord Highest, set in my heart your presence. I am in need. The storms of sin are unrelenting, and I am drowning. Yet, I lift my eyes to you."

"Oh," moaned the devil's voice. "*Michael—*"

Immediately, the chief prince drew a breath, his hands fisted into the flimsy fabric over the poor excuse for a bed he'd been offered by the demons, the devil's thousand of children. He felt his body peel itself off the bed, and he ignored the throb between his legs to stumble over to the clothes he'd removed mere minutes earlier. Harshly, he grabbed and yanked his tunic over his head, then wrapped himself up in his reddened cloak. 'I'll kill him.' Michael stumbled back, turned on his heel, and headed for the way in. 'I'll kill them both.'

He wasn't certain of the way to Satan's chambers, but it had to be nearby, perhaps against the wall he'd been beside of. Firmly, Michael put a hand on the stone adjacent the entrance to his room — the 'broken things' room, where the devil had placed him — then walked stiffly. A corridor was soon at his fingertips, and he twisted into it, shuffling through. What he found was a simple wooden doorway, nothing like the extravagant entrance into where the devil hid his nest. However, all the noises he'd earlier heard were obviously coming from the other side, clearer and louder than ever. Shoving the door aside, the chief prince stomped into the room, ground his teeth, prepared to grab the two demons and pummel them to pulp.

Michael stopped; his heart stopped with him. On a large bed, at the center of a muraled wall ahead of him — he realized that this was not a typical bedroom, as it was far too bare and there were streaks on the ground trailed behind the wooden legs below the bedding — the devil and his favorite demon were sinning. Lucifer was on his hands and knees, facing the chief prince, his lip curling up prettily at the sight of him; his body was draped by a sheer, crimson tunic that was less clothing and more like a bloody tint over his naked body, up until his waist where it was hitched up. By Satan's hips, Baal's talons were dangerously gripping over rattling chains of gold; with each rock of his body forward, he dug himself deeper into the beautiful one below. All of Lucifer's jewelry chimed and sang as he moved, and it was a lovely addition to his gasps, pleasured moans — then cruel laughter. Baal, like the chief prince, immediately froze, his eyes widening, face reddening, before his jaw clenched and gaze flared with fury.

"Oh, Baal," Lucifer teased, though he was facing Michael, "why ever did you stop? I don't remember you ever being shy about us having company." The demon duke tried to say the devil's name, but he grunted when Lucifer arched his back, rutted back against him and let out a long, sweet whine.

"Stop this," Michael managed to grit out, his chest aching like he'd been hit there. "Beast. *Beast!* You will burn because of what you've done. Do you think you can tempt me by whispering my name while you sin?"

"Your name? Why would I moan *your* name?" Lucifer quirked an eyebrow, and Michael blinked, once, twice, before a horror settled over his soul. 'Did I imagine it?' he thought. Had he projected his dreams onto Lucifer's fucking with Baal? 'Have I sinned?' The sin of desire.

Baal, however, laughed and said, "We thought it would be funny." And though Lucifer said nothing, Michael almost fell to his own knees in relief that he hadn't been delusional. "What, didn't you enjoy it, prince?" He gripped Lucifer tight again and returned to thrusting, except this time maintaining eye contact with Michael. "His voice is perfect, and he's beautiful. You don't know that his body is better than a thousand Heavens."

"Be silent," Michael hissed, turning his face away, refusing to see though that didn't save him from Lucifer's moans. 'I shouldn't have believed him for a second. He is the father of lies. He is the king of the demons. He is responsible for sin.' But his feet may have been rooted to the ground below; he could not move anything more than the heart in his chest to beat, to beat, to beat far too quickly. 'Lucifer.' His noises. His body. 'No.' He shut his eyes, remembered the blood on his armor and the humans he'd killed to smother the tightening in his gut.

The devil, however, was now moaning loud, languid. Baal, too, was grunting in pleasure. In between, the slap of their bodies was constant and horribly dirty, wet. Michael breathed out, harsh, and thought to leave, but his anger was bubbling up in his throat again. There was, too, a certain disgust twisting his stomach as if around a finger; the revulsion directed itself at Baal. Baal, the bull of a monster rocking into Satan, who was certainly not Lucifer but had his sweet face. 'This makes me sick.' It didn't matter that this was the devil; he still cried out like the angel of beauty and his hair was still his and that pretty body was still his. Michael opened his eyes again, saw it for himself.

The fallen angel of worship shuddered, then chuckled, reaching back, taking Baal's hip and forcing him to stop. "Why," Satan giggled, "are you still here, archangel? Do you like to watch? Are you a voyeur like your Father? Do you want see how a demon fucks the beautiful angel you adored in Heaven?"

"You sicken me," Michael snapped. "The filth that you partake in will be the reason you burn one day." He listened to Lucifer laugh once more, push Baal away, then sigh as the sin pulled out of him and leaked. "But, before I leave," Michael forced out his mouth, "I wanted to tell you that, tomorrow, I will lead an attack against the easternmost tribe." He didn't know why he was saying this; he supposed he'd planned to inform the devil of this since yesterday.

Satan huffed but seemingly ignored the prince, craning his neck back and murmuring something that Michael didn't quite catch. He was perplexed for no more than a few seconds, however, as Baal settled to sit, clawed hand coming to grip high on Lucifer's waist, then guide him back. Stiffening, Michael saw the devil settle onto Baal's lap, facing the angel prince still, teasingly swing his hips, before sinking onto hardened sin. "*Oh,*" Satan whispered lovingly, one hand delicately trailing down from his chest, his stomach, to his own groin. "Mmhmh," he hummed, then placed his hand on his own arousal, beginning to work his fingers. "Easternmost... you said?" Satan smiled, mischievously, stroked himself, rose a few inches, and lowered his body again with a sharp gasp. "No... You should take the one by Mount Hermon."

Michael's face was burning, and the fury clenched at his pelvis was so strong his knees almost buckled. "What—?" left his mouth dumbly.

"Mount Hermon," Lucifer cooed, grinding down on Baal. "That's where the leader of the Watchers is." He tossed his head a little and some strands of his impossibly long hair fell over his front. "And that Azazel is there too... Don't waste time. You should attack them first."

"The— The—" Michael coughed as Lucifer more earnestly began to ride Baal, who was behind him making all kinds of pleasured noises with a deep, rumbling reverb that, horribly, also tugged at the prince's building, burning need. "The people in the east— They worship their giants. They must be... punished." 'Damn you.' Michael's hands were turning fists once more but the pain of his nails cutting into his palms was not enough; in fact, the sting nearly made him whine pathetically. 'Damn you both. Damn you, Baal, for corrupting Lucifer.' He was not angel Lucifer. 'Oh but he looks just like him. The way his body moves. The way he sings. His sunny eyes, his smile.'

"Mm, yes, but the east is prepared for you at the moment. You must wait for them to starve, so that they're adequately weak enough to fall quickly." Satan glanced down as one of Baal's hands raised to his sternum, then to one of his nipples to rub at the piercing there. Humming again, Lucifer put his fingers over Baal's to squeeze them encouragingly. "Don't— Don't be so hasty." Michael stared; he stared. "Oh, sweet little angel. You're so hard."

"Don't," Michael said but he didn't know what he meant. "Don't you... put your eyes on me, Satan!"

"I can't help it. It's rather prominent... and, really, it's so easy to pity you." The devil tugged Baal's hand up, then kissed his index finger, flicking his tongue against it. "You should touch yourself." Michael clutched at his cloak, tried to tug it over his tunic to hide himself. "It's very easy. I can guide you, Michael." The chief prince tried not to think of Baal, tried not to look too hard at how the demon was thrusting up into the angel he'd once kissed everywhere he could. "Come closer."

Michael lost himself, for a moment, in the fantasy. He was seeing sweet Lucifer in his mind, the shy thing. 'I remember you fighting against me in a secret garden. I remember you pouting each time I pinned you down. Beautiful Lucifer. You were so ashamed of yourself. The innocent, lovely smiles you gave me. Your voice.' The prince took a step forward, and he released his cloak from his grip. Inhaling, trembling, he saw the ghost of angel Lucifer before him slow down on Baal's length, then reach out with both hands, pull up the archangel's tunic.

"Good, good," Satan purred before kissing the wet beading at the tip, and the little touch of sweetness made the prince shiver. "Stroke it." Without his armor, Michael wasn't remembering where he was, who he was. His hand took himself, and a pitiful whine fell past his lips. This horrible thing was sensitive. "Pump it." Michael did, his hips jerked forward, and he rasped at the pulsing sensation that climbed up into his head. "Yes, like that. How naturally it comes to you, angel." Satan grinned and, for a moment, the dream shattered; Michael saw the beast, saw the grotesque beneath his angel. "Slap it against my mouth."

He shouldn't. He shouldn't. 'God forgive me.' Michael, weak, did as told, tapping his hardness against plump, parted lips, saliva coating them. It sent bolts of goodness across his body. "Satan—" He wanted to say that he will kill him, but instead, he merely whispered his name again. "Satan."

The devil's tongue peeked out, lapped against the head, then swirled. After this, the gorgeous being in between angel prince and demon duke returned to riding with vigor, not wasting any time to breathe hot against the prince's stiffness. Just the drag of his lips against it made Michael see stars; yet, when it slipped past them, slid across a tongue to strike against the back of the devil's throat — it was Heaven that he saw. Or, perhaps, it was a hundred Heavens, a thousand of them. "Mm," Lucifer moaned around it, the feeling forcing Michael's hips forward, back, forward again, without thinking.

"Satan," he panted. "Satan." The devil sucked, like it were a candy in his mouth, dipped his head forward, then back to the tip. All the chief prince could do was surrender, take Lucifer's hair in a grip too gentle and weak. In a haze, he felt himself roll forward, fuck a perfect mouth sloppily, amateurishly. It was such an overwhelming euphoria that he could be drowning in it; his vision blurred and his hearing grew muffled. He could hardly hear Baal's laughter or Lucifer's suffocated, mocking moans.

Once, Michael remembered, then devil had begged to have this in his mouth, to taste it, and he had denied him. It had occurred in Heaven, in the prince's own house. How stupid Michael had been. How stupid.

"Satan," Michael gasped a final time before he felt a goodness so strong that it turned painful, that could have made him believe Lucifer had ripped off his length with his teeth. With how wet it was, how hot, he could have believed he'd bled into him. Instead, looking down, he saw the devil pull away to reveal a smile with white dripping past his bottom lip the color of Heaven's gates. His eyes flashed with victory and, below him, Baal was groaning in what must've been finish too.

Satan, lazily, reached down to stroke himself again, and he said, "Attack Mount Hermon." Dread was sinking into the prince's heart, his eyes widening in horrific realization over what had just occurred. "Listen to me," Lucifer added, "or else I'll tell God what you've done."

SURRENDER

They were wrestling one day — Michael and Lucifer. Roughly, the chief prince pinned the most beloved angel in Heaven to the grass, threw one leg over him, set himself against Lucifer's back at the same time he twisted a delicate arm behind him. "Ah!" Lucifer cried, but Michael laid his weight over him some more with a rumbling, happy chuckle. Blonde hair had been tied back into a thick braid that nuzzled Michael's cheek, a few stray leaves tangled in the threads after so long they'd spent rolling over the dirt. Distantly, they could hear angels chattering, chirping, moving along the roads and doing what they always did, their usual routines in eternity. *"Michael,"* came a gasp, tight and desperate.

Michael found himself grinning broadly. "Yes, Lucifer?" Instead of replying, the angel of beauty kicked his feet angrily, thumping them against the ground, but Michael caught a leg between his own, squeezed it with his strong thighs. "Do you surrender?"

"No– Agh!" Lucifer shuddered when Michael pulled on his arm just a little more.

"Are you sure?"

The caught angel thrashed like a butterfly trapped between

someone's hands, though he kept his wings within his flesh; they had forbidden using them while Lucifer was still learning the basics of wrestling, and an angel would certainly never go back on their word, of course. Thus, Lucifer could only struggle against him, letting out a frustrated roar that Michael found horribly adorable; Lucifer was adorable. "Get off of me," he insisted. Michael told him to surrender. "No!" His wiggling only grew more desperate, and the chief archangel met it with a laugh until, in a frantic attempt to escape, Lucifer rolled his body back, rubbing.

Breath hitching, Michael almost lost his grip, and Lucifer must've noticed because he continued, grinding back more incessantly. And Michael, not meaning to, not wanting to, made a noise like pain but higher, softer. With it, a warm flush spread over his cheeks, and his legs twitched, terribly conscious of where his body pressed to Lucifer's below the navel and the shape of himself, there, and the shape of Lucifer, there. Unwillingly, he could feel himself pressing *more* against him, though the rest of his body was frozen in place.

"Lucif–" The beautiful angel had just halted his moving, perhaps because he could feel the hardness against him. Michael feared, instantly, that they would remain petrified like this forever — he didn't want to move, and all the other angels were far from them — but within seconds, Lucifer returned to thrashing some more. He pressed his hips back, beginning to kick his legs again. "Agh, *Lucifer*—"

A giggle, light and amused. "What's wrong?" The beautiful angel ground against him, a thin tunic doing little to shield Michael from the soft press of his curves, Michael almost slipping in between. He moaned again, shamefully, lowly, but breathless, feeling his own hips twitch. "I've never—" There was a new hitch in Lucifer's voice. "I've never heard you make noises like that—" The chief prince whispered his name, that wretched name. "I like it." Lucifer managed to lift his head, and Michael was soon breathing hot against the nape of his neck, the stray golden lines that had escaped the braid, and some few chains.

"Please."

"Please what?"

Michael gasped as Lucifer rocked his hips from one side to the other, teasing the eager stiffness pressing whereas the rest of the chief prince's body could only tremble. "We should..."

"Do you surrender?"

Where had Lucifer learned such cruelty? It made Michael grimace. "No."

The angel of worship whined, pouting. "Let go of me."

"No."

"Mmm." And Lucifer continued to grind back, the most vicious and teasing he had. "I won't surrender either." A little pleased noise escaped him, then, and the sound was so sweet in Michael's ears that he almost went blind, his hips rocked forward, trying to pierce through the fabric that separated their bodies, cut through, into the flesh of the angel beneath him. Wound him. Stab him like Michael was really wielding a sword that he couldn't put down. God's sword, he'd once been called. "Ah–" Another slight moan; Lucifer wiggled his body against his, urging him to keep going, keep stabbing.

Michael felt hot, tight, like when he had first sprouted wings, and his lips parted finally, ready to give in, but he did not. Instead, he gripped Lucifer's arm even tighter, yanked, removed his weight for a moment. Harshly, he flipped the younger angel onto his back beneath him, then planted his hands at either side of Lucifer's head, snatching his wrists almost hard enough to snap them, and Michael was trembling, heaving, meeting the soft flush on the angel of beauty's cheeks, the beads of sweat, the wet, plump mouth. "*Lucifer*," he said sternly.

And, ever briefly, the younger angel flinched, in Michael's shadow, his eyes a little frightened, like the archangel was really God about to punish him. But Michael wasn't angry, wasn't sure that he could be. So, he took a deep breath and saw Lucifer relax with great relief, but he couldn't find the words to continue speaking.

"Michael?" came Lucifer's soft voice, timid in a way it hadn't sounded like since they'd met.

"Maybe we," Michael whispered, "shouldn't do this."

"But you liked it, didn't you?"

"Lucifer..."

"Didn't it feel pleasant?"

They stared at one another, and Michael glanced down at Lucifer's own groin, wondered if he felt the same painful need in that place as him. With a slow exhale, he rolled his hips, experimentally, dragged newborn hardness against the other, and the beautiful angel opened his mouth, made a sweet, languid noise. The prince could feel dampness in his tunic, could feel himself leaking like he'd been cut and now bled. He had a strange urge in him to put his own blood in the younger angel, fill him with it, to have a piece of himself inside him forever. It frightened him — the desire. Desire made him ill. Yet, he allowed his body to continue to rock forward, and Lucifer parted his legs so that he could move in between them properly. When Lucifer sighed and shivered, Michael asked, "Does it feel good for you, too?"

"I like the way you feel." Lucifer rubbed up against him, as well, the warming friction making Michael grunt. "But I feel odd, almost painful." As the chief prince began loosening his hold on his wrists, Lucifer added, "Don't let go of me—" His voice cut off with a soft, desperate moan. "I haven't surrendered yet." And Michael did as told, tightened his grip. "Mmm."

Michael heard his own grunts increasing in volume, but he couldn't stop himself, rubbing his need against Lucifer's pulsating own. He wanted to swoop down, to shove his face in between the angel of beauty's legs and gnaw at whatever sweet thing he'd roused from sleep. Instead, when Lucifer let out a wanting whimper, he took the beautiful lips that pressed just right against his own, softly, warmly, invitingly. They continued rocking, but Lucifer giggled again with a touch of joy. Their hips were losing their rhythm, going at different paces, but the uneven friction was eclipsed by the pleasure of feeling closer, *closer*, to relief on the horizon. To surrender.

Moving his mouth to Lucifer's jaw, his cheeks, his nose, his neck, tasting the cold metal of jewelry in between the heated skin, Michael moaned deeply, rumbling, hardly lucid. Lucifer's beauty was too much, too mesmerizing, *intoxicating*. And Lucifer cried out for him, his legs shuddering and trying to shut from the intensity of the pleasure, but Michael was in between, and it only pulled the prince closer with perfect, shapely thighs caging him. The touch drew a shiver up the archangel's entire body, and he had been leaking so much that he didn't immediately realize when his finish was pulled out from him. He merely felt his hips thrust forward, not much like rubbing his hardness on the other angel's divine body anymore but like trying to sincerely pierce into him. Distantly, he felt Lucifer free a hand that Michael had clumsily lost hold of.

Lucifer reached for Michael's tunic, tugged it upward to expose the girthy flesh to the cool breeze of Heaven; he did it just in time for the moaning, whimpering prince to spill. In between them, he did, the white like the lilies that Lucifer was so fond of and onto his pale tunic, over the visible, unfinished roused flower at his own groin. But the angel of beauty soon smiled wistfully, his sweet laughter filling the space in between them, space rapidly increasing as Michael drew back as quick as he could. He staggered onto his feet, wavered.

"I'm sorry–" the archangel blurted. "I didn't mean to." He had bled on him, he thought. "Forgive me, Lucifer." Michael took another few other steps back, wondering if he should run away as fast he could, hide in his house forever from the young angel.

Lucifer must've read his mind; he raised his body up to sit, then lifted his gaze, and smiled. "What are you afraid of, Michael?"

"I've never— I've never done this in my life, Lucifer."

"But it felt good, didn't it?" Michael stared, not wanting to reply. "It's alright." With one hand, he tugged on his tunic, with the other he scooped some of the seed splattered onto him. He exposed his need to him, like he wanted them to be naked together, like they could be in an Eden of their own. Michael stared at Lucifer's nudity, and he felt oddly ashamed of his own in comparison, the shape and size of it. "Look."

"Should I," Michael whispered, "help you?"

"I was thinking of how badly you wanted to stab me. I thought maybe you should put it in my mouth, or I should cut a hole into me that you can thrust into. I thought that, maybe, if I press my thighs together, slipping in between them might satisfy you too. But—" Lucifer lifted his legs, leaned some of his body backward, exposing perhaps the only part of himself that Michael had never seen. "What about here?"

Nervously, Michael shook his head. "That's too—" He was still thinking of how reprehensible the shape of need in him was.

Lucifer hummed. "How do you know? My mouth is small, too, but I can stretch it wide." Just one step forward; that was all Michael could muster. "Look." With the hand still dripping Michael's seed, Lucifer touched his entrance, then began pressing in a finger. "Mm–" Michael felt himself twitch at the sight, the in-between of his legs beginning to rouse once more. "Mmm." Lucifer hastily pushed in another finger, also wet with Michael's salty release, then released another lovely moan. With his other hand, he began to fondle himself at the front, stroke delicately.

All the rest of Heaven was disappearing; Michael could only see the most beautiful angel, the favorite, fucking the cum of Heaven's prince into himself. He could only listen to his cries like they were his psalms of worship for God. 'God?' Was He still with them? 'Is this right, my Lord?' Perfect, pretty Lucifer, staring back at him, some hints of timidity still there but shadowed by a gleam of love and nubile excitement. The angel of strength was so weak he wanted to fall to his knees, to crawl to him, to mouth at him all over. Lucifer whined as he inched closer and closer, whispering Michael's name.

When the finish came, the beautiful angel's entire body shook, his voice high, his back arching sweetly, like pleading for a pair of hands to take hold.

Michael surrendered to the urge; he moved forward, finally, after Lucifer had made a dribbling mess of himself, and he tugged down on the young angel's tunic. Lucifer stared at him with wide, nervous eyes as Michael took him by the waist and the back of his knees, lifting him. "Come," the archangel said, "we should leave this place." There was a hint of terror in the angel of beauty, so Michael spoke again gentler, more lovingly: "I'll take you home, Lucifer."

Lucifer, tiredly, echoed: "Home?"

CHILD

A story about Lucifer and Michael running away from Heaven before the war can occur and having a child, somehow. Told in two parts.

ONE

Michael felt fingers running through his curls, on his scalp, then felt the warmth against his left cheek. Without thinking, he cracked open an eye, realizing that his face was rested against Lucifer's stomach, his whole body draped over the beautiful angel's legs. With one hand, Lucifer was reading the chisels on a stone tablet while the other worked through the prince's hair. A ditzy smile began to wiggle across Michael's lips before he rumbled against his lover's belly, "Hello." Lucifer hummed. "I don't remember falling asleep here."

"You weren't thinking," replied the perfect angel; he was on his back over a makeshift sofa — some plant-fiber cloth bundled around a heap of feathers. "You were bleeding everywhere when Phanuel dragged you back in. He said one of the beasts got you into its mouth, almost ate you. I wonder what would have happened if it managed to swallow you down. Would you have to live in its stomach forever? Or would you die? Is that how an angel can die?"

Michael crawled up Lucifer's body, pecked his plump mouth, and smiled despite the somberness in his lover's face. "I wouldn't dare die without your permission, beloved."

"So you say," said the beautiful one, then tossed the tablet to the wooden panels of the flooring, which creaked. "I had some angels bring water from the river, and I did what I could to heal you. Does anything still hurt?"

"No, no." Michael hesitated, concentrated, searching for any part of him that stung or throbbed. "No. You did well." He reached for the hand Lucifer had just freed, then lifted it between their faces, kissing a finger, then two. "And how do *you* feel? Any pain?"

Chuckling warmly — "Only on my legs. You're very heavy, prince."

"Shall I remove myself?"

"No." Lucifer pressed his mouth to the other side of his finger in between them, then shut his eyes. "It's quiet for once." It was true; Michael only realized now that he wasn't hearing all the usual noise that the wooden walls muffled. "There must be... a storm coming." No birds', no beasts' howling, and the glassless windows of the cottage were streaming in faint light, though it mustn't be too late in the day. He couldn't be sure. "We should board the windows, or maybe we should go out and gather the angels and fly elsewhere for a day." He paused and, seconds later, there was a small, pitched babble at the other end of the room. Immediately, Michael turned his head, saw a pile of Heaven cloth on a high tree stump, the fabric circled by an assortment of twigs almost like a nest, though it was really meant to be a crib. There was, after all, a baby in the middle of it, kicking one of their stubby legs in sleep and fluttering pale wings beneath their body. "Your baby misses you. Go wake him."

Michael huffed but obediently peeled himself off his beloved angel of worship. "Our baby," he corrected.

"So you say," Lucifer echoed, shifting his body so that he could lay back comfortably, his eyes still shut.

As the chief prince took the few steps necessary to reach the crib, he listened to the infant mumble again, saying syllables, mostly vowels. Michael lifted a hand after he reached them, then lingered it over their face, afraid to touch any part of the baby's delicate features. Their eyes, though shut, were a distinct brown-green color, like Michael's, and the small tufts of dark hair on their head were like the archangel's as well. 'He'll look like you,' Lucifer had said once, and Michael had frowned, not liking that distant tone his lover's voice took on. But Lucifer had seemed distant for quite some time.

Just some years ago — Michael had hurried to see Lucifer after returning from Earth, on one of his Father's strange commands. What he'd found was the beautiful angel with a wide, deep gash running down his body, a kitchen knife in one tremoring hand. The sacs and strings of flesh that make an angel up were all gushing out from him, though Lucifer had cried for the prince to stop when he tried to hold him down, to force him to stop hurting himself. 'There is something in me,' Lucifer had wailed, hoarse as if he were speaking through a burnt throat. 'There is something inside of me. A garden. The Lord put it in me. I'm trying to get it out.' Then, the broken angel had choked up, 'Michael, Michael, Michael— You promised you'd *save* me—'

At first, the prince suggested speaking to God, and Lucifer had shouted that they can never return to Him. Michael, coward that he was, tried to argue, but Rosier had stepped in, seen them, then grimaced, his brows furrowed.

'Earth,' Lucifer had pleaded, breathless as if in panic. 'Let us go to Earth, Michael. Take me to Earth.'

Rosier agreed: 'Take him, Michael. Run away from here. I saw— I never dared to say but— I saw our Father hurt Lucifer when he tore out his voice. Take him to Earth. I don't know what will come out of it, but— I'm certain God has hurt him again. I don't want Lucifer to hurt anymore. Run away with him.'

Some days later, Michael had escaped Heaven with Lucifer. He would have done it immediately, but he'd wanted to tell Phanuel and prepare him for whatever Uriel might do, and he wanted to pack some cherished belongings. 'I can't stop you,' Phanuel had said, 'and I don't understand, but I will trust you, brother. Please be careful.' They'd embraced tightly, and Michael promised he'd either return soon or call for Phanuel to climb down to Earth as well. 'I love you, brother.' Michael had wanted to say it back, but he'd opted for kissing Phanuel's cheek and squeezing him instead.

What followed were the first years on Earth. Lucifer had changed. He didn't sing or dance anymore. He didn't even seem to smile. Michael tried many times to ask whatever happened between him and God, but Lucifer would respond with either silence or an explosion of anger. When the pretty angel first climbed onto him, speaking of sin and pleasure, Michael had almost flown right back to Heaven in fright, scared of this stranger that Lucifer had become, scared of whatever the fallen angel of worship wanted to do with his body. But he'd had no choice but to stay, to try to talk Lucifer down each time from his spells of fury. He reminded Lucifer of grace, of purity, of love that was good for them both. But Michael gave in, eventually. One night that they were in the grotto — Lucifer had been touching his body, as he occasionally did, then the prince had turned his head, kissed him deep, then deeper.

'Create with me, Michael,' Lucifer had breathed against him, 'and let's call it sin. Please.' He'd tugged on his robe desperately.

'I don't know how,' Michael had said. 'I don't know how to do it. I'm sorry.' But he'd given in.

Within months, Michael indeed returned to Heaven to call for Phanuel, and then some other angels, particularly Lucifer's old friends. He'd worried that Lucifer seemed so weak, suddenly, and he'd like a healer angel to visit and confirm if there was something in Lucifer broken that Michael couldn't see. When Uriel appeared, there was a great confrontation between them, but the oldest archangel hadn't been able to stop them when other angels declared they'd follow their chief prince in an exodus out from Heaven. It was only a hundred, but Michael, terrified, tried to reject them all. He didn't want to provoke God's wrath — he knew already that he was acting foolishly, disobediently — but he'd wanted to return to Lucifer as fast as possible. And, eventually, the runaway angels had built something akin to a village on Earth.

Michael, finally, picked up the child and rocked their small, delicate body against his front. Craning his neck back, he could still see Lucifer quietly resting. 'I wish I knew what happened to the Lucifer I used to know.' Since the exodus, the prince had many times been subjected to Lucifer's sudden, violent whims on Earth — his shrieking and breaking things and even striking Michael himself — but oftentimes there remained a lingering sadness on him, even when most things were well. He'd thought the baby might help; after all, Lucifer had seemed the happiest he'd ever been after holding the child in his arms for the first time. He did seem a bit livelier these days, but Michael feared the grief in Lucifer was now a permanent fixture. 'Angel of grief.' Turning back down, he saw the baby's eyes begin to flutter open.

"I think it's time to tell the others where the baby came from," said Lucifer quietly.

Michael sighed. "I don't— I don't think so. Why should they need to know?" They'd had this conversation before. He wanted to say they'd done enough of angering God, that His silence was even scarier than if He'd already punished them.

"An angel," mused Lucifer, his gaze opening a sliver, "is meant to be an eternal thing, an obedient thing. We were meant to be constant. God never wanted us to create our own lives or own paradise. It is very nice here, isn't it? We're all doing very well on our own. Maybe we ought not to be angels at all anymore, and the others must know of sin to stop being angels." Michael rather disliked when Lucifer talked like this. "You're irritated with me."

"No, no," Michael said, then watched as the baby in his arms opened their mouth and cried out shrilly. "Oh— He's hungry."

"We should feed him." Lucifer, slowly, moved to sit, then tilted his head over. "And... Michael?"

"Mm?"

"I love you. God will not come after us. I'm of no interest to Him anymore. All of us on Earth will learn to be happy here, sinning."

"I... love you too."

TWO

Recently, Lucifer had warmed up to carrying the baby around, had even begun showing it off. He — after the angels had returned to their humble village following a rough storm in the vicinity — marched with the infant held tenderly to his chest, heading toward the makeshift plaza where their largest rain-collecting fountain was and their greatest bonfire, as well as some wooden benches with stone bases. Settling on one, Lucifer smiled at the other runaway angels, allowing each to come coo at the beautiful baby with brunette curls and fluttering, pale wings. He nuzzled his child's face, peppering kissing on their round cheeks, and eventually allowed his dear friend Rosier to hold the bundled little angel.

When Michael arrived, the sun was setting, and he saw how a crowd of adoring angels was gathered by Lucifer — as if he were God — and listening to every pretty word from his pretty mouth. He did, really, look very nice today: his sunny hair carried a few minuscule braids and a crown of dried Heaven flowers was perched not far above his brows. His outfit was a blend of a paradise silk tunic and an earthly fur coat, whereas his sandals were leather and tied high by his knees. "Oh?" the beauty called when he noticed the prince, who'd seemingly been standing there a few seconds, admiring how much his beloved angel was adored by the others. "Are you here to tell me to sleep? I suppose it's late."

"Yes," said Michael, stiffly, a bit too rapidly. "Yes," he echoed himself. "We should let the little angel sleep, as well." He smiled, knowing it was unsure, but the dozens around Lucifer didn't argue, simply frowned and began to scatter. Before him, Michael watched as Lucifer leaned toward the angel of fruit sitting on the bench with him, whispering some words in his ear to make Rosier laugh, then finally rose to his feet.

Lucifer adjusted the baby in his hold, then walked toward Michael elegantly. "Let's rest then, prince." He moved past the archangel, leading the way back to their hut as Michael dutifully followed close behind. "I had the thought earlier that tomorrow I'll go to the river to bathe. Would you like to come with me? If not, I'll bring Rosier. It's not safe to be alone with such beasts roaming as recklessly as they have been. It must've been the storm; it's confused them." A soft, pleased smile tugged on his lips as Michael settled a hand on his back. "Is that an answer?"

Face warming, Michael said, "You're in a very pleasant mood today."

"Does that frighten you?"

"Perhaps."

"If you're so scared of me, I could go and sleep in Rosier's cottage instead tonight." Lucifer chuckled as Michael's hand moved to touch his wrist. "I see."

Michael asked, "How is the child?"

Gently, Lucifer handed the infant to the chief prince, who took it in a careful hold, rested the little angel against his biceps and chest, and stared down at their yawn, then the baby's restless kick. "Well, I imagine. I'm not sure why he's so quiet."

Raising his gaze, Michael stared at their home as they reached it, wasting no time to enter past an open wooden door with Lucifer, to pass by the living area, to bring the baby to their nest-like bed right at the archway that led into the bedroom. Lucifer stopped, staring at Michael as he lowered their child and began re-bundling them in their blankets. As he did so, the prince breathed nervously, then mumbled, "Animal children are very quiet too."

"But we're not animals," Lucifer replied. "We're angels." He touched Michael's upper arm, then leaned his head on the archangel's shoulder. "I'll convince him to start speaking soon... The other angels love him. They tell me he's beautiful. I think some are... jealous." Michael swallowed. "I shouldn't hide him away so much. The other angels must know him well." He leaned to peck a loving kiss on the curls over the baby's forehead.

Michael stepped away slowly, then said, "Come, let's sleep." Hastily, he entered their bedroom and reached for his gray cloak, shrugged it off, then draped it over a wooden chair. There was a window beside them with no glass — thankfully, insects didn't seem to stomach angelic blood well — where all the distant buzzing and howls and rustling trees crept in, as well as some dim moonlight that shined directly onto their bed. With a rough tug, the angel of strength pulled off the last of his clothing, leaving himself naked, thinking to reach for the shorter tunic neatly folded nearby that he wore for sleep.

But Lucifer strode in between Michael and the drapery, settling down onto the mattress, settling his hands beside himself, then tilting his head up at the archangel. Distant, his eyes shone some of the moon's glow. "You already know what I want to say, Michael."

The prince stalled for some seconds, standing there, naked — but he knew he had nowhere to run to. "How would we? We can't. They should learn how it can be done on their own and if they can't, then–"

"If the angels here have many children, then we can raise them all to fight, and we can return to Heaven to take on God. We can rule all that exists, Michael. We can sit on that Throne, together. All we must do is show the other angels how to do it." Michael parted his lips, but Lucifer answered before the prince could ask the question: "We'll do it as they watch." He leaned forward a few inches, then added, softer, "Though…"

"Though?"

"I do like the thought of… the other angels never knowing too." Lucifer extended a hand, fluttered his fingers over Michael's as his voice dropped to a whisper. "All the others would be so jealous of us, able to create while they can't. They would worship us." 'I don't want to be worshiped,' Michael wanted to say. "Us and our… children."

Michael, nervously, swallowed, staring at Lucifer's face now, his parted lips, his steady breathes. "You mean… child," Michael found his own hushed voice replying at the same time there was a twitching, tight sensation between his legs. 'No,' he scolded himself. 'No.'

"Wouldn't it be nice to have another?" Lucifer's hand, suddenly, began to trail. "Don't you enjoy creating with me?" Sweetly, his touch climbed towards his abdomen, trickling down. "We could have as many children as God does. All you have to do is give them to me, Michael." His fingers found Michael's arousal, stroked circles, then began to tug, encouraging it to grow, to harden like a blade.

The chief prince trembled. He liked sex with Lucifer; in fact, he loved it. Ever since feeling the inside of his beloved angel, ever since experiencing holding him in place and kissing him and rocking in deep and listening to the angel of worship gasp in plea-sure, he'd been certain that this was what he was made for. He was made for Lucifer. He still believed, and really prayed, that God had done this all purposefully and that He would soon reveal that this was a part of His loving plan — but Michael didn't dare to say that to his angel, who would suddenly yell and throw things and snarl when the prince mentioned the Lord above. And so he always hesitated to sleep with Lucifer, no matter how good and perfect it felt.

And when Michael fucked Lucifer, Lucifer was always right. If he wanted an army, Michael would give it to him. If he wanted to take on God, Michael would promise to tear off His head with his own hands. If Lucifer said sin was wonderful, Michael would swear his eternal life to it.

"Mm," Lucifer moaned, sugary, lovely, as he took the prince in his mouth. Between his own legs, he began to stroke himself, but Michael shut his eyes for now, grit his teeth. Already, he was thinking of giving the beautiful angel everything he wanted. It was just so wonderful to see Lucifer's smiles, his brightened eyes. He deserved everything he wanted. 'Yes,' Michael wanted to surrender, 'anything. Anything you want, beloved Lucifer. Sweet Lucifer.' He took a fistful of Lucifer's hair, feeling some of the dried flowers tickle his wrist, but Michael didn't dare control how Lucifer dipped his head to take more of the hardness into his hot, wet mouth.

Michael bit his lip to stifle a noise when he felt himself slide into the tightness of Lucifer's throat, the younger one gagging on it in such a way that only squeezed the archangel's length enough more, to nearly make his knees buckle. "Lucifer," he panted. "Lucifer, Lucifer." 'Sweet, sweet Lucifer, beloved Lucifer, anything you want.'

The angel of beauty pulled off, pink lips wet, swollen, then hazily looked up at Michael through his long lashes. He flicked his tongue against some of the beading on his bottom lip, then said, "I want you to fuck it inside of me, Michael." The prince shivered, watching as Lucifer reached for his flower crown, tossed it away, then yanked off his coat. Gracefully, he pulled his tunic over his head before dropping it with the rest of his clothes. "Please. Please—"

Tightly, Michael took Lucifer's legs at the lower ends before pulling them up, bending the younger one nearly in half. The prince swept down, dragging his hands slow toward the Lucifer's thighs, then placed his mouth on the exposed entrance to drag his tongue desperately against the forbidden heat the Lord had tried to deny to him. Sleeping with Lucifer could do away with the guilt, however momentarily — staring at this body twitch at a wet appendage trying to slip inside and listening to his pretty hums. For a few seconds, Michael really *could* turn his back on God and think, 'If you deny me Lucifer, then I will deny you. Destroy worlds, destroy paradise; I won't bother myself to grieve anything at all if I can just have my beloved angel.' His reasonable mind drowned, all the knowledge left him that God might very well destroy only one of them, that He was capable of worse than what Michael could even imagine. He really shouldn't provoke Him. They should both return to Him and ask for mercy.

But the prince swirled his tongue at the edge of Lucifer's entrance, then pressed it inside, his eyelids falling shut. The encouraging purrs and coos of such a charming angel could make him forget anything about God and Heaven at all. 'Lucifer, Lucifer, Lucifer.'

Even less than usual could Michael deny Lucifer; oftentimes, when Lucifer wanted sex, he'd become rather erratic. He would demand, he would swing as if on a pendulum between sadness and fury. Once, the two had been grinding on each other over the ground, and when the prince had hesitated, the beautiful angel had suddenly snapped at Michael, called him an idiot and coward and useless; 'Idiot. You're useless. You never want to fuck me.' Michael hated that word; he'd grimace each time. 'You're a coward. Fuck me.' 'No,' Michael had said, 'not if you're acting like this.' 'Don't mislead me. You want to. You want to, more than anything. I know that you do. You're toying with me.' 'Lucifer.' 'Do you want to wrestle? Is that how you want it? Idiot, idiot. Do you want to hold me in a headlock while you do it?' And other times, he had simply choked up in the midst of it, and then asked Michael quietly not to stop, even if he cried. But right now — Lucifer seemed so sweet. He wasn't asking for much, just a child. Another one.

"Kiss me," Lucifer whispered, clutching at the bedsheets, his head tilting to the side, his hair a perfect, river sprawl on their mattress. "Kiss me."

Slow, Michael inched his face back, fluttering open his eyes, licking his lips. As if on instinct, he almost returned his mouth to the wonderful sin he wanted to tear into with his teeth, to swallow, to eat — but Lucifer wanted something, a kiss. The prince rubbed his face against a thigh, revering it, before forcibly reeling himself up to stand and move in between the angel of beauty's legs, crawling over his body. The urge to pray, whenever he positioned himself above Lucifer, strum at his heart; in Heaven, he'd struggled to worship and it had been Lucifer, the youngest, who'd taught him how to. 'Let me show you,' Michael mouthed, or maybe even said, 'how well you've taught me. With your body, I'll show you how I can worship.'

Lucifer's face was serene, but the ends of his lips twitched, a brief amusement, almost arrogance. When Michael leaned down to kiss him, to moan helplessly into his mouth, he felt the rumble of a laugh. Lucifer must adore it, the frailty he brought to the prince. He must know all the power he holds in Heaven and Earth. "Michael," he breathed harshly against the archangel. "We don't have to tell anyone. They'll worship us and our children. They'll think us gods." Inching back, Michael pressed his forehead to Lucifer's, his mouth so terribly wet, his body shaking, his hardness aching and leaking. "Fuck me."

Michael didn't like that word, but he didn't complain. He lowered his gaze, reached to take hold of himself, then began to rub the tip against the entrance he'd just tried to devour. "I love you," he tried but Lucifer was quiet, or at least he was until the prince shifted his hands to either side of the beautiful angel's head, fingers threading the golden strands — and he began to press in.

"Ah," Lucifer gasped, "I love you too."

Watching himself disappear into the other, Michael clenched his jaw, feeling the tight, warm hold that now cradled his sin, before he lowered an arm to wrap around Lucifer's waist, hoisting some of his body an inch off the mattress to better angle him. At that, the younger angel breathed out again, his eyes half-lidded in bliss, as one of his own hands climbed down to rest over Michael's fingers, squeezing them. "Is that comfortable?"

'I don't care,' Lucifer's eyes said, but his mouth hesitated. He ordered softly, "Deeper." Then he shuddered as the archangel pushed in the last of himself and brought his face to Lucifer's temple, pecking a kiss. "Mm," was the lovely response. "There. When you finish, spill your seed there." Michael didn't like that word either — seed — not how Lucifer used it. At the same time, he was throbbing, and the inside of Lucifer was trembling his hips, wanting to drive in, to do exactly as he said, to give him the child, to fuck him. "Fuck me," Lucifer was pleading once more. "Please, Michael."

Michael's hand by his angel's head was a fist; he loved this, he loved Lucifer, he did. But he was scared. He realized he would always be. He didn't think another child was a good idea. He didn't want the other angels to worship them. And yet — he felt his hips begin to rock, and he made no move to stop himself. Instead, he panted against Lucifer's head, grunting, holding him more firmly. Every little move, no matter how small, was a bloom of utter delight at his pulsing groin but, maybe even more so, in his heart, his head. It felt good. Lucifer felt better than anything. He truly did, and his moans were even better than they'd been before, higher, needier.

He was murmuring, "Create with me, Michael. Create with me." One hand went to scratch at Michael's back, in between the wings that were unfolding instinctively, fluttering, then hanging over them protectively. "I want to create. Help me." He cried out at a particularly hard thrust and, after a few more, Michael pulled out, to the angel of worship's immediate gasp in protest, before the prince lifted Lucifer with the hand on his waist, then sunk him back into his hardness, and listened to Lucifer moan, longer, slower. He wasn't quite on Michael's lap, instead being held firmly against the prince's chest as another hand groped Lucifer's bottom to hold him in place, practically impaled. The angel of beauty bit his lip as Michael began to thrust again, up into him, making his body jostle and have his arousal rubbed in between them. "Create with me," he continued hazily. "Michael. Michael, Michael."

Nuzzling his face against Lucifer's neck, Michael tried to keep himself upright, ignoring the almost-painful strikes of goodness that were making it impossible to see, to hear. He wanted to watch his beloved angel's face as he finished, wanted to hear his cries. Before long, he found himself going faster, trying to ride this to completion already. He turned his face and kissed Lucifer again, pressing into his mouth deep like he did the lower end of his body. Suddenly, it was not enough to fuck or to kiss; he wanted to crawl inside him entirely. He loved and he adored so much he couldn't stand it anymore. "I love you," he said again, and Lucifer laughed, stretched his own wings, and cocooned them both in violet feathers, intermingled with Michael's brown.

Hours passed, and when Michael finally returned to his senses, he was back to laying over Lucifer on the bed. He was crashing down from the euphoria, as if falling from Heaven — as the angel of worship weakly ordered Michael: "Stay inside of me. Be patient." As always, regret was forming a knot of the chief prince's organs, and he was gasping, his skin sweated, all of him too warm. "I wanted to tell you— I have a name for the child. I thought of it... this morning. Sin. That is a pretty name, isn't it? And our second child can be... Pride. Or maybe... Wrath."

Michael mumbled, "Let's sleep, Lucifer." He kissed his cheeks tiredly. "We can discuss more tomorrow."

"You do," Lucifer asked softly, his voice suddenly delicate, "want another child, don't you?" He turned his face, looked into Michael's eyes with his starry own. There was a juvenile fear there, like he was also a child. They were not, Michael was sure, and yet he felt immature in a way he hadn't felt in centuries. The longing for easy food and a proper house he didn't have to worry so much over and the sudden talk of children made him terrified, made him realize that he had no idea how to be a chief prince quite at all. He'd never actually led anything. He'd never *done* anything at all. He had been an angel in an easy utopia.

"I do," Michael replied, and Lucifer traced the bridge of his nose quietly. "We'll have more children. And we can rule." He'd hoped the younger angel would brighten up at that, maybe offer him a happy kiss, but Lucifer soon lowered his hand, shut his eyes. And it wasn't long before he was breathing softly, snoring. Michael had thought it so silly once, but now the sound only saddened him. How abruptly everything had changed. How abruptly Lucifer had changed.

Soon, Michael pulled away from him, wiping himself off, then reached for the clothes he'd earlier discarded. 'I need to walk.' His knees knocked together, then he stumbled, but he caught himself against the doorway. The baby, the child, was right nearby, sleeping the same as Lucifer. 'Sin,' had been the proposed name. Michael hesitated, then moved toward the infant, lowering his face to kiss their head, their cheeks, their soft abdomen, their stubby limbs. Giggling, the child kicked, but they didn't rouse from sleep. 'I wouldn't mind another,' he told himself. Maybe it wasn't the baby he was afraid of, he was afraid of what the children seemed to represent to Lucifer — creation, god-ness.

The prince left the cottage, realized dawn was still an hour or two away. Aimlessly, he walked. Michael made his way toward the center of the angels' makeshift town, traveling past some homes that still had chatter leaking out through their windows and the light of torches. Their distant laughter instantly raised some of the weight off his chest, which he hadn't realized had been there in the first place. At the same time, he noticed how sore his muscles were from how tense they'd been most of the day. He turned away from the village, saw two figures by the river they'd all settled near to. Raising a brow, Michael exhaled some cool air out of his nostrils, then hurriedly walked in that direction.

As he called out, one of the figures — who'd been crouching — shot up to his feet; it was an angel, tall and lanky with a ribbon in his straight hair. The one beside him, on the other hand, had lighter-brown curls and more build on his upper torso. The curly-haired one swiftly turned as Michael reached them but, before the prince said a word, stood and growled and threw out his hands, shoving Michael back. "I saw it— I saw—"

"What—?" Michael stumbled, so startled that he almost lost balance and fell over. "What did you–? Baal–?" Of course, he realized; looking into Baal's wide eyes, his brown skin paled a shade, Michael realized. "No," he blurted, all his blood cold, all his muscles stiffening once more. "You didn't see anything."

"I saw," Baal echoed. Over his shoulder, Asmodeus was stepping away, and Michael's gaze flashed to him frantically, realizing the angel of flight had likely been telling him, given Asmodeus' perplexed, cautious expression. "I saw, and Lucifer saw me watching."

Michael said again, "You didn't see anything. You—" He stepped forward, grabbed Baal by the collar of his tunic, then hissed so sharply one would think he's the devil — "*You didn't see anything.*"

MARRIED

Since they married, Lucifer and Michael have been severely troubling. Their hands are always interlocked as they walk through the streets of Heaven, and they always exchange kisses between words. They always cocoon with their wings when they want some privacy in public. And they are often staring at each other when their attention ought to be anywhere else. The angels all think Lucifer has become far too spoiled — he whines and demands and grows enraged when attention is shifted away from him — all the while Michael continues to give him everything that he wants. When Lucifer wants a kiss or a new outfit, Michael will arrange for that without question. He worships him, adores him.

Right now, they're kissing again, Lucifer sitting on Michael's lap on their couch, hips teasingly raised to avoid brushing against the chief prince. He's holding the strong jaw of the angel of strength, flicking his serpentine tongue along Michael's own. His gaze isn't quite shut, so Lucifer gazes hazily at a shelf on a wall where his collection of St. Michael figurines sits. They're all from Earth, human-made little sculptures for their religions. In all of them, Michael is vanquishing his greatest foe — Satan — with a mighty sword and chains, a foot set over the devil's back. Lucifer doesn't mind how ugly they depict him; his beauty is only for angels to have, for Michael. Michael.

Many times before, Lucifer has commented on how Michael looks in the figurines, how cute. They make him so dainty, so skinny, so blonde and curly-haired. If they had a child, Lucifer giggled once, perhaps that's what it would look like. He thinks of mentioning that again, but the prince pulls his mouth away from Lucifer's and drags his lips along his throat, one firm hand on the angel of beauty's waist.

"Mm," Lucifer sighs happily. "You should make love to me."

Michael presses a slow kiss to his cheekbone, then says, "I was supposed to leave an hour ago, Lucifer." But his voice is gentle; he doesn't care how Uriel might punish him.

"But I don't want you to go," the spoiled rotten Lucifer says, leaning away from Michael, then undoing the front buttons on his long tunic, revealing an opening sliver of brown skin, embraced by chains of gold and speckled in gems. "Stay here with me. Let me taste you. My mouth feels so empty."

"The humans... Lucifer..." But Michael stares at the angel he's married to, his angel, the body that offered to join with his for eternity. And he doesn't struggle when Lucifer tugs his head closer, nimble fingers in his dark, loose curls; he kisses over where Lucifer's heart would be, lips brushing a pendant that he'd won for his angel many centuries ago. Maybe it was wrong to treat Lucifer like a trophy at times, like an object — but Lucifer seemed to want it, want to be an object, so long as it was of worship.

Lucifer shushes him, then takes Michael's hand and brings it between his legs, where his arousal is already evident. "Mm." He laughs a little. "We're married. You shouldn't leave me alone. What if someone steals me away? I wouldn't fight them, Michael. I want to be with someone strong enough to keep me."

Furrowing his brows a little — "Lucifer, you're so... strange."

"If you make love to me, I'll stop acting like this." Lucifer begins to grind his hips against Michael's tough hand, breathing slower.

"Love only makes you stranger," Michael whispers, but he squeezes Lucifer, then he turns them around, setting his angel spouse on his side over the couch. "But I know better than to argue with you." He was smart enough not to provoke a tantrum from the angel of scheming.

"You're so good to me, Michael," Lucifer purrs.

Michael sighs, but he lifts Lucifer's tunic to his hips, then grips his angel's bottom, staring at the entrance to him and those perfect thighs pressed flush together. One of the beauties of living to Michael had been slipping in between those thighs after waking up with Lucifer in his arms, then sleepily getting off on him; Lucifer loved it too, loved drowsily stroking himself to Michael rutting on him like a dog.

He presses in slow. It's been centuries since Michael has felt any shame regarding himself, but occasionally, the grimaces return. So, he leans down and nuzzles his lovely angel's neck, breathing in that lavender scent of his, as Lucifer scratches soothingly on his scalp and moans at the stretch. He coos, "Good... You're so good to me, Michael," quietly.

"I love you," Michael murmurs, listening to the pulse of his angel like its a hymn. "You're everything to me."

Lucifer reaches down to squeeze the inch or two that still hasn't been pushed inside him. "You're beautiful, Michael. Do you realize that?" Michael whimpers a little when Lucifer's nails scrape a bit too harshly. "I love you too. I'm yours. Have me. Keep me."

Michael presses in the last of himself, feels Lucifer lift his hand from there to the chief prince's bicep to squeeze. Often, he worries about crushing Lucifer beneath him, but Lucifer said he loves the feeling of the massive archangel on him. He especially liked when Michael was in his armor, a few times managing to convince Michael to mount him like that, to even press his sword against his neck as he made love to him.

Lucifer always joked that the humans were right about Michael dominating Satan, but they were wrong about the fall. He was still here, still in Heaven, a pretty angel with a knack for whispering scary stories to the gullible humans on Earth and getting himself prohibited from visiting again anytime soon. However, Lucifer always argued he had the right to be a mean trickster to humanity; that planet used to be his and Michael's perfect getaway. They'd even spent their honeymoon there.

Michael's thrusts are always careful, like this was the first time. It doesn't matter how much Lucifer insists for the chief prince to love him mercilessly, Michael is too gentle beneath all his strength. He kisses Lucifer's cheek as he rolls his hips into the warm embrace of the most perfect angel in paradise, taking his hip like earlier and squeezing tenderly.

"Good," Lucifer returns to cooing. "Worship me."

Michael pants as he builds up to a faster, steadier pace, his other hand skimming up from Lucifer's belly to his chest, rattling all the jewelry there. "Lucifer, Lucifer," he whispers, almost chants. "Beloved Lucifer." He scrapes his teeth on him, a part of him wanting to taste blood, to have this body and blood, to be saved by Lucifer. "I love you, I love you." Saved from what? Maybe from Lucifer as well. That was the nature of having a god — to be damned and saved by the same hand.

"More," Lucifer begins to gasp, throwing his head back and squirming. "Please."

If Michael could go any deeper, he would, but he's already pushed far enough inside that it concerns him. It's like the inside of Lucifer is endless. "Fuck," Michael grunts; he never swears — he's a good angel — but Lucifer manages to pull the worst out of him. Maybe the humans were right, maybe Lucifer is the devil, seducing even the highest of angels to fall into sin with him. But Michael can hardly care. He's ramming into what amounts to a temple; he loved his god, his angel Lucifer, he wants to be useful to him. He'll give him everything. Anything he wants. Lucifer is crying out now, the hand of his in Michael's hair raising to clutch at a cushion by his head.

"Fuck me, fuck me," he pleads. "Pleasure your god." Michael can feel himself pulsing inside, the need at his lower belly so great that it hurts. "Michael, Michael, Michael."

Michael kisses him before Lucifer continues to run his mouth. He can be so strange, and he only gets stranger the closer he gets to release, starts blabbing about creation and sin and so on. Swiftly, Michael plunges his tongue inside the way he's still thrusting in, his thighs shaking, his sweat cold as it runs down his face, the curve of his chest. "I love you," he manages to grunt as he finishes in a series of spurts, collapsing on top of Lucifer, who moans wonderfully as he finishes against his own teasing fingers. "I love you, I love you." His hips are still twitching.

Lucifer is trembling, gasping for breath, but then he smiles. He laughs. "You're cruel to me."

Michael turns up his head instantly. "What? Cruel?"

"I asked for you in my mouth. You never listen. Go ahead and travel to Earth, then. I'll stay here to be angry with you."

A HALLOWEEN SPECIAL

At a Halloween party, in a cramped bathroom, there was a young man dressed like an angel — in a pale dress that hugged his upper thighs with lace accents at the hem, mirroring the wispy sleeves that billowed out at his wrists. Over his hair, dyed a gaudy blonde, there was a halo of glittering gold, a few specs of which occasionally landed on his face painted with white freckles — the work of his frenemy Azazel. Azazel was in the living room, probably with his partner, some student from the other college in town who'd recently traded his goth outfits for nurse scrubs; Azazel had been in the bathroom with the blonde an hour ago, touching up his makeup and grumbling at him but not mad enough to leave him looking subpar. The fake-angel, the fake-blonde, could still feel the cold taps of the brush on his face, even as his mouth moved hotly against another.

He was kissing a wrestling star. A guy the fake-angel had thought was vaguely bi-curious once, but the wrestler held him too firmly around his waist now to be unsure of his sexuality. He'd thought he was a friend once, too.

When the fake-angel pulled back, letting his tongue slither out of the wrestler, he caught some fear over the other's half-lidded eyes, a sort of brown, maybe green. "Michael," the fake-angel chuckled. The wrestler wore large, plastic red horns and a similarly colored tail that dangled from the belt hugging his jeans. It was such a lousy costume — Michael had a plain white tank top and regular sneakers on — but the entire wrestling team had seemingly coordinated the outfits. Baal and Phanuel were dressed like demons in the living room, too.

"I should leave, Lucifer," the fake-demon murmured, his gaze on Lucifer's white stilettos over the checkered bathroom tile. "I promised my dad I'd be home before midnight."

"Ugh." The fake-angel reached to comb his fingers through Michael's curls, noting some glitter over the fake-demon's mouth, surely from the gloss over Lucifer's lips. "What are you, in high school?" He nudged him with a knee, felt Michael's leg twitch. "Come on. A big guy like you doesn't need to answer to him. Give me another kiss." Furrowing his brows, Michael lifted his face, revealing worried eyes, and parted lips just as Lucifer trailed his hand to them. "If you're so scared, you can move in with me and my friends."

"Rosier wouldn't like that."

"Oh, Rosier wouldn't mind. It's his shitty boyfriend we have to worry about." Lucifer leaned forward, pecked Michael's mouth then traced the shape of it with his finger. "But who cares? I'm paying half the rent anyway." Typically, Lucifer was being an enormous hypocrite; he, Michael, Asmodeus, Rosier, and Azazel all had terrible fathers, as is the nature of having a father at all, and Lucifer had hardly cut himself off from his own father, not eager to lose the generational wealth. Not yet. He still called his father for allowances, then spent it all on Asmodeus and Rosier's place they were struggling to pay for recently — Rosier worked at a grocery store, Asmodeus worked in construction and had dropped out of college years ago — and drugs. But Lucifer wasn't high today or even drunk; Michael had shown up too early for that. "They're here, you know. They're probably by the drinks. Rosier is Red Riding Hood; Asmodeus is the wolf. I can talk to them right now."

"No, no." Michael exhaled through his nose, then shut his eyes and leaned forward, Lucifer's hand slipping away, to bury his face in the fake-angel's warm neck. "I'll go home soon. But after I kiss you a little more."

Lucifer wanted to call him a coward, but he instead waited, listening to the bass of the music. 'Whose house is this?' He didn't know. He typically never asked. Beside them, the door-knob jiggled, and then there was the muffled groan of someone telling another that the bathroom was occupied. "Mm, sweet-heart," Lucifer whispered, turning his head and rubbing his nose against the fake-demon's hair. "Come home with me, at least."

"Not tonight."

"Well, I have a condom in my pocket." When Michael's entire body tensed against him, Lucifer couldn't help a chuckle. "Mhm, this dress has pockets. It's the only one I could find with them." The fake-angel took Michael's hands in his own then moved them over to his hips, guided them, slow, down to slide into the pockets of the costume. "Can you feel it?" He felt his white, plas-tic, synthetic feather wings sweep the sink behind him. "Take it," Lucifer whispered huskily, tilting his head toward Michael's ear, "and use it. Or, go back to your dad."

Michael, his voice stiff, answered: "*God*, Lucifer."

"If you don't like me, you can leave." Smiling wide enough that Lucifer was sure the fake-demon could feel it against his earlobe, he added, "But you love me, don't you?" Michael's hand was curling into his pocket, gripping something. "Come on. Stop wasting my time." Firmly, he pulled Michael's limp hand out of his pocket and guided it back, toward the curves of his ass, then giggled when the fake-demon gave him a nervous squeeze. "Don't you miss me every time your dad makes you go out with a girl? Do you ever fuck them and think of me?"

Harshly, Michael sighed, not replying, then pulled his other hand out from Lucifer's pocket with a square wrapped in blue plastic in between two fingers. "I'm going to hell." He was so scared of that, he really was. Michael's father was a pastor.

"We're all going to hell, baby," Lucifer said, "might as well try to deserve it." Then, he kissed him again, slithering in his tongue and locking an arm around Michael's neck. "Mm." He pressed his body up against Michael's, relishing in every inch of that strong build, and was just about to swipe the condom from Michael's hand before he felt himself grabbed around the waist and a thigh. Confusedly, Lucifer's stilettos kicked the air as he was lifted and sat at the edge of the sink. "Agh—" Michael's hands came onto his thighs, tugging them apart and forcing Lucifer's costume to ride up.

"Really?" Michael said, quirking a brow. "Nothing underneath?"

Lucifer shrugged. "I couldn't decide between jockstrap or panties. Wasn't sure which one you'd like more." With a grin, he spread his legs wider. "Which would you rather I wear?"

Michael visibly gulped, his gaze flickering in between the fake-angel's arousal and his lovely face. "Were you really thinking of me? I don't believe you."

"Well," Lucifer admitted, "I actually didn't have anything that didn't fold the dress weirdly on my ass. I did think of you, though, when I decided to come to the party like this. I figured I'd fuck Baal if you didn't show up too." He tilted his head. "I could still fuck him once you're done. Or we could call him in here. You two could fight over me."

As he inched away for a moment, Michael brought the condom to his mouth, tearing it open, and muttering, "It's lubed?"

"Not much, but it's a little vanilla-flavored." Lucifer chuckled and watched as Michael went to unzip his pants, then began tugging them down, along with his briefs, to allow a half-hardness to swell between them. "Mm, you keep ignoring me. You don't like vanilla? You don't like the thought of Baal coming in to join us?"

"You're so... full of yourself." Carefully, Michael began to roll the condom over himself, his shoulders twitching, a tiny grunt leaving his mouth.

Meanwhile, Lucifer reached over to rummage through a cabinet over the toilet, instantly finding a slim, but short, green bottle of CBD oil. "When you're this pretty, you have to be." He rocked the oil from side to side as he brought it between then, and there was a quiet sloshing noise within. "Didn't you tell me that once, Michael? Three-four years ago?" The fake-demon in question exhaled through his nostrils, avoided Lucifer's gaze. "I still remember." 'The day you heard me crying in the bathroom of the library, and you talked to me through it, told me not to do anything stupid. When I finally stepped out, your eyes went wide, and you told me a pretty boy like me shouldn't be crying like that. When you're that pretty, you should be able to do whatever you like.' He unscrewed the tap, then began to pour the oil onto his fingers. "Been a while since I've had you in anything besides my mouth."

Michael murmured something, then he repeated himself, a little stronger: "I haven't slept with anyone since you."

"Not even the girls your dad sets you up on dates with?"

Huffing — "Why are you bringing that up? Are you jealous? You're the one fucking Baal."

"I'm pretty," Lucifer argued, "and that means I can do whatever I want." He smirked, then pressed his slick, cold fingers to his entrance and twitched. "That includes being a hypocrite." Michael's eyes had fallen now to the intimate part being coaxed to open; and with the hand that wasn't holding his cock still, he took Lucifer's thigh again, squeezing it.

"Let me help," said Michael, soft again, then trailed his hand to brush at Lucifer's scrotum, then up his bare hardness, the drag making Lucifer's toes curl and his hips shudder before he could help it. "Please, Lucifer."

"Angel," Lucifer corrected. "I'm not Lucifer right now. I'm an angel, and you're a demon." He pressed in another finger and breathed softly right into Michael's approaching face, the same Michael who was now taking hold of Lucifer's cock along with his own, hugged in wet latex. Instantly, Lucifer had to bite down a needy, wanting whimper. The bottom of his spine ached from how pressed it was to the sink and how it was supporting all of his weight, but he couldn't bear to move or even ask the fake-demon to set him down as Michael began to pump his fingers. When their mouths met again, it was deep, frantic. The pumping of their lengths together — so different in size and girth — made the both of them shiver against each other and pass moans and grunts between their lips. "Won't—" Lucifer panted because he could never stop talking, "—your dad kill you if he finds out you dressed up like this?"

"Stop talking about my dad," was the now-stern reply.

"I like pissing you off." Lucifer grinned against him. "Is it working?"

Michael removed his hand, but then lowered his face, opened his mouth, and bit down at Lucifer's neck, hard enough to hurt. At that, Lucifer gasped and jerked a little, but as he did — he accidentally pressed his fingers into a sensitive cluster inside himself that made him moan helplessly, tilt his face up, let Michael eat away at him all he liked. "Hmm," Michael grunted, his voice rumbling against Lucifer's flushed skin. And then Lucifer felt a hand come over his wrist, tug at it until his wet fingers slipped free, dripping little beads of oil onto the tile below them. "I won't give you what you want." As thicker, larger fingers pressed in, Lucifer breathed out slow, staring dizzily at the ceiling. "You want me to hurt you, but I won't."

"You bore me," said the fake-angel, licking his dry mouth and gripping the sink as Michael curled his fingers inside and brushed his sweet spot. "Just get on with it already and go home to your dad if you won't be any fun. You're so exhausting. I bet you won't even have the drinks here. I bet you won't even have a cigarette."

Michael murmured against him — his fingers thrusting

steady, loosening — "Can you stop arguing with me for one second?"

"Why? You want me to be quiet? You want to fuck me like I'm just a toy for you?"

"What I want," said Michael, pulling his hand out, then taking Lucifer's waist with a firm grip, clutching at the folds of the lifted angel dress, and holding one of Lucifer's thighs up — "is for you to enjoy having sex with me." Lucifer pouted at that, then lowered his face, eyeing Michael with something of a weak glare, but the fake-demon looked back, a shy smile blooming across his lips, dimples deepening right by. "Are you going to call me boring again?"

"Don't smile like that. Just fuck me and go." Lucifer put a hand on Michael's neck and tugged him down, but not for a kiss, just to press their foreheads together and breathe the same air as the fake-demon rubbed his head against the entrance for a moment, almost lazily.

Lucifer didn't rush him, nuzzling his nose against his, thinking of how he'd return reeking of sex and Rosier would frown. Asmodeus would laugh it off, but then he'd notice Rosier and change his demeanor. They wanted Lucifer gone, of course, but Rosier refused to let the beautiful young man go until Lucifer had found a safe place to stay with a safe roommate. He supposed that he'd been waiting, hoping for Michael to pick him up and save him, but Michael lived with his father. Once, the two of them had sat at the sidewalk with cups of corn and talked about how they both grew up motherless, with no family except for a father. But they responded to the mistreatment differently: Lucifer wanted to kill his father for his freedom, Michael wanted to kill for his father's love.

The cock pressed in easily, sliding right into place, almost like it would lock.

It had been Halloween when they met, too. Freshmen in college — Lucifer coming from a penthouse in the city, Michael from a quaint town an hour away — both in the library bathroom. When Michael found Lucifer crying, the younger one had been dressed like a pop star, or at least an attempt of one. He'd been hugging his body, apparently overcome with shame over how much skin he'd exposed. Michael had dressed as a wrestler, which was his last minute decision when he realized he had nothing else to wear. And that night with the corn cups had been another Halloween — they were both dressed like ghosts, which had just been a coincidence. Junior year, they hadn't seen each for Halloween. They'd been fighting. Neither of them could remember why now.

Suddenly, they were kissing again, slow, tender as a bruise. Their bodies met over and over, Michael burying in, then pulling nearly back out. He was careful, like if he removed himself, he might never be allowed back in. It annoyed Lucifer at the same time that it endeared him. A part of him wanted to reassure Michael that he could really come move in with Rosier, Asmodeus, and him, or he could even move in with his friend Phanuel; Michael didn't have to go back to his father tonight. He could stay here with him. He could find a life with other queer people and stop trying to live the life his father had planned for him. Michael could spend the rest of his years biting down moans against Lucifer's mouth. But — Lucifer had long given up trying to save Michael. Michael had never saved Lucifer from his father, so why should Lucifer save Michael from his own? Lucifer had saved himself, and he was better for it. He was being fucked against the sink at a Halloween party, spitting into the mouth of an old friend — right where he belonged.

Michael was a good lover; Lucifer always detested him for it. He jacked the fake-angel off as he thrust hard into him, using his other hand to rub at one of Lucifer's nipples through the thin fabric of the dress, and he refused to take his mouth off of him. It wasn't long before Lucifer whispered that he was close, then took Michael's arm and dug his nails into him, trying to muffle his whine as the coil of pleasure at his lower stomach twisted tighter and tighter. He shuddered when he finished, cursing because he always cursed when he came, but also thinking of washing this stupid costume tonight. Lucifer imagined Rosier trying to help him with laundry, tilting his head at the semen stains, then sighing.

'You can't judge me,' Lucifer always said, and Rosier always insisted that he never would, but Lucifer would repeat himself anyway: '*You can't judge me.*'

"Fuck," Lucifer gasped. "Fuck—" Michael hadn't stopped rocking into him, but his pace was slowing, sweat was dribbling down his brow.

When Lucifer started thrashing, the fake-demon instantly stopped, stumbling back, pulling out his still-throbbing cock without hesitation. His eyes widened, the look in them so sincere and scared, so worried he might've hurt the fake-angel. He really does care. Michael cared so much about him. 'You're so annoying.' "Are you okay?"

Lucifer didn't answer, instead planting his hand on Michael's chest and pushing him back a step. Swiftly, Lucifer moved to crouch, somehow managing to do it in his stilettos, and then he took the fake-demon's cock in a tight grip. He rolled off the condom, tossed it vaguely in the direction of the trash beside the toilet. Then, he squeezed tight and began to pump. Low, rumbling, Michael moaned in response, a hand going to Lucifer's hair.

"Don't," said Lucifer, "knock over my halo." Still, he leaned forward and pursed his lips together on the head, beginning to suckle, before taking all of the tip into his mouth. With how his cock twitched in Lucifer's mouth, Michael was teetering on the edge of release, so the fake-angel didn't drag this out very long. He shut his eyes, listening to the muffled EDM outside the bathroom and the wet, hollow sucks as he bobbed his head.

"Lucifer," Michael whispered helplessly, "Lucifer, Lucifer." The wrestler had to lean over the sink, his knees buckling, his hand yanking on the fake-angel's hair. Just as his hips thrust forward a handful of times, erratically, he began to spill, and

Lucifer pulled back so that he could have it land on his tongue. He liked the taste, not that he'd admit that, especially not to the boy who will only ever do this with him in bathrooms, in closets. 'I'm too old now,' Lucifer thought, 'to be ashamed of loving who I do.' "Thank you." 'I don't want to be with someone who is ashamed of me.'

Lifting a hand, the fake-angel wiped his mouth of saliva, then elegantly rose to stand. "We should go back to the party." He turned to the mirror above the sink, just as Michael removed his grip on it, and adjusted his hair, his halo, and noted the smeared mascara, the swollen lips, the fade of the white angelic freckles. The others would know exactly what Lucifer was up to. They'd probably call him a slut. 'But who cares? There are worse things to be.' He caught Michael's twitching, conflicting face in the mirror as he zipped his pants back up. 'I'm not unhappy.'

"I have to go back home— I really do."

"Don't let me stop you." Lucifer reached for some toilet paper and began dabbing it on the inside of his dress that he'd stained, accidentally brushing his sensitive cock in the process and flinching. "I have ket to do." But he paused, waited to see if Michael would say more or would confess something, anything. If he planned to, the fake-angel didn't have the patience for it. Lucifer turned on his heel, brushing past Michael, and finally unlocked the door. Just as he stepped out, he heard the fake-demon behind him call his name and felt the brush of a hand on his arm, but Lucifer kept walking. Hurrying down a sparsely populated hall, he approached the living area with the blaring music, chatter, and laughter.

"Lucifer, wait." Michael grappled him tighter, forcing the other to stagger to a stop. "I'll talk to my dad. I'll do it this week." Lucifer stared ahead of him; he could see the hint of the front door behind a group of other students with red plastic cups and styrofoam plates of pizza. "I will. I'll tell him about you."

"What are you going to tell him about me, Michael?" The urge to shove the other away was strong enough to make Lucifer clench his teeth, and yet he couldn't bear too. He liked the feeling of his hand. He wanted Michael to hold him more.

"That I love you," Michael whispered; it was barely audible. "That I," he said stronger, "want to be with you."

Hesitantly, Lucifer turned to face him, the fake-demon, the wrestler, the old friend he'd just been kissing. "Then do it. Don't come and see me until that happens." His eyes flickered to Michael's lips. "I don't want to see you until you've stood up to your dad." But he gave the fake-demon a parting kiss on the mouth, a quick one, so that no one in the party started more than the usual rumors about their star wrestler and Lucifer. And drawing away, he noted the flame of hope in Michael's eyes, and the fear, and the want.

"Lucifer? Lucifer!" Rosier — coming up beside the fake-angel. "Where have you been? I've been calling you for an hour." He was in a red-hooded cloak, a woven basket the color of cream-heavy coffee hanging from one of his elbows, and he wore a worried frown. "Are you okay?" He turned to Michael, then blinked a few times in surprise. "Oh... Michael. Are you okay too?"

"Goodbye, Michael," Lucifer bid him farewell, and Michael nodded with a sad smile, before Lucifer took Rosier's hand and began tugging him away. "Come on, Rosier. Are we leaving? I haven't even gotten any ket yet." He didn't turn back to Michael.

Rosier huffed but squeezed Lucifer's fingers. "Well, you'll have to wait. Asmodeus told me that the cops are on their way, and we should leave now just to be safe."

"Mm, is someone dead or just disturbing the peace?"

Outside, Asmodeus was already leaning against his car, stubbing out a blunt, and already mostly out of his costume — having removed his wolf mask and top, so he was merely in an undershirt with furry gray paws on his feet. Baal was at his side, dressed just as Michael had been, blathering away. "Hurry it up," Asmodeus called the moment he caught Lucifer and Rosier over

Baal's shoulder. "Baal's coming with us. Got in a fight with his roommate."

Lucifer snorted a bit but figured he'd hear all about it at the apartment or maybe in the backseat while squeezed in beside him. He was a decent guy, Baal — just clingy. When he saw Lucifer, he lit up on every feature of his face and opened the door for him, offering his hand to help the fake-angel climb up the step. Lucifer took it easily and slid onto the seats, crawling over all the clutter of tools and trash Asmodeus had in the back.

He'd left his phone in here, but Lucifer was trying not to spend so much time on it, so he'd figured it was a good thing. Picking it up, clicking it awake, he saw that Michael had texted: *I hope you get home safe. I'm sorry we're always fighting. I'll make it up to you. Next time I text you, I'll be out to my dad. Goodnight, Lucifer.*

Lucifer replied: *Goodnight, Michael.* He wanted to add the heart emojis he always used to, but he figured they weren't appropriate right now. He lifted his gaze just as Asmodeus and Rosier had shut the doors, the older one turning the ignition and immediately trying to wiggle the car out of the parallel-park cage.

Childishly, Lucifer folded his legs and hugged them, resting his chin on a knee. He was already a little sore, but he'd deal with it tomorrow. For now, he stared at how Asmodeus was reaching over with the hand that didn't grip the wheel to play with Rosier's fingers, and Lucifer listened to Baal excitedly shouting to Asmodeus about the fight he saw in the backyard. "Ooh," Baal said, "that reminds me that Azazel asked if I wanted to join his little gay club."

"His LGBT Undergraduate Committee," Rosier corrected.

"Yeah whatever," said Baal dismissively. "But how did he know about me? Who spilled?"

Asmodeus barked out a laugh. "That earring probably did."

Faintly, Lucifer smiled then closed his eyes; it would be a long trip back.

A few weeks passed and no message from Michael ever

arrived. Lucifer didn't see him on campus either, but their senior schedules had been incredibly mismatched, and he was unsure whether he should seek him out or not. He was told to wait, and he was rather busy at the moment anyway; Lucifer had an honors thesis to put together for his politics, philosophy, and economics BA degree and the stage-act to snatch that useless BFA in Music Performance that he wanted so terribly. So, Lucifer busied himself— looked into getting a real job and re-downloading social media to post his face on, hoping for brand deals. His father had once wanted him to be a model, and Lucifer was still in recovery from the attempt that'd been made in his childhood. But, it'd be nice to have money besides what his last name entitled him to.

Lucifer did run into Phanuel, at one point, and thankfully, the wrestler told Lucifer, unprompted, that Michael had left on a trip with his father, but he should be back soon.

Some time passed, and Lucifer became certain that Michael hadn't come out to his father. If he had, then he would have heard the gossip by now. He checked their texts frequently anyway, waiting, hoping. As graduation approached, he tried to think about it a little less, to focus on his finals. He buried himself in work again, and the perfect distraction came when Asmodeus was fired and fell into depression, which of course caused Rosier to be depressed too. Lucifer's father spamming him with calls about a proper reconnection between them also drew his mind away from his situationship with that college wrestler. Michael. He would see him at graduation, probably, so he didn't need to worry. Except, graduation day came and the massive student body drowned out any recognizable individuals in the venue. He looked for Michael, made a sincere attempt, but he couldn't even find Phanuel, whose number he didn't have.

Lucifer called, a few times. No answer.

Eventually, Asmodeus, Rosier, and Lucifer moved to a new place. Life became busy again. Baal confessed to wanting to be exclusive with him, and Lucifer spent several nights staring at the ceiling, wondering if this was really life, if you really have to let go of loves that feel like your entire world in one second then quietly fading the next. He tried asking around for Phanuel's number, but his number must've changed because an old woman answered when Lucifer tried, and Lucifer took that as a sign from heaven. He signed for a modeling gig, then started dating Baal. Years passed. Modeling unsurprisingly went sour, and Lucifer struggled to continue ignoring his abusive father. He wondered if it would just be easier to play nice with him now and wait for him to die; he was tired of fighting.

He ended up marrying Baal and was beginning to feel a little happier. He even started going to a therapist. He tried a few more jobs before deciding on a low-paying position at a local theater and living off his father's wealth. After the wedding, Lucifer and Baal moved in together, and the conversations about adoption or surrogacy started early. They decided to adopt a little girl, and then Baal asked if they should move to the suburbs. Lucifer said absolutely not. All his friends were here, and the children would probably enjoy the city atmosphere more. Already, he was speaking in plural, wanting to adopt one or two more kids. He realized he loved children, or at least *his* children. Baal was a good parent, too.

One day, though, it was Halloween again and Lucifer was walking beside some townhouses with his daughter; she was dressed like a bat and kicking orange-yellow leaves as they walked. He hoped Baal would be home soon, so they could all have dinner as a family. As he was thinking this, Lucifer looked ahead and saw a figure dressed as a ghost, sitting on the sidewalk. It was the stereotypical white-sheet with cuts for the eyes, but the sight sent an odd child down Lucifer's spine. And when the ghost turned his head at them, Lucifer stopped, making his child halt too. Once, Lucifer had dressed as a ghost and sat on a sidewalk with a boy.

"Michael?" It'd been years since he even thought of that name, that boy in undergrad who loved him but was too scared of his father to ever date him, even secretly. "Is that you?" He wasn't sure how he recognized him. "You're... okay?" The sinking feeling in him was frightened at the same time that it was happy. "Where have you been?"

"I'm sorry," said Michael, but his voice echoed. "I meant to come back to you sooner. I got lost. I've been lost."

Without thinking, Lucifer started walking closer, dragging his daughter behind. "What happened? Did you dad send you to conversion therapy or—? You completely disappeared. *God*, Michael, it's been... eight years? Nine?"

"Who are you talking to?" asked the little girl, and Lucifer let out a tragic breath.

BIRDS OF A FEATHER

A story where some of the angels are princes in a strange high fantasy world. Told in three parts.

ONE

The hawk prince Michael had heard all about the dove prince Lucifer, of course — the way one might hear about a gruesome natural disaster or a great miracle. Lucifer was beautiful, it was said, and those who adored him called him the angel of Catepetl, which was name of the mountain that crowned the dove's kingdom. And it was known that bird-folk royalty traveled from every continent to court him with a hundred servants behind them, hauling hills of jewelry and precious stone to offer. Accordingly, it was also said that Lucifer was always in golden chains and gems, so strung everywhere on his body and wings that one might think he was bound like a slave, but they were all presents from fellow royals, betrothal offers Lucifer or his father had all rejected.

And it was odd, to Michael, that Lucifer was unmarried. He was quite old now, at nineteen or perhaps twenty.

Before Michael's parents had passed on — bless their souls, God — they had asked twelve-year-old Michael if he had any interest in the prince of the doves, similarly aged though likely soon to marry already. Michael hadn't answered, then, too concerned with practicing the swing of his wooden javelin, and now nearly ten years later, he still had yet to meet or even see

Lucifer. He didn't bother. His kingdom wasn't wealthy enough, he thought, nor was their territory expansive enough.

In fact, he had been caught up for several years in a dispute regarding control of the peninsula across the thin sea that separated Michael's kingdom from the southernmost continent, a land that had traditionally belonged to hawks for centuries, up until the death of Michael's parents. The only achievement Michael had as the young crown prince was retaking their territory. He'd rapidly strengthen the army and, in a now infamous battle, slaughtered the invaders. In the aftermath, Phanuel had patted him on the shoulder, cheering, then embracing him. It was the happiest Michael had ever been, the day he no longer felt so insignificant, felt strong the way his dead parents had urged him to be.

There was another reason he'd never bothered to court beautiful Lucifer. Michael was a hawk, a bird of prey, a raptor, and carnivorous bird with an herbivorous one was taboo. Of course, royals could break any widespread customs that they like, but if mourning dove Lucifer could have anyone, he would surely choose a bird-person of his own kind.

And yet, one day, Michael received a letter. He'd been with Phanuel, eating skewers of meat and discussing governance on that peninsula with a new minority population of owls, when a messenger stepped in with servants and offered a folded, stamped paper to the prince. Before Michael had even opened it, he noticed a printed dove emblem with curious blinks. There were other dove kingdoms — for no kingdom is truly *of only one species* nor the *representative for all of a single species*, despite every kingdom's individual nationalisms that proclaimed such — it could have belonged to any other minor dove kingdom than Lucifer's. However — this emblem was very particular, very official, ancient.

"It's," said Michael after he'd opened it, skimmed the few lines, "an invitation to meet Prince Lucifer."

"Prince Lucifer?" Phanuel picked at his sharp canines with

the wooden stick that had pierced some beef a minute earlier. "Not his father?"

"No," Michael answered quietly, turning the page to see nothing on the back. "It says he'll be away, in fact."

Phanuel laughed, but it tinged with apprehension. "That's odd."

"Odd."

"Will you go?"

"I don't see why I shouldn't."

"Hm. Well, you do need to think of marriage, Michael. You cannot be king until you marry." So the laws proclaimed. "Now that the war is settled, you should think of heirs and love. Not all of life is praying and wrestling, friend."

"Unfortunately," Michael mumbled, though his cheeks warmed at that. "But, as you said, it's very strange. Prince Lucifer shouldn't need to invite anyone to court him, so this must be about something else." He was so certain of it, in fact, that he decided not to bring anything that could be mistaken for a romantic offering.

Nevertheless, when the day the invitation had indicated arrived, Michael had himself dressed in his best furs and had his hair styled back as he wondered incessantly what the most beautiful bird in all the land would think of him. Briefly, he fantasized of the dove prince confessing to be in love, but each time, Michael would shake his head shamefully and tell himself to be honorable. He must announce his departure to his people; he must hurry to make the journey before dawn faded.

Though bird-folk can, of course, fly, royal confrontation were typically conducted through foot marches as a sign of peace, and Michael had a small legion with him as he ordered for Phanuel to be left in charge of matters for the weeks he'd be absent. This was hardly a transition of power, as Phanuel had been in control of the court for all the time Michael was too young to utter a command without stammering. It was because of the high advisor Phanuel, really, that the kingdom hadn't fractured following the death of Michael's parents. One day, Michael would have a statue of Phanuel erected — he was already planning — with a golden plaque detailing how his lone effort had likely saved the kingdom of the hawks.

But that is enough words about the journey. When Michael arrived to the kingdom of Lucifer, he did it with a slow exhale of juvenile wonder at the sheer age of each stone wall, each mosaic, and the cobble roads. Fountains, in every direction Michael turned, celebrated the doves' impressive and vast irrigation system — though there were obvious signs of weathering at the edges of the sculptures pouring water. In contrast, all of the colorfully patterned clothing of the kingdom's residents, as well as their abundant jewelry, were as bright as if they'd been weaved just the day before. Wealth in everything but decrepit in many corners — golden fixtures on hundreds of buildings, all now crooked or slouching. Once, this had been the center of the world.

The capital of an empire, but that had been centuries ago.

At the castle of ancient stone, Michael was welcomed in, told exactly where prince Lucifer was, and offered empty barracks for his soldiers to sleep in. They were very luxurious, he was reassured; a guest's army ought to be pampered like royals if the visit is friendly. Michael didn't quite understand the sentiment, but he removed his top layer of furs as soon as a servant offered him their hands. The bird-folk of the castle were of extraordinarily diverse sizes and features, as had been the case with all those out in the streets. Michael had heard of this, the same as he'd heard of Lucifer all his life — the kingdom was great, populated with bird-folks of all kinds, though they must all heed the royal doves.

In a lounge, the beautiful prince was waiting for him.

Golden-haired and rosy-lipped, he sat with one leg crossed over the other on a velvet sofa lined with golden decals, not far from a portrait of the kingdom's landscape and a window that provided a hint of what must've been a garden. Lucifer had a chalice in his hand, but he was setting it down on a golden table before him before uncrossing his slim legs to lift his body, to stand. He had the build of a dove — delicate, lithe — though he was in abundant, white frills that might've been modest if they weren't tight around his waist and partly open at his chest to display each of the perhaps two dozen necklaces he'd been gifted by candidates for marriage. Pants ended at his mid-thigh and left the rest of his legs to be protected by mere socks, more chains, and heeled boots.

As beautiful as the legends said; he could have been an angel. He made your chest ache, made you hurt for him. And his gaze was boundless.

"Your Highness," Michael breathed in greeting. "I thank you for the invitation to your beautiful land."

"Prince," said the prince of the doves, a smile curling his plump lips pleasantly, his voice like the most alluring bird's song. "The pleasure is all mine." He stepped toward him, and Michael felt his jaw clench at how the dove swung his hips a little as he walked. "You're as large as I was told." He tilted his head, spiraling and heavy earrings rattling. "One of my guards is a hawk, but even he's not as well-built as you— Oh." Lucifer ran his gaze up Michael's body, and the latter tried not to shiver. "You didn't bring me a gift."

Michael hesitated, only for the second of silence, before he cleared his throat roughly. "No, I thought that would be inappropriate." Faintly, he heard the door thump behind him, then click — a turning lock. "You invited me, and I didn't want anyone to misinterpret this as a courting visit. I didn't think you'd appreciate that."

"So you have no interest in marrying me?"

Coughing, spluttering Michael tried to stammer that he hadn't intended to come off like that. Lucifer was gorgeous. Michael could marry him. Would be the happiest bird alive to have him. Who wouldn't?

But then the dove was giggling, and he fiddled with a small braid in his long hair. "I was only teasing. Sit, please sit. I'm glad you arrived safely. My father says that there's some unrest down south, and I know you were at war for some time."

Again, Michael didn't reply immediately, but as Lucifer returned to his seat, he followed and soon settled on a couch parallel to Lucifer's. "Oh, yes. I was, but the land is secured, and it's been quite peaceful for a year or so. I'm not typically one for aggression, but the invaders were persistent. And owls, too." Amicably, he laughed. "Battle after battle, and all of them had to be in the dead of night. It's only through God's will that victory was possible at all."

"Hm." The braid Lucifer had been playing with slipped through his fingers. "We have the same religion."

"Hm?" Michael tilted his head a little, confused at the sudden mention of faith. "Yes. I believe so."

"Your kingdom used to be a province of the old empire," answered the dove prince mundanely. "Because I'm interested in you, I read about your people and your land in our libraries. The hawks were very rebellious, the histories say, but you never quite broke away from us, and you accepted the doves' religion easily."

Waiting, allowing those words to sink into him, Michael then swallowed coarsely. "Not so easily. We... worship differently, I hear. There are some things we don't agree on."

"Oh, yes, I read of that as well." The dove smiled. "Your God is much kinder than mine, and yet he's the same God."

Beginning to furrow his brow, Michael asked, "May I ask why you invited me here, Your Highness?"

Lucifer stared at him, then sighed and leaned back into his seat, crossing his legs again. "I heard," he began, "that you were ruthless on the battleground. You beheaded the invading king, and you had his loyalists crucified."

Grimacing. "I had no other choice."

"Often, it's only violence that works," Lucifer replied, quietly, his hand working through his hair like a comb; it looked lovingly soft and perfect to pull. "Some can't be reasoned with. Some deserve fates worse than death." Michael stared this time, levelly, waiting and waiting. "Prince Michael of the hawks... I did invite you here romantically." In his chest, Michael's heart stopped and hurried to hide in his throat. "I want you to marry me." Before the other could even vomit the gasp in his mouth, Lucifer added, "After you murder my father."

Michael's breath then left him.

"After you murder my father," the dove continued, "I want you to conquer my kingdom and force me to marry you. I want you to do it violently. Kill the king of the doves in public, slowly, make him suffer, and then you'll grab me and lay your claim on me."

"What," Michael choked out, all of his blood chilling, "are you saying, Your Highness?"

"Should I say it another time? I want you to kill my father."

"Why?"

"You'll gain this kingdom and all its wealth, and you'll have me as a bride."

"Why," Michael demanded again, voice strained, his throat aching, "are you asking me to do this?"

"Your army is strong, and *you're* strong. I think you could do it."

"But why do you want him dead? It's the greatest sin to bring harm onto one's father, Lucifer—"

"That's why you will do it and not me." Lucifer smiled, long, then rose to his feet again, even slower than he had earlier. "You must've been awed at this magnificent kingdom when you arrived. Wouldn't you like it?" Again, he made his way around the table, toward Michael, who was looking all around only to realize they were indeed completely, utterly, alone. "And me, Your Highness. You can have me. Any other prince would kill to be you."

"I don't—" Michael whispered, but he didn't know what he wanted to say, his last breaths spilling from his lips as the dove maneuvered a leg over him, setting on Michael's thighs, not quite his groin. Michael wore sheep skin pants and a belt, and the dove's nails soon began to scratch at the silver buckle. "I couldn't do that. I was protecting from invaders during that battle. I'm not an invader myself."

Lucifer hummed. "You're being difficult." He unclasped the buckle, then tugged slowly at the belt, letting it slide past the loops, and Michael didn't stop him.

"Lucifer, we're... not married." But Michael shuddered as the dove tugged down on his pants. "This is a sin, too."

"It surprises me that you're unmarried," Lucifer replied, not touching him yet. "I would have expected you with multiple children already. You're very beautiful, very handsome. If we have children, they would be the greatest in all the land. This could all be an empire again." Michael's hips twitched, eager to plunge into the dove and establish the heirs that Phanuel had told him of. "Wouldn't you like to rule an empire, Michael?"

"Please," Michael whispered.

"Will you kill my father?"

"I don't want to," Michael still said, "but I want you."

"You can only have me if you do as I say."

Finally, the dove touched him, worked his fingers, trying to urge him to grow into an adequate size. "I've been told that you birds of prey are better endowed." Michael was nearly whimpering, realizing how starved he'd been of amorous strokes. "Mm, it's growing fast. I suppose it's true." He took one of Michael's hands, lifted it to scratch at his top, and the hawk's shaking fingers barely didn't tear it off Lucifer's body. "Will it fit inside me?" He tugged Michael's hand downward, made it palm between his legs. "I'm just a dove. I wasn't built for you."

"I'll do anything," Michael started begging. "Please. I'll do it." He surrendered. "Whatever it is you want." He rubbed Lucifer's crotch, feeling for the exact shape hidden beneath the shorts, licking his lips, thinking of sucking on a dove and hearing beautiful Lucifer's songs of finish.

Suddenly, Lucifer smirked, and he pecked the edge of Michael's mouth. "Good." He climbed off of him, leaving

Michael's hardened cock between them, and then adjusted his earrings, humming thoughtfully. "Dinner is soon. You should relieve yourself, so we can head there and feast. I even had meats prepared for you. Aren't I considerate?"

"What—" Michael gasped, thighs shaking, his tip already beading. "You're not going to...?"

Wickedly, Lucifer laughed. "My father has some concubines you can use, but if you'd rather use your hand and finish quickly, then you can stare at my face as you do so. I'll even stick my tongue out for you, Your Highness." He took Michael's chin, delicately turned up his face, and there was some autumn sunlight streaming in from the window, shining on pretty, pretty Lucifer. "Don't look at me like that. Did you really think a beautiful dove like me is an easy whore? Do as I say and then you'll earn it. But this isn't an eternal offer. I need him dead by spring. Come spring and you must torture him to death; then, you may have me. Do you understand?"

Michael yielded, again, his voice weak: "Yes."

"Yes, hm?"

"Yes, Your Highness."

TWO

My father's very upset about our meeting, began the letter.

One of the servants informed him, despite my instructions not to — but it's no matter. I knew this would happen. My father only screamed at me, said that I'm never to speak to you again, then he went off to drink. I can't say the king's always been a drunkard, though I'm not certain enough to say that he has become this way recently either. When I was young, he would often ask me, instead of his servants, to serve him wine; and when he drank, I never thought that he couldn't stop. I thought that the pleasure to him wasn't the wine but the sight of me following his commands. This occurred in the same years that I wasn't allowed to leave the castle, too. The imprisonment did nothing, however, to keep my beauty a secret. I started receiving marriage proposals at eight years old; I was the fruit of a legend before I was a person. I feel the need to say that it troubles other birds when I tell them I'm well aware of how lovely in face and body that I am. I suppose that if I were ignorant to it, then I would be delightfully helpless. But I'm not an idiot, and I'm not a child, and I can do anything I like now. My father is elderly, and I should be married already. You should be married too, Michael.

When you were here last, I was curious why you're not a king yet. Word of your victory and the strength of your army has spread so far. Surely, others have sent you proposals or jewels. Why haven't you taken a wife, or a husband? With your strength, I suppose all the world has assumed you're to be the husband of a pair, but I think you'd be quite a good wife too. You're very gentle, though no one seems to know, and that brings me pleasure. I feel that I'm carrying your greatest secret.

I'm inviting you again. The servant who snitched will be put on trial for execution, and my father will be gone again in three months — the eve of Narzo, 3 Ak'bao. He's headed for the kingdom of the lovebirds. They're in plenty of peril there, economic and social. They've tried to cut their trade to the owls again, how silly. But what can be expected from such backwards people? They were never integrated into the old Empire, you see; they still believe in their pagan gods.

You will come meet me in the main garden. The daisies should be blooming. We'll discuss more of what I told you about. Write back to me soon.

Yours, if you're brave enough,
   Lucifer.

A week later, Michael replied, though without telling Phanuel because his shame since he'd returned to his land had still proven too much:

Lucifer, your Highness.

I'm happy to write to you, but don't you think this is dangerous? I know the dove king is your father, so you may not see how dangerous he is, but you must know how far his influence extends. If he decides I'm his enemy, he could cripple me. It's true that my army is strong, but an army is only as strong as the silver behind them. If he acts to threaten access to our usual trade routes, such as you speak regarding the lovebirds, then my kingdom may fall into ruin.

All of this said, I would like to see you again, but if possible — not in secret. Can't I meet with your father? You said you were interested in me romantically, so allow me to court you. There's no need for this elaborate plan of murder and conquest. If you no longer want your father to rule, then all you have to do is marry so that you and your spouse have the dove throne instead. And if we married, I can allow you to rule your land with no influence from me. This war you're flirting with is unnecessary, Lucifer. You're beautiful, and my heart has been full of you since I saw you. Allow me to court you. That's all I want now. You've stolen my breath; allow me to have it back through a wedding kiss.

Yours,
  Michael.

Only days later, Lucifer's response arrived, short and without signature:

I have no interest in you if you do not kill my father and take my kingdom. If you won't do it, then don't come on the day I've invited you, and don't send me another letter.

And this, of course, created quite the predicament for the prince Michael. He needed to speak to Lucifer again, not only for courting purposes — Michael was self-aware enough to know he was merely suffering a seduction-induced fleeting yearning — but he felt he had a duty to encourage the dove to not try to have his own kingdom conquered. Though Lucifer's kingdom, and broader territories, should be of no concern to him, Michael couldn't help but worry about an unnecessary loss of life; his faith forbade allowing for such. Thus, he knew that their conversation couldn't end on that final letter, but if Michael sent a messenger once again denouncing Lucifer's plans, he felt that the dove would likely ignore him and find someone else to convince of leading an invasion. There was no other choice but to meet in person, however weak seeing the dove's beautiful face might make Michael, again.

None of these thoughts did he dare share with Phanuel. One evening, he merely informed his friend, "I'll be leaving tomorrow with the army to speak with Prince Lucifer again," over dinner and, when Phanuel spluttered, he added, "I can't explain it now. I don't know if I'll ever be able to explain it to you. Forgive me." Michael was fiddling with his cut of meat, talons peeking out of his fingertips though he was calm and had no need for them. "But it's not a courting. If you're asked, you should tell the court that it's a trade deal and nothing more. You can tell them that the doves are interested in our furs." That wasn't outrageous; one of the most lucrative hawk exports was furs, and the doves imported everything from everyone. "Am I clear?" The doves had lost an empire of violence, but their empire of commerce remained.

Phanuel hesitated, sitting at his end of the table, his eyebrows furrowed together. At either side of him, there were long torches screwed high into the stone walls, their flames casting his shadow onto the long wooden table between them, carved extensively with various animal faces on the legs and down its surface. "I... suppose." The kingdom of the hawks was mostly temperate, though it had been a little colder than usual in the past few years, and it was composed of a dominant city and its village territories along some very forested hills. "Am I allowed to ask for more information from you, Your Highness?"

"I plead you not to."

"I see. Be safe, then, Michael. God be with you."

"Thank you."

Michael didn't explain himself to his army either, even as he gathered and set them on the march north; he even considered leaving them behind for secrecy, but the hawk prince was tradi-tional above all else. Additionally, he didn't have anyone to answer to — or so he told himself. Michael was the crown prince. He will be king. The court was composed of elders that were mere advisers and law enforcement on peasants; the actions of the hawk king could only be judged, investigated, and persecuted by himself. He was a tyrant, or, rather, he could be.

'Your father,' Phanuel had told the young Michael once, 'was a tyrant. All of your lineage has been made up of tyrants.' His voice had been tight, almost angry, and if the crown prince had been older and wiser, Michael would have asked why Phanuel didn't kill him now. Why not end the cruel dynasty that Michael was the heir of? It was the perfect moment to do it, and Phanuel was so easily secretly governing that he might as well just slice open the prince's neck and crown himself. Why didn't he?

Upon arrival — weeks later — the people of Lucifer's city looked at Michael with curious tilts and whispers about, clearly, a courter who wasn't taking no for an answer from their perfect, beautiful prince. The hawk stared back at them; they really were so different from his own kingdom's people, in this sort of posh manner that they carried themselves with across the streets and toward the markets. The hawks themselves hardly had any internal markets, still preferring communal hunts and resource-pooling for the majority of necessities. Michael was sure the dove kingdom's people would call the hawk's lifestyle a remnant of the ancient past, perhaps even Lucifer would think so. And so Michael tried to take his mind off of it, lifting his chin to look at the castle down the cobblestone path that he marched toward, seeing the peak of stone towers perfectly in line with the tall mountain at the horizon.

Lucifer was, as promised, in the garden. Michael went through the routine of leaving his army at the luxurious barracks of the doves, then he went to the castle's servants, asked for directions, then followed a small bird person — perhaps a finch? — down a few corridors. The finch was heavily jeweled, just about rattling when she walked — such jewels were a sign of a married, submissive partner. According to Phanuel, before the doves' religion took over the world, there was no social distinction between being the dominant or submissive partner in a marriage, and there was no way to know outside of visible pregnancy. He'd said this a little quietly, but not with any longing. Maybe he thought it was pointless to yearn for such a distant past. Michael felt similar, though he remembered his conversation with Lucifer the last time he'd been here regarding religion just as he found himself stepping back into the open air and down a few slanted steps. The hawk religion — a product of dove colonial rule.

The dove prince was facing a fountain with an angelic face carved into it, water spilling down its open mouth. All around them, there were daisies, white petals open and facing the sun overhead. With his arms tangled in a shawl as pale as the flowers, Lucifer turned his head slowly, staring at Michael in silence, his face expressionless, so empty in fact that Michael began to worry something was wrong before he heard the door shut behind him. Instantly after, Lucifer laughed, shaking his head, saying, "I didn't think you'd come."

"I haven't changed my mind," Michael said quickly.

"Trust that I know that, Your Highness." Lucifer pulled his arms out from under the shawl, exposing a thin, leather-bound book that he, taking some steps toward Michael, instantly began pressing into his hands. "Here."

"Hm?" Michael clumsily took the book that was being shoved against his fingers, nearly dropping it. "What? What is this?"

"The history of your kingdom." Lucifer nodded his head at it, then turned up his grin to Michael. "The hawks are savages." Michael almost immediately sighed. "Or so that's what it says, but I don't believe that's true. One of the issues with writings from the empire days is that it says every non-dove bird is a backward savage, but I think it's especially amusing in this text, because our kingdoms have a more similar history than you think." Just as Michael opened his mouth, Lucifer interjected: "You're from a bloodline of evil tyrants. The way in which your ancestors secured power was by killing and banishing the non-hawks from the land. I read how you've been violently suppressing rebellions for centuries, before and after the old dove empire collapsed."

Grimacing, Michael tried to push the book back into Lucifer's hands. "I'm not proud of that history—"

"History is what you are, Michael."

"I am not my father." He said it harshly, but hardly meant it because though *yes*, he'd heard these awful words of his father before, he had only ever known the soft, kind side of the dead king. Michael loved him, even though he'd been a monster to all others. "Now— Why are you saying this? Lucifer, if you planned to use this as some kind of way to guilt me into starting a way with you to follow my legacy—"

"Oh, can't a little dove just read some history books? I told you." Lucifer took the book back into his arms and hugged it to his chest, almost childishly. "I find it fascinating that our histories are really quite similar. I started comparing all the histories of royalty that I found. Do you want to know what I discovered?"

Michael didn't really want to know, but Lucifer was beautiful, and he had a brilliant smile, so he yielded: "What did you discover, Your Highness?"

"Well, incest," Lucifer joked, "but also war, conquest, assassination, and that there's never been a peaceful ruler, Michael. Not one. Every story you tell about good kings and queens is a lie." He tilted his head, then leaned in and murmured, "You don't find that a little frightening? No matter how moral you try to be, Michael, you will have to commit atrocity. There's no other way to rule." Blood running a little colder, Michael shook his head. "Oh? Do you think you'll be different? You're not the first oppressive tyrant to declare that. And you won't be the last."

"Lucifer, I," Michael cut in, his face twisting, "I'm here to urge you not to do this." He looked away, just to try and stop staring at the dove's beauty, just to try and focus. "I can't only tell you to stop speaking to me because I fear you'll trick another prince into doing this. So, I must ask, why do you want this to happen? Whatever it is you want, surely there's a way to do it where there won't be so much bloodshed. You said that if I do it, I can marry you, but I don't want to marry you with blood on my hands, Lucifer. And no one should."

"There's already blood on your hands, Your Highness," said the dove, slow and cruel.

Swallowing down his heartbeats, coming quick and quicker, Michael admitted, "You said it yourself: we have the same religion. You know God calls upon us to be good." He, without meaning to, looked back at Lucifer, his perfect, long-lashed eyes, his perfect lips, his golden hair tossed by the breeze. "Don't do this." Michael's gaze flickered from that mouth, to his eyes, mouth, eyes, mouth. "Please."

"You want to kiss me." The dove said it calmly.

"Can't I court you the proper way? Whatever it is you desire, I can give it to you as king." Michael reached, put his hand over Lucifer's. "I want to be good, and I want you to be good too." The dove's fingers were cold, and though Michael expected to be shoved away or even slapped, Lucifer just stared at him.

"Why you?" Lucifer asked simply. "I can have anyone I want."

"You could," Michael admitted, his hand drifting along to the dove's wrist, then up his arm. "You could deny me and find another bird to play with."

Lucifer snorted. "Play with, hm?" He tossed his book haphazardly aside, then put his hands on the fountain behind him, leaning against it and tilting his head at Michael curiously. "There's something else in the books, in all the books about birds of prey like you. Long ago, before even the empire. You used to attack the herbivorous birds all that you liked, used to raid our villages and kidnap us. Even eat us, at times."

Michael began, "Those stories are greatly exaggerated."

"It's nothing to be ashamed of. If I were a bird of prey, and you were the pretty herbivore, I'd want to eat you too." Lucifer smiled at the hawk's face, warming rosy at the cheeks. "Come, let me show you the castle." He brushed past him, heading for the short stairway and door. "I'll even show you my bedroom. You should become acquainted with it. You'll be spending a lot of time there." Michael made a little grumble, feeling his wings puffing up in shyness. He was never good at being flirted with, but as much as he'd like to sink into the flustered feelings — he was afraid to. What was Lucifer doing? What was he planning? "Come, come." And so Michael followed.

Hours later, it was time for dinner, and Lucifer insisted they eat in his room as the final stop in their tour. Michael had never been very interested in history, especially in any history that didn't pertain to his people, but Lucifer had a way of maintaining your attention. He had funny anecdotes about every little trinket in the hallways, knew the gossip behind the royal portraits, and even offered the real stories behind architectural details in an oddly compelling way. While riveting, it wasn't helpful for Michael's growing feelings for him. He knew now that Lucifer's ideas about ruling were nothing less than frightening, and Michael knew that maybe he *should* allow the dove prince to capture another bird in his web of terror just to clear his own conscience while he could. However: Lucifer was pretty. He was brilliant, too. He fascinated Michael. That was the most terrible part of this for Michael: he knew better. He knew better than to follow the dove prince up the steps of a tower as he continued listing off some details about the windows they passed.

He remembered Lucifer's letter, where he'd mentioned being locked up by his father in the castle. Michael had the urge to ask if this is why the dove knew so much, but he wasn't sure if now was the time. He chose to merely keep listening, to keep obeying.

At the door, Michael stopped and, glancing to his side, noticed there was a heavily armored guard who was nearly his height — almost certainly another hawk. There were hints of brown curls, though tighter than Michael's, beneath his helmet. "Baal," Lucifer greeted him. "Be a dear and open the door for us."

"Does your father know about this, Your Highness?" replied a curt voice.

"Mm, I suppose not," said Lucifer, "but he would kill me if he found out..." Dramatically, he sighed. "So we should very well hope that he doesn't find out, Baal."

"I see."

"Now, may you open the door or should I say it a third time?"

Grunting, the guard took the iron handle and wrenched it wide open, but his gauntlet grip was visibly shaking, as if his anger would overcome him at any moment. Again, Michael kept quiet, or at least he did so until after he and Lucifer stepped inside and the shut the door behind them. This time, Michael locked it himself, his brows furrowing, as Lucifer waltzed on ahead, over to a golden platter of food over a long couch. He took it by its marble handles, then headed toward an archway with jewels hanging down it, acting as a makeshift curtain that cut the bedding area from the lounge. "Baal," Michael echoed to himself.

"Come, come," Lucifer urged once more, slipping past the curtain of colorful gems. "We'll eat on my bed."

Michael followed behind carefully, not looking around much but still lifting a hand to touch the jewels and think of how much each little stone cost. He was a crown prince, so he was well-acquainted with wealth, but the dove kingdom was so much richer, so much more decadent in every aspect. "That guard... He was a hawk?" He stepped into the bedroom — or what birdfolk liked to call the "nest," which Michael refrained from doing because he'd always found that word unnecessarily sexual. For a bird of prey, he was a bit of a prude, whereas the pure dove before him was the machiavellian seducer — if the public knew, they'd probably become the punchline of a joke.

On a massive, overly pillowed bed with far too many blankets — very low to the ground and with a circular shape, as all bird beds typically are — Lucifer settled, fluttering his wings behind him a little and setting the platter beside him. "Hm. You mean

Baal. Yes, he's a hawk. There are a few hawks working as guards, soldiers, and so on around here. Some vultures and eagles too." He shrugged out of his shawl slowly, then tossed it aside to reveal that he was in a heavily embroidered tunic over his pants. "But not so many birds of prey live here, most are those banished from their home kingdoms or the children of the banished. Baal's parents were banished, I believe, and they ended up here, birthed him here. He's been my guard since both of us were very small."

Michael, slowly, sat on the bed by Lucifer, staring at the rolled meats, realizing now that he had no appetite. "And does he know what your plans are?"

Lucifer hummed. "I wouldn't trust an idiot like him with any plan of mine." His words were more venomous than Michael was expecting, but the dove took his rolls of vegetables and grains with an elegant two fingers, then brought them to his mouth to bite, chew, and swallow. "You should eat before it gets cold."

"I will," Michael promised, though he wasn't sure of that. "Now, Lucifer, may we— May we discuss this situation again?"

"Mm, what's there to discuss?" Lucifer licked his fingers, slow, swirling his tongue around. "You said you wouldn't do what I asked, and now I have no interest in you. You're going to leave tomorrow, and I'm never going to contact you again. I'll find another bird who will do what you're too much of a coward to do. Hmm. Maybe the vulture prince, but I hear such awful things about him. Do you know him? His name is Asmodeus. He's inheriting the strongest weaponry in the world, but they say all he does is smoke and drink and fuck concubines." Lucifer chuckled, then nodded his head at Michael. "What do you think? Do you know any mightier princes than you? One that can commit a conquest and fuck me?"

Michael narrowed his eyes. "I just want to know why you refuse to marry anyone that's not a conqueror."

"Why do you want to know? This is our second time meeting and you've made it clear that you don't have enough of an interest in me to do as I say. If you really loved me, then you'd do it." He shoved the entire roll in his mouth and began playing with his hair over a shoulder as Michael sighed angrily.

"I came here to help you, to talk you down from this."

"I never asked for your help."

"You're going to destroy your kingdom and yourself."

"And why does that matter to you?"

"Because..."

"Because?" Giggling, Lucifer pushed aside the platter and leaned his body closer. "I like this. I like seeing you angry." Michael hadn't realized his hands had curled into fists, but they were there on the mattress between them, almost shivering. "There *he* is. There's the hawk that crucified those invaders. That's the hawk I heard such scary stories of." Michael tried unclenching his jaw but couldn't. "That's why I haven't given up on you. I can see what you can become, what I can make of you." His voice was dropping, falling to nearly a whisper. "I could make you a God-king."

God-king. Michael wanted to shake his head, to say that was blasphemous, but the dove was inching closer, closer, and the hawk's furious breath was stuck in his throat. Paralyzed, he stared at the hungry look fixed on him, a stare like Lucifer was the predator rather than himself.

When Lucifer kissed him, it was soft, a little bird's peck — but as he leaned back, Michael hopelessly chased his mouth, hurrying to brush his lips on the other just a little more. The dove smiled again, giggling again. Lucifer opened his mouth invitingly, scraping his teeth on Michael's bottom lip. And then Michael pounced on him, surging on top, pinning the dove down and crashing his mouth onto Lucifer's, thrusting in his tongue and moaning against him in a way that couldn't be described as anything other than pathetic. He immediately started moving his hips as throbs worked their way down from his belly to even his legs. Lucifer's hands moving all over him weren't any help: they tugged and pulled at the hawk's clothing, then found his wings and yanked on the inner feathers enough to make Michael whimper and rub himself on Lucifer's lifted knee in desperation. It was almost like a trance, but he couldn't do anything more than pant as he lifted his face away from Lucifer's burning, wet mouth. Blinking rapidly, he tried to return to himself, to his body.

With hair sprawled over the pillow, Lucifer gave him a brilliant smile, and instantly, Michael forgot, forgot who he was, where he was. He felt like God. He felt like Lucifer could make him a God-king, after all.

"Do you need some help, little bird?" The dove brought his hand to Michael's waistband, pulling free the buttons, then slipping his hand inside to immediately stroke his fingers on him. "Do you need me to guide you?"

"I know," Michael gasped weakly, "what to do." With one hand, he reached into Lucifer's pants as well, and he rubbed his finger amateurishly, then he tried gripping and tugging, wondering how large Lucifer was. Michael was not a virgin, however much his behavior might indicate; he'd gone through various hawk breeding seasons in horrible pain but never alone. He was quite the fan of frotting or rubbing on any willing soldier in a tent. But the dove prince made him feel exceptionally weak to his own instincts. And Lucifer's sweet cries as he began grinding his hips up into Michael's hand, now clutching a cock more surely, had his soul half in heaven and half in hell.

"You can't," Lucifer grunted, "penetrate me." Still, he tugged Michael closer with his free hand, and soon he was freeing both their cocks and trying to guide them to slide against each other. The first sensation of Lucifer's length against his own sent a shiver of pleasure all along Michael's body and made his wings tremble behind him, and he couldn't stop himself from placing his full weight on Lucifer, burying his face in his neck, the warm heat and pulse and locks of sunlight hair. He couldn't control himself, either, from thrusting wildly — his shaft rubbing against Lucifer's own and rubbing against Lucifer's entrance, dampening the head of his cock with each slide. "Ugh, idiot," Lucifer growled, clutching at Michael's wings again but spreading his legs wide to accommodate the big hawk between, only to wrap them around his waist a minute later, thighs pressed plush against Michael's hips.

"I'm sorry," Michael whispered. "It feels too good. You feel too good."

"It's like you're in heat," Lucifer grumbled only to lean his head back and moan soft, rhythmically. "No," he hissed when Michael tried angling his hips back, trying to get his body to come to its senses. "Don't stop." He rolled his hips, trying to create more friction. "You started this. End it."

"I want to finish inside you."

"Don't." Lucifer's legs were still locked tight around him, pulling him so, so close to slipping inside. "But you can try—" He gasped, shuddered and whimpered out a stifled moan. "Not inside. Just... on my stomach. And don't finger it in either. Do you understand?"

"Yes." And Michael finally went back to kissing him deeply, taking Lucifer's waist in his hands, imagining how the inside of Lucifer would feel if the outside was this good, thinking of how tight and warm he'd be, of how he might have to be gentle with him, to not accidentally claw at him or bite at him or eat him. "Mmm." 'God-king,' he'd said. Michael knew better. He knew better than that and this. Lucifer was trying to scheme a war that could cause his own destruction, and Michael felt like he was being tempted right into self-destruction too. He should leave. He should pray. He should tell himself stories of good rulers. Instead, he kissed Lucifer one last time, a little peck, and he allowed himself to listen to the dove finish — beautiful and loud and honey-sweet — before he spilled over him.

Instantly, Michael flopped on top of the dove, and he could feel exhaustion tugging him down, making his eyelids weigh. God-king. That's not what he was. But Lucifer, smiling, blissful, and laughing wonderfully, could convince him, for just a moment. God-king Michael.

THREE

The vulture prince Asmodeus had gone through some four, five, wives already by 26 years old. The first had been a noble, a gorgeous fellow vulture practically raised to marry him, but Asmodeus had been utterly uninterested in having children, which he found loud, stinking, and aggravating. An excruciating few months passed of the noble nagging at the lazy prince, then there had been a scandalous divorce that the kingdom gossiped about for a lifetime. Shockingly, Asmodeus' parents had managed to restrain themselves from killing him, then paired the prince with another noble, an excited replacement. This one found less of an issue with Asmodeus' dislike of children but was disgusted by his opium addiction and his preference for the royal concubines. The catalyst for divorce this time was Asmodeus snidely commenting that he couldn't get off with someone so prissy.

The third marriage went marginally better, this one involving a prince from a small principality of lovebirds — not the true, largesy kingdom of lovebirds that had an entire religious revolution decades ago. Unfortunately, this spouse was suddenly, mysteriously, poisoned a week after the wedding during a visit to his homeland. Certainly, it was the work of the large lovebird kingdom, crushing what it considered rebellious off-shoots of itself. It was all very complicated, and Asmodeus had no interest in politics, so he requested not to be married to another lovebird if it could be helped. He added that he wasn't interested in doves either; he'd meet the beautiful dove prince once, felt in his soul that something was terribly wrong with him, then decided he wanted nothing to do with it.

So, his parents found him a fourth spouse — a sparrow. This one went the same as the first two marriages. Half a year in, the sparrow forced Asmodeus to sign the divorce agreement, though not without snarling at him publicly about him being a drug-addicted, concubine-loving infertile cretin. This time, Asmodeus' parents were furious. They demanded that that their oldest child make the next marriage work, and that he have a dozen children, and that he quit the opium. Asmodeus agreed to only the marriage part, for now. Unfortunately, the fifth spouse — a royal from an owl kingdom — died during a storm while on the way to the wedding.

"I'm cursed," Asmodeus told his parents with a shrug. "What is there to do about that? The spirits don't want me to marry. You must have my younger siblings assassinate me and take the crown instead."

They were not happy about this, as one might expect, and so he wasn't surprised when he received news one afternoon that his parents had found another match for him, but he was shocked when he heard the wedding would be the following morning.

"What the fuck?" he'd laughed at his mother from a seat in his favorite living area, tired from sex with his least favorite concubine. "With who? Another noble? I don't like the nobles, and they don't like me."

"A finch prince from Guateru. His name is Rosier."

"What? Guateru?" It was an immense island off the northern coast of the continent to the east — rather beautiful, but underdeveloped in terms of economy. "Hm." Then, he snickered again. "This is to take control of their fruits, isn't it?" He received no answer, and so he decided to smoke and not think much of it. "Fine. As you wish, mother. We will see if he divorces me once you start destroying his rainforests."

The next day, as promised, was the wedding day. Asmodeus treated it like any other morning in his life — waking up late, eating, fucking, going out for a stroll, and playing a ball game with some cousins and nobles. Once sunset approached, however, he allowed for his servants to lug him back to the castle, take him into his cleaned bedroom, then begin dressing him in elaborate, silk robes, tying back his hair, outlining his eyes with dark paint. The vulture was so bored with weddings by now that even the anticipation was gone. All he could consider looking forward to was being intimate with a new line in his mental list of different bird species he'd slept with. But he didn't even know what his new spouse would look like, and so he feared the worst.

Asmodeus' people, the vultures of Ceprea, didn't have temples or churches, only some monuments and shrines; thus, sacraments, such as weddings, were done in homes. They had a god-less religion, which prioritized unity and spiritual balance above all. Marriage was about balance, creating a new balance. And Asmodeus was not a spiritual person, but he did rather enjoy his few beliefs, especially compared to the weird religions he knew both the western continent, where the doves still culturally dominated, and the eastern continent believed in. Long ago, Ceprea had been engulfed by the dove empire but avoided its religious influence for all the centuries under its power, largely due to Ceprea being an island and largely due to vulture stubbornness. Ceprean gunpower and rebellion had been helpful too. Thank the spirits. Asmodeus wanted nothing less than to believe in a god.

Thinking this, he made his way to the royal hall, pausing by the concubine quarters and seeing all seven of them lined outside, fanning themselves, before they quickly bowed together, some not able to stifle their laughter enough to avoid the prince hearing. They'd likely bet on how long this marriage would last, but

Asmodeus couldn't blame them; personally, he was estimating three to four months, so long as this new spouse wasn't also assassinated.

Before him, servants were pulling back double doors, and he breathed in as he saw the crowded hall, where dozens of tall, lanky vultures stood at one side, whereas there were dozens of smaller finch people standing at the other. At the center, right at the foot of the staircase that led up to dual golden thrones — there was the vulture spiritual guide that had been there at every wedding of Asmodeus' thus far with a sullen face, standing beside, seemingly, a shaman of the finches. Asmodeus' new spouse stood there, as well.

Rosier. He was stout, adorned with a heavily embroidered cape, wearing what amounted to tens of wooden charms around his neck, hanging from his wrists, wrapped at his ankles. His tunic was also colorful, and as were the many ribbons braided into his hair. In his hands he was shakily holding a few flowers — bright and large, a species Asmodeus was sure he'd never seen before. When Rosier turned to the prince stepping into the hall, his cheeks visibly warmed, but he looked away quickly, which was a shame. Asmodeus was relieved that he had a very pleasant face, one that would be easy to kiss. As he approached, the vulture did make note of their ridiculous difference in size, but that didn't detract from how pleasing the finch was to look at.

The instant Asmodeus reached them, the spiritual guide and shaman began the joint ceremony. Royal weddings that involved culture mixing could sometimes be so awkward, or even tense, but Asmodeus listened to the finch religious leader with an interested tilt of his head. He was saying something about the gods of love, prosperity, and fertility, maybe calling on them to bless this union. At that, Asmodeus shifted, then glanced back over at the stranger he was marrying. Rosier seemed nervous, flinching occasionally, and Asmodeus realized this was probably his first marriage, then pitied him. Rosier was naturally beautiful; he had warm brown skin and long dark hair with neat bangs. He should be getting married to anyone other than an opium-addicted vulture with parents who wanted to drain the finches' resource wealth. He was no good for him.

And, yet, once they were given the gesture, Asmodeus took the one of finch's cheeks, careful with his talons, tilted Rosier's face up. Maintaining his eyes on his new spouse's soft lips, the vulture kissed him with a patient, careful slowness. Rosier hummed against his mouth, but only seconds later, he shuddered. Asmodeus drew back, instantly, and stared at the curious, fawn-like look the other offered him. Around them, there were cheers, clapping, and the first notes of a song. The two gazed into each other's eyes for a moment, until Asmodeus smiled, and he said, "My name is Asmodeus, in case you weren't told."

"Oh—" The finch jumped. "I'm Rosier." His face was still flushed. "It's a pleasure to meet you... husband."

The typical festivals followed. Some canopies were built beforehand outside, and all the vultures celebrated in the streets, as well as the hundreds of finches that'd come to watch their prince be married off. They'd brought their loud music and dance with them, and if there was one thing Asmodeus still managed to enjoy about his million weddings, it was the party. Taking a few shots of liquor, he immediately joined the crowds, dancing and smoking and eating with them. Rosier, meanwhile, sat on one of the ceremonial chairs meant for the wedded couple before the crowds, fiddling with his hands often.

When Asmodeus attempted to ask if the finch prince would like to join, Rosier, softly, replied, "Thank you, but I'd rather sit here. I don't like festivals much."

Asmodeus, beneath the rising moonlight and against the glow of ceremonial torches, hesitated, then said, "Well, I'd still like to offer you some food from the table past all the dancers. How does that sound, wife?" Faintly, the finch prince smiled, then laughed. "Is that a yes?"

"I wouldn't mind. Thank you, Asmodeus."

The night continued with the vulture bringing Rosier whatever he liked, food and beverages and even the flowers that caught his eyes, as well as drinking as much as he could. Eventually, it was almost dawn. Eventually, also — Asmodeus was vomiting dinner by a rosebush and staggering around enough that his mother ordered for him to be taken to bed.

Rosier immediately intervened, hurrying past the growing crowd of soldiers, officials, and a few civilians, before wrapping an arm around the vulture prince's waist, setting his other hand on his lean stomach. "I have you," he reassured. "I have you... Walk with me. One foot, then another. I'll bring you to bed." Slowly, he managed to drag the groaning prince along the field, headed toward the castle. Other drunken birds hollered at them, teasing for the royal couple to enjoy their night together.

Neither the finch or vulture replied to that, though Rosier lowered his gaze with a touch of deep sadness and left it there until they'd reached the guards at the door. Once they were allowed to step into the cold interior of the castle, all the clamor of marriage celebration become suddenly muffled. All the music, all the singing, the dancing, the laughing — gone in an instant. Except, the silence lasted a mere few seconds; Asmodeus, whose head was slouched forward, croaked, "My bedroom's down the hall to your left."

"Ah." Rosier turned his head, then back to his husband. "There.... is no left?"

"Oh, I lied then. It should be right."

A disbelieving laugh, then the finch prince chirped, "Now, please keep your eyes open. If you fall asleep atop of me, I won't be able to hold you up."

"Alright, alright... You're very good at telling me what to do."

The sound of a smile in Rosier's voice — "And you're good at listening."

"What can I say? What can I... say..." Asmodeus trailed off incomprehensibly.

Soon, Rosier guided Asmodeus to the prince's bedroom, where long, burning candles had been placed around a rounded mattress, which itself was decorated with flower petals. The smell of incense was thick too, misty and drowsy. It was all very romantic, but Asmodeus ignored it all to shift away from his spouse, staggering toward the bedding, then collapsing onto it with a hefty groan. With a hiccup, afterwards, the vulture twisted onto his side, vaguely feeling the the other bird climb onto the bed beside him. "Are you," Rosier was calling, "alright?"

The room was twirling around him, but Asmodeus answered, "I've been worse." He patted the bed, even though Rosier was already there with him. "Welcome to my nest."

Again, Rosier laughed, but he quickly tried to smother it by talking: "Yes, it's very nice. It is. Your kingdom is very nice."

"I'm very pleased you like it. I built it."

"I don't believe you did."

"Everything you see," Asmodeus went on lying, "is my blood and sweat and soul. It wasn't easy." With a grunt, he turned onto his back, then felt his face cringe when a tide of nausea teased his throat. "Hngh." He noticed the beautiful prince Rosier sitting beside him, peering down. "Oh, right. We're supposed to be having wedding sex."

Rosier instantly startled, shifting back. "Oh." He didn't sound enthusiastic. "Yes. We are."

"Well, I won't lie to you, darling. If we try anything now, I'll vomit on you, so your virginity will have to live another day. Forgive me."

At this, Rosier laughed the loudest he'd had yet. "No, no," he said, "please don't apologize. I don't think I wanted to lose it today, regardless. Thank you... for not attempting."

"I'm going to sleep now."

"Wait, you should stay up and drink water instead— You'll wake up ill if you sleep like that—"

"Good thing I have a wife to take care of me now. Goodnight, darling."

"Goodnight...?"

As Rosier had predicted, Asmodeus was horribly sick in the

morning, though he didn't vomit again. He merely laid on his back, groaning and groaning, as his new spouse poured him multiple glasses of water, then spoon-fed him a hearty soup of bull tongue, a vulture delicacy. "Fuck," Asmodeus grumbled, "thank you." An hour after waking, Rosier had shoved the prince of the vultures toward the baths, and now Asmodeus was in a damp, cotton robe, his hair still wet and tied back. "I should apologize again." Rosier lifted his face, eyes wide and curious as he swirled the last of the soup in the painted porcelain bowl over his lap. "This is your first marriage, right?" He realized he'd assumed since Rosier was younger and, frankly, seemed so shy the day before. "I'm sure you imagined something much more romantic than this. Once I feel better, I'll try to make it up to you."

"It's really no problem," Rosier said lightly, then scooted to set the bowl at the bedside. "I was so nervous that I felt ill too yesterday. You're right that this is my first wedding. If I may be honest with yoy, I always did want to get married, but in recent years..." Asmodeus quirked an brow, watching Rosier's sunny wings flutter behind him anxiously. "It's difficult to put to words."

"I'm here to listen," said Asmodeus. "You have a nice voice." He smiled when Rosier let out a flustered sigh. "I suppose that is no surprise. Finches love to sing, don't they?"

"Yes," said the younger one. "Though I've never been good. I have a lot of siblings, and they're all better than me. My father has... a lot of wives." Reaching for a charm hanging from his neck, Rosier took and fidgeted with it.

"Multiple?" Asmodeus realized how little he knew about the finch kingdom. "Your kingdom was unified... very recently, wasn't it?"

Rosier nodded. "We were ten separate tribes thirty years ago. My father told me that we only unified to try to counter invasions. He told me, too, that all the other birds are jealous of our land because there are no other rainforests as fruitful as ours." Asmodeus agreed but hesitated to say that; he was not in the state to admit to what his parents' plans regarding those rainforests were. "My mother was from the smallest tribe, and my father's other wives... aren't very fond of me or my mother's other children with my father. They were the ones that convinced my father to marry me to you. They told me I'd be of better use as a present to some foreign prince."

Asmodeus, thickly, swallowed. "That's cruel of them. They can go fuck themselves."

Solemnly, Rosier shook his head. "Don't talk ill of them. No matter how they treat me, I want to be kind to them. My patron god encourages me to be good to everyone, and I'm willing to forgive them if they ever see the error of their ways. I really hope that they do." He paused, then shifted the discussion slightly. "I was very frightened of you. Everyone warned me that you were a scary, old vulture, that your kind are strange and vicious. They said that if I didn't satisfy you in bed, you'd eat me whole. But, you seem kind. Very reckless. Are you feeling better?"

Asmodeus, suddenly, noticed that his head wasn't pounding as it had been for hours. "Oh, yes. I'm feeling better." Slow, he lifted his body, supporting himself on his elbows behind him, then looked at Rosier more seriously. "I know that I'm not... a good soul, but I won't eat you. Not unless you ask for it," he joked dryly. "And we accept divorce here. We believe in balance, and if you think I'm harming you, then you can fly away from here." He paused. "But I would miss you terribly. I did enjoy kissing you during the ceremony."

Rosier's expression faintly brightened. "I think I'll remain here, at least for some time more. But you'll have to be patient with me."

"Only if you're patient with me, as well," Asmodeus replied coyly, then reached to fiddle with one of Rosier's jade earrings. "Hm. Now that I feel better, we can move forward with consummating, if you like. Do you want the flowers back? I can have the servants decorate the room to be as it was last night." Rosier's mouth twitched, then his gaze fell. "Or are you… not interested at all in me?"

Shakily, Rosier breathed out. "Can I ask something of you? Please?"

Asmodeus blinked a few times, then lowered his hand. "Anything you like."

"I don't want to consummate, yet." Instantly, the finch grimaced. "Is that alright?"

Bewildered, the vulture was quiet for a moment, but then he shrugged. "I suppose so. My parents will ask whether we've been fucking though." Rosier's cheeks reddened again. "You can make up the details. And if they ask about heirs, you can blame me. Tell them my cock won't harden, and I'm a terrible spouse, but you're so kind that you won't leave me… yet."

Rosier grinned, looking both relieved and amused and sincerely happy. "Can I say that you vomited on me while we were consummating?"

"Of course, why not? My reputation cannot get any worse."

Then, the finch leaned over him, kissing the vulture on the lips — sweetly, loving. "Thank you." At that, Asmodeus' chest warmed; he couldn't recall if any of his past marriages had ever inflicted this feeling on him. He wasn't certain if he'd ever felt this way at all. As Rosier curled up against him, nuzzled his face against his, their bodies pressed together — the vulture exhaled tensely, tried not to let his mind wander into the erotic territory it often did.

For the first time in his life, Asmodeus feared losing something, someone.

Many months later, sex did eventually happen. It occurred on a night like any other, entirely unplanned. The finch, surprisingly, had initiated it with a tepid kiss, then a roll of his hips against the vulture's. Realizing what was happening, Asmodeus had leaped at Rosier like the animal he partly was only to hastily try to be gentle instead, afraid to frighten his already nervous spouse. Once inside, all he'd been able to do was press his face to Rosier's throat and rut helplessly into the warmth. Airy gasps from the finch's mouth were like music to him, better than any royal orchestra arrangement. For once, he cared about a lover's pleasure, purring in Rosier's ear, stroking him in time with the thrusts.

"You're everything to me," Asmodeus was groaning against Rosier's skin. "You're all that I want."

Breathless — "I am?"

"Yes—" the vulture stumbled. "You and your fruit pies." When Rosier immediately laughed, trying to ask what Asmodeus could possibly mean by that, the older one turned to kiss his giggling mouth. Afterwards, Asmodeus managed to coax him to finish with a stifled cry. Asmodeus' release was quick to follow, sweeter than he could have ever imagined.

In the aftermath, Rosier said, "I'm not sure... if I want to do that again any time soon." He was fluttering his wings anxiously, as he often did, and Asmodeus would be lying if he said he wasn't disappointed, except the last thing he wanted was to see the pretty finch frown. He would learn to bear this, swallow it down. For Rosier, he would. "But I really did like how it felt to be that close to you. I hope you understand."

Asmodeus nodded. "Whatever you wish, darling." He was determined to make this marriage work, to make Rosier be the last love of his life, the same way that he was the first.

"And I do want children... one day."

Offhandedly, the vulture said, "After five marriages, I'm finally starting to consider it."

"What?" Coughing. "Five!?"

THE ALTAR BOY

A story where human Lucifer is an altar boy and human Michael is not. Told in three parts.

Additional content warning: mentions of CSA.

ONE

"Why did you follow me, sweetheart?"

Michael's feet, Michael's heart, stopped, tripped. Shuddering, he inhaled without thinking, his gaze flashing upward, catching from up close the hints of black at the roots of the boy's blonde hair. 'Well, he's not much of a boy,' Michael corrected. Despite the blood-red, wispy cassock — almost like a gown — and the white surplice on top with a lace hem that made him look extremely boyish — he had the sharp face of a young man, as well as aged eyes. Of course, it was beauty that had made Michael's eyes drift away from the Eucharist to the altar boy holding it, offering it to the priest, but it was the gleam in his eyes that made Michael draw a breath the first time.

"I'm sorry," Michael blurted, his hands holding each other nervously at his back as he glanced behind him at the bathroom door that had just shut. There was a simple, rusted, and tiny hook attached to the wooden planks that composed the door that he could use to lock it, not that he had any intention to. "I didn't mean to give off that impression." He turned back to the altar boy and realized that he was just an inch or two taller than him. "I was just— I was just in a hurry to go to the bathroom."

"Lying is a sin, don't you know?" The altar boy turned back to him, a long smile on perfect, faintly pink lips. "Who are you?"

Michael swallowed; he'd thought seeing him this close would make him snap out of the persistent daydreaming, would make him catch flaws in the boy's face. Instead, the beauty that had become the object of his obsession for weeks now was only more gorgeous at a meager distance. "I'm Michael." His voice was quiet and echoed off the tiles where his boots were planted. "I really didn't mean to make you uncomfortable." The altar boy's eyes brightened in coy amusement. "Can I ask your name too?"

"It's Lucifer, sweetheart." But before Michael could speak, he added, "I can't believe you waited so long to come after me. How long has it been? Three weeks?" A jovial laugh, then he leaned back against a thin window engraved into the stone wall of the couple-centuries-old church they were in. "I hope you don't think I never noticed you here."

Clenching his jaw, Michael murmured, "I sat near the exit. I didn't think you'd see me."

"Three people showed up yesterday, and you thought I'd miss you somehow." Lucifer tilted his head, but he was still smiling. "And no boy your age is coming to Mass in the middle of the week."

"You don't know how old I am," Michael answered a little stiffly, his white button-up feeling a bit damp, his tattered jeans feeling a little too tight.

"You're too young, I can tell that much." Lucifer took a step toward him, his black dress shoes pointed and made of leather, but they were severely chipped all along the front. "I don't like boys my age." Another step, and now he was too close, in between Michael and the window and the single urinal and the sink. "Why are you here? Hurry and tell me."

Michael wasn't sure, really. "I just thought it was strange. I don't see your family anywhere. I've never seen you in town. And you're..."

"Beautiful?"

Oddly, it embarrassed Michael to know the pretty altar boy was well-aware of how pretty he was. "You also," he continued regardless, "sing very nicely. I didn't mean to start coming to church again. A few weeks ago, I just came by with my grandmother because she wanted me to walk her in. I don't think I ever stopped believing, or I never realized that I stopped believing, but yes, I came by then, and I saw you." He realized his talking was jumbled, but Lucifer stared at him too intensely to think. "I liked your singing, and I wanted to see you again. I started coming to Mass a lot, like you said. I don't think you did it on purpose, but you brought me back to God. Thank you for that. I forgot how nice it is to pray."

Lucifer's hand reached out, so quickly that Michael flinched then froze as the altar boy's hand snaked past the collar of his shirt, the top button slipping out of the slit to reveal more of his chest and, especially, his rosary. It was made up of wooden spheres, trailing down to a plain wooden cross, but it had once belonged to his father; in Michael's mind, it still did, and he was wearing his father's grip around his neck at all times. "Oh." Lucifer's fingers' light brushes on Michael's bare skin were like the touch of flame. "What a pretty rosary." It wasn't particularly nice, but Michael didn't argue. "I just wanted to see it." He tugged, and Michael felt the yank on his throat, felt his feet stumble like when he'd walked into the bathroom. "You said I brought you back to God?"

"Yes," Michael said, his cheeks warm, his gut coiling. "Like an angel."

A low, bitter chuckle, then Lucifer brought the cross of the rosary to his mouth, kissed it. "Like an angel..." He lingered his lips before slowly inching back, the beads slipping from his touch. "That's very sweet of you, Michael." His hand fell, landed on Michael's belt. "But I'm not sure if I believe you. Can you pray for me? Pray for your angel?"

Michael's blood was growing cold, but his gaze dropped, looked past his dangling rosary and fluttering chest. "I can pray."

Lucifer unclasped the buckle. "Our Father?" Lucifer made a humming noise of affirmation. "Our Father." He needed something to lean against, so he shuffled backward just enough to lean against the door, to reach for the cold hook and jam it into the hole and pin attached to the wall. "Who art in Heaven." Following him, Lucifer undid the button, tugged down his zipper. "Hallowed... be..."

"Mm, go on." Lucifer cupped him through his jeans just as there was a twitch of life, then a dull pulse hardening him. "Hallowed be what? Don't disappoint your angel now."

"Thy name..." Michael clenched his eyes shut just as Lucifer lowered himself onto his knees how he always did after taking the Eucharist. "Thy kingdom come—" Michael gasped when Lucifer squeezed him, as if to feel for his size, then tugged down on his pants. "T-Thy will be done." The room was so much colder than he'd realized; his cock was almost shivering, beading at the tip already. 'Pathetic,' he wanted to snap at himself. "On Earth as it is in Heaven. Give us this day our daily bread and forgive us—" Lucifer giggled before his soft hand came around the throbbing flesh and his scorching tongue flicked at the very tip. "*God, forgive me.*"

"That's not the next line, sweetheart." Lucifer tugged back on the skin, then rubbed his lips against the exposed head, smearing them as if with holy water.

"Isn't this a sin?" Michael breathed, finally fluttering open his eyes, forcing himself to face the gorgeous boy on his knees for him.

"You said I'm an angel." Lucifer smiled at the cock pressed against his mouth. "A pretty angel can't sin, can he?"

Michael shuddered. "Fuck—" A wet, hot mouth embraced him, reeled him in, and he felt the slide of a tongue underneath. 'I think he's really the devil.' Still, his hand shamefully went to the blonde waves of hair that were too long for a boy, especially at their age, and Michael's knees almost knocked together, almost buckled, when Lucifer sucked harshly, his gaze through his eyelashes both loving and hellish. "Forgive... those who trespass against us," he forced himself to keep praying.

Lucifer's hands rose to Michael's hips, tugging a little in need.

"Lead us... not into temptation." Michael paused to pant, to lean his head back and stare at the ceiling. He clutched tight Lucifer's hair, and he surrendered — his hips beginning to rock forward into the choking, adoring suckles of the altar server. "But deliver us from... evil..." He accidentally rammed into the back of Lucifer's mouth, hated how good it felt when he jerked and tightened. "Please." But Lucifer didn't pull back, and after a second of catching his breath through his nose, of holding only the head in his mouth, they both pressed forward. Michael slid into his throat, and he shut his eyes again. "Amen."

Just a few thrusts forward, and then Lucifer was reeling off and Michael arched his back against the door, raising his free arm over his face, embarrassed and sick to his very stomach. Shame didn't kill his lust. He, shakily, came in Lucifer's mouth and onto his serpent tongue. And, worse still, Lucifer hummed delightfully, his fingers digging into Michael's hips, sure to leave blotches of red or perhaps even purple.

"Amen," replied Lucifer as he removed his mouth. "Good. I see I really did bring you back to God." He turned his face, rested his cheek on Michael;s thigh. "But I can do much more than that." Michael, painfully slow, looked downward to meet the beautiful altar boy. "I can make you *like* God." His eyes were dazed but sweet, tempting. "Just have me, and you can have everything..."

TWO

Michael should have waited; he should have taken some months to spend in bliss with the altar boy Lucifer. Every couple days, he was climbing out of the house after sunset, sneaking the beige mare out of the stall, then leading her into a gallop past the wooden gates of the ranch where he lived, right outside of town. It was quicker and safer to go through the narrow pathways on horseback than to take his parents' car, which shrieked to life and coughed out from its engine whenever it moved; Michael didn't mind the horse, either. He liked the feeling of riding into the center of town, approaching the church in the plaza, and seeing a figure outside — Lucifer in jeans and an inconspicuous white button-up that was too large for him. It was always romantic slowing his mare into a steady walk in the dark, then climbing off, going for one of Lucifer's hands so he could help him up. At any moment, Michael liked to think, they could ride off before sunrise, never to be seen again. They could start a new life in a different town or maybe even move to the city.

Instead, he brought Lucifer just outside town, to where there was little more than shrubs and the occasional small house with huffing goats and clucking chickens. Along the dirt road, perfectly in between the distance from Michael's family's ranch and the town, there was a shrine to the Virgin of Guadalupe. And, often, Michael brought Lucifer there to kiss him. He'd hop off the horse, reach for Lucifer's waist, grip it tight, then carry him down. Behind the shrine, he'd kiss him deeply, running his hands all over him, nuzzling his neck. The faux blonde always ran his fingers through Michael's curls, scratching his nails against his scalp, then whispering sin into his ear. With the oil for the lamps of the shrine, Michael would finger the altar boy, then press Lucifer's front against the back wall of the shrine, then rock into his entrance.

It was bliss, though Lucifer hardly spoke at all afterward, always choosing to sit wrapped up in a blanket with Michael and smoke a cigarette in mostly silence.

However, one day, Michael's parents told him that they were going on a trip to the city to visit his aunt and beg for money, and they'd be gone for a few days. Michael should have simply nodded his head, promised to feed the two horses and three chickens and check on the four goats and milk them if needed, care for his grandparents, tuck his baby brother Gabriel to bed — but he decided to say, "I'll invite a friend to help me with things." His parents didn't seem shocked by this, but they asked to meet this man before they left. And Michael had agreed.

"No," Lucifer had said immediately.

"Why not?" Michael asked as they sat with their backs against the shrine, sharing a quilt on such a windy evening. "They won't suspect anything but... if you could maybe remove the dye or cover your hair... I can lend you my hat. My dad will think your hair is too long anyway, but as long as you're respectful, there won't be any problem."

"But why should I meet your parents? Do you think I'm a girl you can marry? Don't waste my time."

Eventually, though, the two boys were at dinner at Michael's ranch. The house was quite quaint — entirely composed of a middle room with a kitchen and living area, then a bedroom to the left that belonged to the parents and Gabriel, and finally a room to the right that belonged to Michael's grandparents and Michael. At the center, a square table had been draped with an orange cloth, a candle had been set beside their radio and lit to cast a rather ominous glow. Michael;s parents sat at one end; Michael sat opposite, with the altar boy. For the first time, Michael had picked him up in his father's car, dressed in clean pants, an ironed shirt, and a hat, praying Lucifer had dressed up for the occasion as well. Out in the street, not far from where Michael always came for him on horseback, the beautiful Lucifer was, thankfully, in similar clothes as him. His hair was not covered, however.

And it was the blonde locks cascading past his shoulders that Michael's father, of course, commented on over his plate of nearly-charred pork over tortillas. "They let you," he was chuckling, though not warmly, "have hair like that as an altar boy?" He was a burly man, but not so old, still had a handsome sharp jaw and large nose, the latter of which Michael had inherited perfectly.

Instantly, Michael had tensed, but Lucifer answered with a pleasant smile and a pleasant, "The fathers think it suits me." Sometimes, Michael was amused by Lucifer's constant references to the priests — how *gay* it sounded to speak of having multiple fathers. "And no, they don't think it's a sin. It's a greater sin to judge a man's hair than it is for a man to color his hair. Oh, thank you, ma'am," he added toward Michael's mother and took the small shaker from her extended hand. "I was just thinking I needed salt."

Michael's grandparents asked if Lucifer had really been raised by the church, and the blonde said yes. He had been left on their doorstep by what must've been a teenage mother. And the bishop, kind man that he was, had Lucifer raised among the priests. At this, Gabriel had begun to babble angrily in the arms of the grandmother. His chatter grew higher, higher, then turned into cries.

"Well," the father huffed. "I'm glad Michael met you. You seem like a nice young man." He nodded at his own food, twiddling the fork in his hands. "Are you going to stay in the church? I've been asking Michael if he wants to study somewhere." Michael frowned a little; he knew that he couldn't place that kind of financial burden on his family.

"I haven't decided," Lucifer replied, then smiled, though it didn't reach his shining eyes. "But I hope Michael and I choose the same place." A hand grazed Michael's knee, and Michael's muscles tightened in fear as Lucifer's fingers began to scale up his thigh. "You've raised a good man. I love seeing him at church."

"That's very sweet of you to say," Michael's mother replied, reaching for little crying Gabriel so that she could set him on her knee. "If you ever need some family, we're here for you. Make yourself at home while we're away." Lucifer squeezed Michael's thigh, right by his crotch, then thanked her.

That night, Lucifer slept in the living room, but the following day — after the parents had driven off into the horizon — he said he'd like to share the big room with Michael. He said it as they went for water from the well and walked along the ranch together. He never helped with the cattle, nor did he even help gather the water, but Michael tried to just be happy to have the boy he was in love with at home. It was the dream to him to be able to do chores in a proper home beside a lover even if it was beneath a raging sun. Lucifer commenting on how strong Michael was, how big and firm his muscles felt beneath his hands, purring and giggling, was also nice.

Wiping sweat from his brow, Michael looked over at him as they walked and approached the tiny home. "Hm? Share my parents' bed?" He flushed a little at that; he'd never actually been in a bed with a guy he liked. "Sure. My grandparents probably won't care. They'll be too busy with Gabriel." And two men sharing a bed for convenience likely wouldn't raise brows if one of them was a good church boy.

"He's cute. Gabriel."

Michael perked up and, without thinking, took Lucifer's hand. "Yeah, he's adorable, and he's really good. He doesn't cry much. I don't know what got into him last night."

"He might not like me." Lucifer gave Michael's finger just a single squeeze. "Babies have good intuition. One look at you and they know if you're going to hell." Michael tilted his head, but Lucifer didn't elaborate, and the two soon searched for a place to sit so they could watch the sun dip behind faraway hills.

When it was finally time for sleep, Michael undressed in his corner of the room, pulling his top off over his head, unbuckling his belt; he faced the only window in the room, staring at the stars freckling the dark sky. He breathed in slow, tugging his pants down to leave himself in the pale briefs he wore to bed; well, he had some striped pajamas, but they were too ugly to put on with such a beautiful boy nearby to see it. At the same time he heard the large mattress in the room squeal, he caught Lucifer reflected in the window pane before him. He was adjusting his golden hair, and he'd removed his pants as well, though also his underwear; over his body, there was nothing but a white shirt. Slow, Michael turned to face him, and he sighed softly.

Lucifer settled down on the edge of the bed, leaning back on his hands, then tilted his head over at him amusedly. "These walls are pretty thick, aren't they? I could barely hear anything when I slept in the living room yesterday."

Swallowing, Michael's gaze flickered down to the flaccid cock between Lucifer's legs, then back up to his face. "They... are," he affirmed softly. He liked seeing Lucifer there, in bed.

Lucifer must've read his thoughts: "You're really loving this, mm? Me being here. How far do you want to take this pretending?" Michael wanted to speak, but Lucifer's brilliant smile and narrowed eyes stole his breath. "Should I act like your wife in bed and act like this is our farm?" Michael felt a frown tug on his lips as he stepped toward the bed, toward Lucifer. "Should we pretend that, come Sunday, you're not going to take the priests' boy to the bathroom and fuck him until he can't stand?"

With a nervous exhale, Michael settled down beside him. "I just wanted you to get away from the church a little."

"I get away plenty, sweetheart." Lucifer's breath moved closer to Michael's ear, caressed warmly. "Or do you think you're the only guy I spend time with?"

Michael already knew that he wasn't, someone as beautiful and experienced as Lucifer couldn't be the virginal, sweet boy he liked to dream that he was. "If you want to leave, you can," he answered carefully. "You don't have to spend days here. I'll tell my parents the priests needed you."

"Your parents... Your dad is very macho." The altar boy raised a hand, skimmed it along Michael's arm. "And he's handsome." When Michael made a face, Lucifer giggled. "Why are you upset? That's good. When you're middle-aged, I think girls will be all over you." Squeezing Michael's bicep — "But you don't like girls, do you?"

Michael murmured, "I don't know." He did know.

"Oh, honey... Not even a little? What are you going to do? Your parents are going to be so sad..."

Flinching. "I don't really want to talk about that right now. What about you? Don't the priests know?" A part of him wanted to ask if Lucifer had any interest in girls too, but that question was too dangerous. Thinking of the golden-haired altar boy in anyone else's arms was already making Michael grind his teeth, and he knew how guys like them are — no matter how distant the tiny, secretive society of homos in town was to Michael; they were uncommitted to any one person when life was this unstable, unpredictable, and depressing.

"Some do. They make me confess sometimes, but most of the priests think I'm a lost cause. Some of us need to go to hell, after all, and why not me? They think I want it. And maybe I do."

"I wish you," Michael whispered, "wouldn't say things like that." And the altar's boy touch trailed down to his wrist, then hopped on over to the thigh he'd been caressing at dinner the night before.

"You're so scared of me," mused Lucifer, and soon he was clambering closer, putting one leg over him, settling down on Michael's lap. "I think it's cute." He pressed onto the twitching groin, then began to roll his hips, allowing the older boy's cock to rouse against his own hardness and ample bottom. "Mmm." Just as Michael reeled in a gasp, Lucifer swept down and kissed him, slithering in his tongue, flicking it against Michael's, curling it to drag against the grooves at the top of his mouth.

Michael tried to swear against Lucifer's perfect, plush lips, but he couldn't get the words out, and he instead wrapped his arms around the boy's waist, clutching tight. Purring sweetly at the embrace, Lucifer smiled, then reached between them to palm at the tent in Michael's briefs. He expertly slipped his hand inside, gripped him tight at the base, and this time, Michael managed to pull back and gasp harshly, his eyes already dazed. The air was warm, but Michael nonetheless shivered when his naked cock was tugged free, given one stroke. His head leaned forward, and suddenly he found himself nuzzled against the altar boy's hot neck.

"I already fingered myself with your cooking oil, but you can find more by the bed. On the other side."

Michael mumbled, "You've been planning this."

"So have you, sweetheart. Didn't you make me come here so we can play husband and wife?" In response, Michael nuzzled Lucifer's jaw. "You're not very good at it." He gave Michael's cock another stroke, then squeezed the head cruelly.

"I don't want to see you as anything but what you are." Michael lifted his face, pressed a slow kiss to Lucifer's cheek. "I don't want to pretend about anything." 'I like you as just an altar boy,' he wanted to add.

Lucifer answered coldly, "You don't know anything about me." He lifted both hands, planted them on Michael's chest, then shoved the boy hard, pinning him flat on his back.

'I like that about you,' Michael wanted to say, but instead he watched the beautiful altar boy in his home reach for the oil he'd just mentioned. 'I think I'm scared of you, scared of who you might really be. I like it like this, knowing just enough to love you.' Maybe he'd been pretending all this time about the two of them.

Lucifer returned with the oil, took his white top and pulled it over his head. They were both wearing rosaries. "Lay there for me." He climbed on top again, spilling oil over his hand then settling the bottle back aside. With his dry hand, he returned to pumping Michael, but the other disappeared behind himself. "Ah," Lucifer sighed, and his untouched cock shivered. Michael saw it, reached for it, and noticed a faint pink on the cheeks of the altar boy as he teased his scrotum then dragged his hand upwards toward the tip. "I told you to lay there."

"I'm laying here." Michael smiled a little. "You're beautiful."

"I know."

"I know you do. But I don't want you to forget."

Lucifer visibly swallowed, then sunk down onto Michael's cock, breathing softly, shutting his eyes. He took it slow, but he didn't stop, taking every bit of the girth even when his thighs shook, and he set a hand over Michael's chest again to steady himself. "Lord." He chuckled a little. "What was God thinking when He gave you a cock like this?"

Michael laid a hand on Lucifer's hip, rubbing his thumb on flushed skin, coaxing. "You believe in God?" It was definitely the wrong time to ask; he was buried in his lover's hot, tight embrace. He was already panting, shaking.

"I'm an altar boy, sweetheart." Lucifer lifted his body, allowed it to drop, then moaned quiet and slow. "I believe in God." He grinned. "That doesn't mean I love Him though." Once again, he brought his face toward Michael's and kissed him deep, sloppier this time. Michael grunted against him, rocking his hips in time with the other, trying to press in just a little deeper. He could hear their rosaries rattling, bumping up against each other at times, threatening to tangle. It was ridiculous, but Michael liked them — their rosaries. They were both wholly naked except for this matching binding. The rosaries were almost like wedding rings.

'God, forgive me;' Michael wanted to do all the things he'd been taught about loving — marrying and having a home together — but he wanted it with another boy.

"Mm, fuck," Lucifer moaned as he continued fucking himself on Michael's cock, his own bouncing needily against his lower belly. "I want you to fuck me where you keep the horses tomorrow."

Michael pulled away from his mouth, took Lucifer's waist and stopped his riding as he gasped and gasped for breath. "You need to be quieter." A little too easily, he was able to lift the altar boy off of him, then twist the both of them around, settling Lucifer over the pillows. "I'll take you home right now if you don't quiet down." His voice didn't sound the least bit threatening, and Lucifer giggled.

"You sound like the priests when you scold me like that. Should I call you Father too?"

Not lucid enough to argue right now, Michael slapped a hand over Lucifer's mouth, then took one of the boy's legs and pressed back in easily into the fluttering, oiled hole. "Just be quiet." Lucifer's clench around him was almost enough to push him past the brink. "Jesus."

Giggling against his fingers, Lucifer managed to say, "Do you remember when you prayed the Our Father for me? I can pray for you too." Michael tried to whisper for Lucifer to be quiet as he moved his hips slow, like rusty gears. "Hail Mary... full of grace..."

Michael shoved two fingers into Lucifer's mouth, making him choke and jerk beneath him. Almost instantly, Michael tried to pull his fingers back out, but Lucifer pursed his lips around, suckling. His cock was beading between them, dribbling onto his abdomen. So, Michael kept his fingers in, and he thought of how Lucifer looked at Mass. He thought of the altar boy stepping toward the priest, parting his wet lips for him to take the Eucharist. He thought of himself as a priest, pushing the wafer into Lucifer's mouth, staring into his intense, yet hollow eyes. The altar boy who believes in God but hates Him, still taking the body of Christ against his sweet tongue.

When he was close, Michael had no choice but to pull free his hand, curl over Lucifer and thrust the last few times messily, weakly. He moved his hand to squeeze the altar boy's cock, milk him until he spilled over his rough fingers. He didn't want to finish inside, but the hold around him was too perfect, made him tear his bottom lip in how much strength it took not to moan out Lucifer's perfect name. Of course, he came inside, deep inside. Michael never had any reason when he was with Lucifer. It would be his downfall one of these days, wouldn't it?

For another two days, Lucifer played pretend with Michael at the ranch, acting like he was part of his family, like he could ever join it. He kissed Gabriel's head and laid on a hill, soaking in the sun with flowers by his head, beside Michael. On the third evening, he left, must've gotten bored. He said, "I have a boy picking me up. He's a lot like you, except his hair is a little curlier, and he carries a gun. I like that about him. Goodbye, Michael. I'll see you at church on Sunday." Then, he had walked out, blonde hair twirling in the wind.

Michael thought he looked like an angel before he returned to his brother, pretending there wasn't an ache in his heart.

THREE

Many weeks later, Michael was walking the streets of town past sunset, though he had no plans to meet with Lucifer. In fact, he was here for a completely different reason; he'd just finished speaking with his uncle, who was in town to visit family. He was a man from the city, and he knew someone who could, allegedly, speak to admissions at the state university about a scholarship. Michael, hands clasped on the table, had thanked him almost forty times exactly, dropping his head forward and feeling his uncle clasp his shoulder. "Mijo," his uncle had sighed, "but do you *want* to go?"

"I shouldn't stay here forever," Michael had murmured, then flickered his gaze up to him. "I *can't* stay here." His uncle asked what was wrong with this place, but what could he say? Could he spill his heart? Could he explain that the devil was in this town, one who'd been raised by priests and who kissed him sweeter than any woman could, than any other man could? "I just can't, uncle." Michael didn't admit it to him because he didn't want to admit it to himself — but he had to leave this place and move on from this. Let Lucifer become a memory, or even a ghost. One day, as Michael dies on his bed surrounded by great grandchildren and relatives, he could confess that he met the devil, and he almost ran away with him, almost lived the life he dreamed of.

So caught up in what had happened with his uncle, Michael didn't realize he'd just ran into a fruit cart until he'd tripped and fallen with it, yelping loud. Luckily, there had been nearly nothing on the wooden surface except for a crate of limes that fell onto its side on the street, spilling only a few green little bodies, as well as three or four papayas. "Ow," he cried, then, "Oh no—" He scrambled immediately after he landed, reaching for the papayas and putting them all into his arms as someone's steps approached. "I'm so sorry," Michael said before he even lifted his chin to whoever it was beside him. "I'll pay for it all. I wasn't looking where I walked."

"Oh, please don't worry." The stranger was pulling up the cart again, then he crouched beside Michael, taking the crate of limes and setting it upright before grabbing the few that had fallen. "I was thinking of having to give these away soon anyway... They're almost rotten." The figure was a young man with long, dark hair and pale top over wide, white pants of a thin material. Over his shoulders, he had a poncho of sorts, and over his feet, leather sandals. "Are you alright?" He set the fallen limes on a side shelf of the cart, then took the crate and climbed back onto his feet.

"I'm fine," Michael replied softly, standing up as well with his arms full of papaya. "I'm really sorry."

"It was an accident," said the stranger kindly, setting the crate over the top surface. "Please don't worry. What matters is that no one was hurt." A warm smile spread over his mouth.

Michael was still frowning as he handed the papayas to the much shorter man's arms. "Were you really out selling this late?"

"Not particularly," was the quiet reply. "But I didn't really want to go home."

Chuckling a bit — "I can understand that. Do you live nearby?"

Gesturing vaguely to his left, the stranger said, "Right outside of town with my family." Michael replied that he could relate to that too, and the young man began to smile again. "Maybe we've passed each other before then. What's your name?"

"Michael," was the answer, then followed with a last name.

"Oh..."

"Oh?"

"I've heard of you." His voice was hushed, but gentle like a hand running itself down the face of a mare before you kiss her nose. "My name is Rosier." And he offered his own surname. "Your... a friend of Lucifer's." Michael blinked, then made a noise like a cough. "Don't worry," Rosier added quickly, "I won't tell anyone. I'm also..." Another gesture. "Yes. Well— Lucifer buys fruit from me to bring back to the priests a lot. He immediately knew... what I was." A homosexual of some sort, Michael assumed and found his muscles relaxing a little. "I don't know how. I got angry at him at first, but then I saw that he wasn't a threat, and so I tried to be his friend. Being Lucifer's friend, though, is... difficult, as I'm sure you know." Michael nodded, his heart in his throat, realizing he'd never really spoken about Lucifer to anyone besides Lucifer. "You're either a lover to him or an enemy. He has no room in his heart for friends."

Rosier's face was turning sadder, and Michael heard himself sigh before he responded: "It's not easy to tell which one I am to him, at times." He slipped his hands into the back pockets of his jeans, furrowing his brow a little though he wasn't frustrated, really — curious, instead. "Lucifer told you about me?"

"He talks a lot," said Rosier, then laughed when Michael did. "It's true. He tells me about whatever man he's after. He told me about how you used to come to Mass just to see him." At that, Michael felt some heat crawl up his face, to even his ears. "And he said you would steal him away." To have sex against a shrine for Mother Mary at the side of the road. "You took him home once for a few nights."

"That was two months ago," Michael replied. "I haven't seen him a lot since." They'd only met a handful of times, three or four, and they'd only run away and fucked two of those times. Most recently, Michael had waited outside the church until afternoon service ended. When he saw the beautiful altar boy, he'd gestured without a word, began walking and listening for the sound of footsteps close behind him. He'd led Lucifer to the car parked a few streets away.

"You're such a bore, sometimes," Lucifer had said as they reached the outskirts, sitting in the passenger's seat, the window open and his hair tossing behind him, the dark roots having grown a little longer. He wore a beige button-up, tucked into his pants, but entirely open to reveal the white tank top underneath, as well as a simple, silver necklace with a St. Michael pendant hanging by his heart. In one hand, he was twirling a lit cigarette, hardly bringing it to his mouth, like he was instead considering to fling it out and start a wildfire among the prickly cactus and shrubs.

Michael's eyes had been maintained on the road, but he stole some glances, staring at the soft lips of the altar boy. "Bore?" He wasn't offended. He knew he wasn't particularly interesting, and he knew it was because he'd suffered some social stunting — being gay in a quaint little town will do that to you. Lord knows he'd spent more time at home building muscle by carrying a thousand water pails and crates on his shoulders back and forth than going to town and talking with men his age for half his life.

"You never do anything." Lucifer grazed the cigarette against his mouth, but he didn't press it inside. "You just do whatever your parents tell you, then you come fuck me. You never tell me about interesting things you do. You don't have any ambition." And the next part was softer, more like a personal muse: "I thought you did when you came after me, the first time. But maybe it was just my own ambition that I saw reflected in you."

Michael tapped his fingers against the steering wheel then turned it, moving the car in the direction off the main road and toward the dirt paths. "I don't know what to say to that," he said frankly. He wasn't angry, but he wasn't happy about those words either.

"Of course you don't," Lucifer grumbled, then finally smoked, breathing in the nicotine and expelling a puff of it from his nostrils. "Where are you taking me?"

"There's another altar, up the mount."

"Another Mary?"

"No."

"I think that," said Rosier in the present, "he likes you more than you think. More than he thinks, too." But then he shrugged and began fiddling with his fruit cart, removing the bag weights that had been around the wheeled feet before it toppled over. He set them on another shelf on the side.

Michael scoffed a little. "He thinks I'm boring."

"Did he tell you that?" Rosier smiled amusedly, his eyes squinting some. "You should know by now that he's a compulsive liar." He shook his head. "That's why I can't recommend that you go after him again, even if I wish he were my friend and even though I feel so bad for him."

"Feel bad for him? Why?"

Michael parked the car as close as he could, but they were still two miles from the altar on foot. It was uphill, and he expected Lucifer to complain but he was surprisingly quiet, even putting out his cigarette safely against a stone before following Michael up the mount and into some of the more expansive, dense greenery. It was no jungle, but it was more claustrophobic than the world they were leaving behind, and so Michael took Lucifer's soft hand to guide him through.

"Everything that's happened to him," said Rosier simply. "It's frustrating. I don't think it justifies a lot of the things he's done, so all I can do is feel bad."

"What happened to him?"

"You don't know?"

Between some trees, there was a long stone altar, high off the ground, tilting in age, grayed, and coarse. Over the top, there were some long dried flowers and twigs, as well as what appeared to be signs of wax from long-ago burned candles. On the sides, there were engravings of a few curled symbols and some figures like butterflies and hands, all deeply ancient; but there was also a figurine there — a porcelain Saint Gregory with a broken face. And Lucifer, of course, said, "What's this?"

"My grandparents showed me this place years ago, but they told me not to touch it."

"Why not?"

"I don't know."

"Then why did you bring me here?"

"My grandparents told me to tell my children about this place, but I don't think I'll have any. I decided to tell you, at least."

Lucifer was quiet, and Michael realized they were still holding hands.

"I know that you've noticed how beautiful he is." Rosier's tone was somber, his eyes on the floor. "The bishop took notice too." Michael released a breath he'd been holding prisoner in his throat, and he felt a chill run over his skin. "He abused him for a year, and then he was transferred somewhere else. The church kept everything really quiet, but it's true. If you can find an honest priest, they might confess about it when you ask." Rosier turned to him, tilting his head. "And did Lucifer tell you he was left at the doorstep of the church? He lies about that too. He's the bastard of a priest and a prostitute." Rosier flinched. "Rumor says it was... the bishop and a prostitute."

They walked all the way back to the car before they slept together. Michael sat on the hood, his jeans lowered to his ankles, the altar boy on his lap. As he rode Michael's cock, Lucifer kissed him and kissed him.

Michael sighed shakily, his heart trembling with him. "God," he managed, his body aching, feeling both hot and cold. Maybe there would be rage later, but for now there was utter emptiness.

And the sensation of being extremely small, shrinking in a world that was growing too big all around him.

"I worry for him," said Rosier distantly. "But what can we do?"

On the drive back, Lucifer had smoked again, staring out at the mountains in the horizon, and he had said, "I like going further away from town." In essence, he was demanding Michael to drive him far again. "I always wanted to live in a big city, but you're convincing me that maybe it's not all hell out here." Michael smiled wide, and Lucifer snorted, then corrected himself, "Maybe I'm too fucked right now to think. I never want to see you again."

"I don't think," Michael had answered, "I believe you."

Lucifer had said, "You better learn to."

"Do you know where he is right now?" Michael asked quietly, his voice unstable, his breath stammering. "At the church?"

Rosier shook his head. "No. He's with one of his other boys. I saw them earlier." He frowned. "But why are you asking? Are you going to chase after him? You shouldn't, especially not now. It's already late."

Michael said, "I need to talk to him." Rosier asked why. "I just do." But both of them stared at one another, eyes wide, partly confused. "I need to find Lucifer."

"You love him," Rosier whispered, then smiled sadly when the other opened his mouth as if to argue. "Don't feel guilty." Twenty minutes before Michael had dropped Lucifer off, he'd considered driving off again, but he had nowhere to go. Lucifer was right: there was no ambition in him, nothing but the responsibilities he owed his family. Still, he'd stared at Lucifer's sleepy face against the window, eyes half shut, the sunset creeping down the horizon. "He has that effect on men like you." The altar boy had murmured a prayer as he dreamt. "But don't think about rescuing him from all the bad decisions he makes. He'll get really angry. Lucifer doesn't want to be saved."

REVELATION

The end of the world has come, and St. Michael and the devil decide to put aside their troubled past. Walking alongside each other, they step through the sand bordering a sea that's turned crimson and thick — blood. In their youth, as angels, the two had often danced and wrestled at a coast, such as this one, in Heaven, tittering and fighting and pecking bird-ish kisses when they were sure no one looked. But that paradise had ended as the Earth will end too, any minute now. The anti-Christ is dead; the true Christ is eager to sound the wedding bells for the devotees he'll marry. On the horizon, there are giant, mangled corpses protruding from the red ocean like splintered bone; they're charred from all the time they spent burning above as twinkling suns. All the stars have fallen, and plague has rooted into each human left, and war has made dust of their history, and it'll all be over soon.

But St. Michael and the devil talk. Michael says that he's done everything wrong in his infinite life. Sighing, his voice breaks. He's hurt the ones he loved most and made a fine wreck of the world for nothing. Michael is dead. He has died. There is just a saint now in his place.

Satan says he died too, long ago. The Creator set him on a

grave of flowers, and the devil saw that wickedness was inside him, as it is inside all of us. He was cast out for knowing, and he burnt in the fall.

Forgive me, says St. Michael.

It is too late, says the devil, to be sorry. The world has ended. God is victorious as we always knew He would be. All the living have left this place, and He succeeded in what He wanted most. I don't love you anymore. And you don't love me.

Lucifer, St. Michael tries to say.

There is no Lucifer. There hasn't been since Heaven.

I love you.

You don't.

I still dream of you.

You dream of an angel. You don't know who I am. You haven't since the fall from grace. God has taken what He wanted. You and I are strangers. He will destroy one of us. Soon. Soon.

The Earth shakes beneath their feet. Then, Michael says, There is no need to be strangers. There is time before the end. And there may be time afterward. It can't be that God can destroy any piece of Himself. If He could, He would've done it to you or to me. A part of you will always live on, whether in another body, another place. I will look for you after each end. I will never allow us to be strangers again.

I loved you, mused the devil, before I'd even met you. I looked for you. And you looked for me.

We can love again, said the saint.

I'm tired of you, said the devil, his voice almost as distant as his gaze. There is fire ahead of them.

Even if you're tired of me, I'll love you.

I'll never forgive you.

I will make everything right whether you forgive me or not. God's sword will turn on Him.

Satan no longer wishes to hear the name of God and asks, You're not afraid of the end?

I've been afraid long enough, answers Michael, then he stares at the fires with his beloved as a hand of his extends without a word. When Satan's fingers slip in between his own, they're as cold as his demeanor. Michael supposes you must be cold to survive the scorch of Hell, and he admires the resiliency.

The devil tugs him closer, and his kiss is like liquor. Softly, it moves against his mouth, and their lips part against each other, in unison, as if to eat. They should, the devil says, fuck. It is what started all of this. They longed for it for a hundred million years, ended the world to know desire. And yet, their clothing remains on their prisons of flesh. It is what everyone is waiting for, says Satan. He presses another kiss to him. It is all anyone has ever wanted out of him. If they don't fuck, then it was all for nothing.

Michael wants to say so much that says nothing. And when he kisses Satan for the third time, the sky has begun to bleed. It is already the end. There is no time. Maybe there will be time in whatever life comes after this one to love, to fumble and tenderly create, in another paradise far from here. Michael promises again to look for him, in another time, another body, another place. He will meet him again. St. Michael will fall, fall in love, with the devil at the beginning and at the end of the world; at the creation and the destruction.

That is what they are — Michael and Lucifer — creation and destruction — the beginning and the end; God.

ABOUT THE AUTHOR

Standing Figure of a Youth,
Giovanni Battista Tiepolo

rafael nicolás is an author of queer fiction. He likes marigolds.